The Darkness Saves

The Bridge Series

Book I

K.L. Rutledge

K.L. Rutledge

The Darkness Saves
The Bridge Series, Book I

Paperback ISBN-13: 979-8-218-84967-2

Some bridges are built of stone.

Others are forged in sacrifice.

K.L. Rutledge

This is for the dreamers who understand that the most meaningful adventures are rarely planned, and that a little darkness often walks beside the magic.

Chapter One

Leyla

Some mornings feel borrowed. Like the world hasn't quite decided whether to wake up or not. That's how this one felt. The air still carried a hint of last night's rain, cool and damp, wrapping the street in fog. I pulled my coat tighter as I crossed Sixth Avenue, the faint chime of *Eleanor's* bells greeting me before I even reached the door. The shop smelled exactly as it always did. Burnt espresso, lemon cleaner, and time.

The kind of smell that clings to paper long after the story's done being told.

Rows of mismatched shelves stretched to the ceiling, some tilting slightly like they'd grown weary of holding so many lives between their spines. It was perfect. Every crooked and carefully planned inch of it. This place was my heartbeat. Half library, half coffee shop, and wholly ours.

"About time," came Mick's voice from behind the counter. "I was two minutes away from declaring you dead and selling your collection of depressing poetry."

"You'd have to find it first," I sat my bag down on one of the back tables. "I've got them hidden with the good pens and my will to live."

"Both endangered species," she said, smirking. Her blonde curls were already rebelling against the messy bun perched on her head. Coffee grounds dusted her apron like glitter. "Are you opening today or staring wistfully at the books again?"

"I can multitask." And I could, but she wasn't wrong. I did stare. Often.

Our regulars were a mix of quiet readers, aspiring writers, and a few people who just came to smell the pages. I never blamed them.

"Did you finish that manuscript?" Mick asked as she poured a coffee for our incoming regular, John.

"The one with the tragic hero and emotional trauma?" I groaned. "Barely. The protagonist had a meltdown, the love interest disappeared for six chapters, and somehow there was a surprise elf… Honestly… was kind of here for the chaos, though."

I complained, but deep down, I loved these side gigs.

Being able to assist writers with their vision, but also still running a business with my best friend, was the dream. *"Was"* possibly being the key word here.

"So… a typical Tuesday," Mick laughed.

"Basically."

I picked up the broom, sweeping absently near the front window, but my mind wasn't on work. It hadn't been for a while. Lately, everything felt like repetition… Words, coffee, sleep, repeat.

I used to crave quiet. Now it felt like the silence was waiting for something to answer it back.

Such a stark difference from Mick and I's upbringing. Mick's mom gave it her best, but she was a single mother and her daughter chose to have a best friend whose stepfather was a drunk. Whose adoptive mom died when she was a baby.

So, she's mom. Plain and simple.

She practically raised us both since I came into their lives in the third grade. Times were tough but we had each other, always. I officially moved in with them our junior year, when Jerry, my stepfather… I shook my head. No longer even worth a memory.

My life looks a lot different than it did. The quiet helps; the simplicity and routine help.

But lately the quiet felt heavier.

When I caught my reflection in the front glass, I hardly recognized myself. The morning light softened the edges of my face, but the faint shadows beneath my eyes didn't lie. My dark brown hair was twisted into a loose braid over one shoulder, the ends curling where humidity refused to obey. My eyes… blue, not bright, more like the color of faded denim and just… tired. The kind of tired that coffee cannot fix.

Mick used to joke that I was raised by caffeine and the Dewey Decimal System, and she wasn't entirely wrong. Books made sense when people didn't. That's probably why I opened *Eleanor's* with her two years ago. We made the plan after Mick's mom passed away just a year prior. She loved books, and she left us both with a substantial insurance policy. We opened *Eleanor's* in her honor, our Eleanor. Always looking out for us, even when she was no longer here. God, how I missed her.

Mick handled the people and the coffee while I handled the stories and the coffee. It worked. The bell above the door jingled, and I glanced up automatically, plastering on my practiced shop smile. It was just the mailman, a friendly older guy who always delivered more gossip than actual mail. He waved, dropped a small stack of envelopes on the counter, and disappeared back into the fog.

Mick began riffling through the pile. "Bill, bill, postcard from my dad, bill, and—" she frowned, holding up one, "this." It was heavier than the others. Cream-colored, sealed with dark red wax. No return address. Just my name.

Leyla.

I took it, running my thumb over the seal. The wax was beautiful with a faint pattern pressed into it and thorns twining around a circle. I didn't recognize it, but something about it felt… deliberate. Old.

"You ordering mysterious fan mail again?" Mick asked. "Maybe it's from your secret admirer." She laughed to herself. "If so, he's worse at flirting than you are."

A laugh escaped, perhaps more out of nerves than anything. I couldn't open the envelope right away with the customers starting to make their steady entrances. Instead, I set it beside the register and went back to straightening the display table. But I kept glancing at it, that little flash of ivory against the wood. It looked out of place. Like it didn't belong to this century, let alone this shop.

Once the morning rush decided to die down, I was finally able to tear the seal.

The note inside was simple. One line written in the same elegant script.

You've been found.

That was all.

I blinked, waiting for something else. A signature, a name, a reason.

Nothing.

Mick peered over my shoulder. "Creepy. Want me to call the FBI, or should we assume it's the world's worst love letter?"

"It's probably a mix-up," I said, though the words came too fast, too defensive. The paper felt warm in my hands, too warm. I tucked it away, forcing a smile.

She gave me a look that said *'liar'* but didn't push it. The rest of the day blurred by in soft light and the sound of turning pages. But even after the last customer left, my gaze kept drifting to the envelope. To the words. To the strange pull in my chest every time I looked at them.

That night, as I closed up the shop alone, I headed towards the exit. I caught my reflection on the way in the front window. Muted light behind me, darkness pressing close outside. For the briefest moment, I saw movement.

A shadow beside me that wasn't mine.

Watching.

The air stilled. My heart tripped over itself. I turned, fast.

And then... Nothing. Just shelves. Just quiet.

Was I seeing things?

As I stepped into the fog, a whisper of warmth trailed across my skin, like the ghost of a touch. I told myself it was imagination. A trick of light.

But deep down, I couldn't shake the feeling that something in the dark had recognized me first.

Chapter Two

Leyla

Sleep didn't come easily. Every time I closed my eyes, I saw the red wax seal, the elegant handwriting, and the words that shouldn't have meant anything.

You've been found.

By morning, the letter sat on my nightstand like it was waiting for me to wake up. The fog outside hadn't lifted. It clung low to the ground, soft and soundless, swallowing the edges of the street.

I stood at my window for too long, watching the world blur at the edges, almost convincing myself I'd imagined the whole thing. But unease has a way of staying. Quiet, steady, and waiting for you to acknowledge it.

By the time I reached *Eleanor's*, the familiar smell of roasted coffee and old paper filled the air. My sanctuary. My routine. The heartbeat of my ordinary life.

Mick was already inside, humming off-key while reorganizing the poetry shelves.

"You look like you've seen a ghost," she said without looking up.

"More like I edited one," I replied, forcing a smile that didn't quite land.

She snorted. "That bad?"

"Worse." I busied myself behind the counter, wiping down surfaces that didn't need cleaning. Anything to keep from looking at the letter now tucked safely, or perhaps stupidly, into my coat pocket.

It was barely past ten when the bell above the door chimed. The sound was innocent… Until it wasn't.

Something in the air shifted.

He didn't just walk in… He arrived. Like the world, my shop, had been waiting for him.

Not in the way our regulars did… with their damp coats and sleepy smiles. But with the ease of someone who rarely asked permission. The kind of man who could walk into any room and have the walls lean closer just to listen. His presence filled the doorway and also, somehow, the entire room.

He was tall, taller than any man I had met before, with a long dark coat that brushed the tops of his boots. His hair was black… not glossy, but a deep matte black, with a slight wave to it. His eyes… I couldn't decide on the color. Somewhere between gray and blue, the kind that shift depending on the light. And when they landed on me, the air in my lungs stalled.

"Good morning," he said, voice low, warm. Every syllable deliberate.

"… Morning," I managed. My mouth moved but my brain had apparently abandoned ship. I continued to stand there. Continued to stare. Mick's pointed cough from the counter pulled me back. "Uh… Sorry. I'm sorry. Would you like a coffee or book?"

He smiled faintly as I fumbled through our interaction. "That depends. Which one do you recommend?"

"Books last longer," I blurted before I could stop myself.

That earned me a quiet laugh, soft but genuine. "Then I'll trust your judgment."

He drifted toward the shelves, fingers brushing the spines like he was reacquainting himself with old friends. His movements were deliberate, not hesitant or even remotely rushed. Like he'd been here before and was testing what had changed. The air seemed to follow him, the shadows softening. The lights ever so slightly dimming as he passed through the shelves.

Mick glanced at me from behind the counter and mouthed, *who's that?*

I shrugged, pretending to focus my attention on the espresso machine. After minutes of cleaning the machine and nothing else to do with my hands, I walked over towards the back library section to start going through a few new books we got in yesterday. Keep my mind busy, try not to look at the man that made me forget how to speak. Yes, that should work.

A few minutes later, the man returned with a worn copy of *The Collected Works of Poe*. He set it gently on the counter in front of me, leaning across the small countertop. "Appropriate, don't you think?"

"For the weather or the mood?" I managed.

"Both," he said, then looked at me with an intensity that felt far too direct for a stranger. "You're Leyla." A statement, not a question.

My hand froze midreach. "How—?"

He tilted his head, feigning confusion. "It's on the sign out front. *Eleanor's* — Owned by Leyla and Mick." I let out a shaky laugh.

"Right. Of course." But something about the way he said my name made me feel like he wasn't lying, just deflecting. He handed me a twenty.

His fingers brushed mine briefly, and a pulse of cold went through me, sharp enough to feel like memory. Internally, I shake my head, *what is going on with me? Talk.*

"What brings you to our shop?" I counted his change.

"I'm just visiting," he replies. "Sort of passing through for work. My company rented a house about ten minutes away and I wanted to explore the area. I'll be here for a few weeks."

"What kind of work?" There was a pause.

"… I'm in the business of books." His lips curved. His gaze lingered a second too long, like he was searching for something behind my eyes.

"Like publishing?" I questioned, trying for steady. "You came to the right place. Plenty of stories here; some worth reading more than others, I'll admit."

"I don't doubt that for a second," he whispered, pocketing his change. "It was a pleasure meeting you, Leyla." The way he said my name, soft and deliberate, made it sound like a promise. Made my stomach tighten.

Before I could respond, the bell over the door chimed again, and he was gone.

Mick appeared beside me almost instantly. "Okay, what was that? Tell me everything."

"I don't know," I said, staring at the empty doorway. "Just a customer." Though as the words came out, I could feel how untrue they were.

"Hmm," she drew out the word. "A customer who looks like a tragic novel hero and makes eyes at you while he's pretending to look for a book. Perhaps learning his name isn't necessary." I smiled despite myself. Perhaps she was right.

Outside, the fog had started to lift, but when I glanced toward the street, I thought I saw him.

Standing there. Across the road.

Watching me.

Then a car passed, and he was gone.

Chapter Three

Leyla

I spent last night with Brad. Well, technically on a date with Brad. It wasn't bad. Just… lukewarm.

He was the kind of guy who talked with his hands and laughed at all the wrong moments, nice enough that I felt guilty for not feeling more.

We went to that new Italian place downtown, the one with the mismatched chairs and candles in wine bottles. He told me about his job at the bank, his fantasy football league, his love for spicy arrabbiata. Every word passing through me like background music.

I smiled where I should have, nodded when expected, but my mind kept wandering elsewhere.

To storm gray eyes, that leaned a little blue just in the right light.

To the memory of that voice that felt like smoke and velvet.

To the way he looked at me like he already knew what I feared most in this world.

Brad had offered to take me to a basketball game in two days.

"Front row seats," he'd said, all proud grin and easy charm. And I'd said yes. Because why not?

Maybe I needed to try. Maybe distraction was what I needed, to drown out the pull of someone I just met but couldn't stop thinking about. I told myself it was just a night. Just a game. Just a chance to be normal for a while.

But even as I replayed his smile, his stories, and his too-loud laugh, all I could feel was that faint echo of electricity under my skin, the kind that didn't belong to Brad at all.

I unlocked the door to *Eleanor's,* and the familiar bell chimed, soft and melodic, like a lullaby for the city's early risers. Inside, the smell wrapped around me: coffee, aged paper, and the faint sweetness of ink. Dust floated lazily in the amber shafts of light that spilled through the tall windows. Mick was already behind the counter, balancing a latte in one hand while skimming invoices with the other.

"Late again," she said without looking up. "If the books start reading themselves, I'll know who to blame."

I muttered a response I didn't mean, dropping my bag on a nearby table.

My eyes drifted to the shelves, and that strange pull returned. The subtle sensation that the shop itself was watching, leaning in a little closer.

And then I saw him.

The stranger from yesterday.

He was in the corner, inconspicuous but impossible to ignore. Leaning against the tall shelf near the poetry section, he held a leather-bound book, but he wasn't reading. His eyes… storm-colored, edged with the faintest silver glint, were trained on me. Calm. Focused. And electric.

My pulse stumbled. My stomach turned traitor. Every sensible part of me screamed to look away, but my body refused to listen. His gaze pinned me there, the space between us thickening with something sharp and electric.

Mick noticed. Of course she did. "Leyla?" she whispered, nudging my elbow. "You okay?"

"I'm fine," I said. A terrible lie. My voice betrayed me, too breathless to sound casual.

"He's been here since right after I opened," she said under her breath, eyes narrowing. "He hasn't moved."

I forced a shrug. "He said he's in town for work."

"Right," her skepticism dripped plainly. "Work. Sure."

There was just something familiar in the way he existed. He didn't smile. Didn't move closer.

Just stood there.

He was magnetic, almost in a predatory way; like he had all the time in the world and the patience to wait while the world continued to spin around him.

Every so often, a customer wandered in, but I couldn't keep from making small glances in his direction. As discreetly as possible of course. Each step the customers took felt like a ripple in the air around him, and he barely noticed.

"Stop staring," Mick whispered, sharper now. "Men like that either write bad poetry or worse crimes. And I am not getting saintly vibes." A snort escaped.

He shifted slightly, sliding the book back onto the shelf with slow, deliberate care. Then, as if sensing my gaze had tightened around him like a vise, he moved toward the front of the shop.

Not too close. Not too far.

The air seemed to bend around him, and each footfall echoed faintly, almost imperceptibly, against the tile. My stomach fluttered. I didn't realize I was holding my breath.

"Did you enjoy your book?" I asked, forcing a smile that felt false, clumsy against the heat that had sprung to my cheeks.

He stopped. Just a few feet away, close enough to see the way my eyes followed him. He tilted his head, and that gaze bore into me like an unspoken question, a challenge.

"Enjoyed? No," his voice filled with that low velvet and smoke sound I couldn't stop thinking about. "My attention was being pulled elsewhere."

A shiver ran down my spine.

"You're… different."

I froze. Was that a warning? Or a compliment? My pulse tripped over itself. I wanted to speak, to ask what he meant, but the air between us felt charged, almost alive. And when he turned toward the door, something in me refused to let him go.

"Wait," I breathed, my hand brushing his arm before I could think.

The contact hit like lightning. A jolt tore through me, hot and cold all at once, blooming beneath my skin. The world flickered around the edges, my breath catching as the hum in the air grew louder, closer.

"You know my name," I managed, trying to steady my voice, "I'd like to know yours."

Instead of pulling away from my touch, he covered it. His touch deliberate, grounding, and far too intimate for a stranger. His fingers traced the inside of my wrist, and my pulse leapt.

"Thalon." He said the name like a secret spoken into my bones.

Before I could speak, he lifted my hand. The motion was reverent and practiced. He brought it to his lips, brushing a kiss across my skin. It was nothing more than breath and heat, but it set every nerve into flames.

And for a second, just a second, his control slipped.

His eyes widened… like he'd felt the spark too. Like he hadn't meant to.

And then he was gone.

The bell above the door chimed once, soft and final, and the rain outside swallowed him whole.

Mick leaned against the counter, arms crossed, a smirk tugging at her lips. "You didn't even try not to stare," she said. "You're either smitten… or you've completely lost it."

"I'm… fine." Even I didn't believe myself. I didn't know what was happening.

Even as I moved through the day, grinding beans, stacking books, and straightening shelves, my gaze kept returning to the empty corner where he'd been.

Interlude

Leyla — The Sound of Breaking Glass

I pressed myself deeper into the corner of the closet, the rough wood pressing against my cheek. Every breath I took smelled of stale whiskey and dust. My heart was hammering so loudly I was sure it would betray me. Jerry's boots scraped across the hallway, dragging, heavy and unpredictable.

"Where is it, girl?" His voice cracked, slurred and jagged. "Where's my…. Leyla! Where are you?" He screamed.

I stayed perfectly still, counting my breaths: one… two… three…

Hoping, praying, that he wouldn't notice me. A glass shattered in the hallway, the noise made my stomach leap into my throat. I clutched my knees to my chest. I hated the way he scared me. I hated that I had learned to flinch at the sound of his voice. I hated the part of me that had already figured out the rhythm of his anger: the build, the scream, the crash. Tonight, the crash came early. Shards of glass rained down from the broken ceiling light, tinkling across the floor, bouncing like jagged stars. A piece nicked my palm. I hissed softly and clenched my fingers over the wound.

I couldn't cry. I couldn't move.

Noise was danger.

I thought of my adoptive mother, gone before I was old enough to remember her smile clearly, gone before I could trust anyone again. I was only five when she died, and now I was ten, and the only thing I understood was survival.

Quiet meant safety.

Silence meant safety.

Sirens wailed in the distance. Red and blue lights flashed against the walls, and I pressed my forehead to the floor, letting the colors wash over me. They came for him eventually, always eventually.

The fear inside me eased slightly, and when his shouts faded, I finally crawled from the closet. The hallway was littered with glass, glittering cruelly under the flashing lights. My stepfather was gone, dragged into the night, leaving me in a strange, uneasy calm. The officers knew to call Mick's mom. She arrived soon after. I wish she was my mom instead.

I knelt and brushed a shard aside, whispering to myself:

Quiet means safe.

Chapter Four

Leyla

Morning sunlight slanted through the tall windows of *Eleanor's*, drifting across stacks of books and settling in golden squares on the worn wooden floors. Dust motes floated lazily, catching the light like tiny sparks, and the aroma of coffee blended with the faint musk of old paper. I moved carefully along the aisles, rearranging novels that had fallen, my fingers brushing against leather-bound spines and glossy covers. Every surface, every shelf, felt alive somehow. Like the books themselves were breathing, just beneath the surface of the ordinary.

Mick appeared behind the counter, balancing a tray of steaming cups like she was taming a wild animal.

"I swear these floors have it out for me," she muttered, swiping at a stubborn coffee stain. "One day, I'm going down, and you're going to have to exorcise me from under the espresso machine."

I laughed softly. "You'd just haunt me."

"Damn right I would."

Her energy filled the room, a small storm of warmth and noise. But even her presence couldn't smother the pulse of something else. Something beneath it all. The hum I kept pretending I couldn't feel.

I bent to adjust a stack of classics and felt a strange tug in my chest, like the air itself had thickened for a heartbeat.

One of the books slipped from my fingers, and time seemed to stop.

It didn't crash to the floor.

Not right away.

It hovered for a fraction of a second, wobbling delicately, before settling softly back onto the table. My heart beat rapidly in my chest, my pulse suddenly loud in my ears. I glanced up instinctively, and there he was.

Thalon.

Standing in the shadows near the back shelves, his presence quiet but impossible to ignore. His coat was dark and simple, but it carried a weight, as if the shadows themselves bent around him.

My pulse quickened, heat rising under my skin, that strange pull in my chest tightening until I could barely breathe.

He didn't move. Didn't speak.

Just watched.

Like a hunter pretending to be still.

Mick passed through my line of sight, humming off-key, completely oblivious. When she disappeared again behind the counter, he was still there. Closer this time. How had he moved so silently?

I turned away to the counters, desperate to ground myself. My hands shook as I poured a cup of coffee, the steam curling into the air. The scent of roasted beans and rain filled my lungs. Ordinary things. Safe things. But nothing about this felt ordinary. He moved towards me like a storm disguised as a man. Quiet, deliberate, with that dark, impossible grace. My heart pounded so hard it hurt. I wanted to look away, but every instinct screamed not to.

When I finally forced my eyes to meet his again, I swear the air between us rippled. He tilted his head slightly, as if studying something fragile. I dropped my gaze to the mug in my hand. The liquid trembled, disturbed by the tremor in my own fingers.

That low velvety voice cut through the silence. "You feel it too, don't you?"

I froze. The words brushed down my spine like a touch.

I turned, but he was gone.

Just the corner of the shop again. The shelves.

The light.

The echo of something that wasn't quite sound.

"Leyla?" Mick's voice broke through the haze. "You okay? You aren't looking so good."

I blinked, forcing a laugh that came out too thin. "You worry too much, Mick."

"You sure? You've been staring at your coffee for a full minute."

"Fine. I'm fine. Just thinking about that manuscript from last night," I managed, and she laughed, shaking her head. But as she turned back to the counter, I looked again.

Nothing.

Only that lingering pull, like a hand had wrapped around my heartbeat and refused to let go.

Even as I swept the floor, arranged books, and moved through the motions of the rest of my day, I couldn't shake the sense that the world had subtly shifted. That something immense had brushed against me, and that I had barely survived noticing it.

Chapter Five

Leyla

By the time I pulled onto my street, the sun was already slipping behind the line of trees, painting the sky in streaks of bruised purple and gold. The glow from the streetlamps flickered on, one by one, casting long shadows across the yard.

I killed the engine and sat there for a moment, staring at the porch light I had forgotten to turn off that morning. The rest of my day at work was mind-numbingly normal, the kind of day that should've grounded me after imagining books floating in the air. But nothing felt normal anymore. Not since him.

Even thinking his name made my chest tighten, a strange mix of heat and unease curling low in my stomach. I hated it. I told myself I was done thinking about him. That the best thing I could do was move on and pretend the electric pull between us had been nothing more than adrenaline and bad timing. Which was exactly why I'd said yes when Brad asked me to the basketball game tonight.

Brad was… nice. Normal. He still said things like *'let's vibe'* but he meant well. We'd gone to dinner two nights ago at that small Italian place downtown, the one that smelled like garlic and burnt breadsticks. I smiled, nodded, and tried to convince myself that the boring and predictable was good. Safe. It was what I wanted, what I craved, for so long.

Now here I was, home again, staring at my dashboard like it might have the answers. The game started at eight. It was seven. I should have gone inside, showered, changed, done something to feel human again. Instead, I lingered, my eyes fixed on the tree line at the edge of the yard.

The shadows there looked wrong. Almost too thick or too still, I couldn't tell.

A flicker of movement.

There, then gone.

"Hello?" My voice sounded small against the stillness. No answer.

I shook my head, forcing a laugh. "You're fine. Totally fine. Probably just a squirrel or something."

Still, when I reached my door, I hesitated before unlocking it. My reflection in the window stared back at me. Wide-eyed, tense, not at all like someone about to go on a date. Inside, the apartment was dim and waiting for me. I tossed my keys onto the gray granite counter, flipped on the light, and kicked off my shoes. The silence pressed in around me, broken only by the low hum of the refrigerator.

I made my way to the bedroom, trying to shake off the unease. Maybe a change of clothes would help. Maybe pretending everything was fine would make it true. I stood in front of the mirror, the faint light from the hallway washing over me. My hair was a mess from the day, my mascara smudged just enough to make me look tired. Jeans and a white sweater, it would have to do. I wasn't trying to impress Brad.

And yet, as I ran my fingers through my hair, I caught myself glancing toward the window. My chest tightened.

He wouldn't be out there. He couldn't be.

But the thought rooted itself anyway. The memory of gray eyes watching me from the shadows at *Eleanor's*. The warmth of a hand that had never truly left my skin. I swallowed hard, forcing a laugh that didn't sound right.

"You're fine," I whispered. "You're imagining it."

But, I wasn't so sure.

The curtains stirred, slow and deliberate, though the window was closed. I crossed the room and brushed them aside. The yard beyond was still. Just grass, streetlight and the quiet tremor of trees. Empty. And yet my pulse refused to settle.

Still, I found myself moving differently.

Slower, more aware, with every gesture deliberate. As if the air itself was watching. I smoothed my hair, adjusted my sweater… and pretended like I wasn't performing for someone unseen. The sound of my heartbeat alone filled the room.

Stop it, I scolded myself. I gripped the dresser until my knuckles ached.

He's not here. But my body didn't believe it.

This is insane. I was being insane. Finally, I grabbed my jacket and purse. When I looked one last time through the curtain, the yard was empty. Only the fading glow of the streetlamp and the soft rustle of wind through the trees.

Empty. I exhaled.

"See? Nothing." I told myself.

But as I locked the door behind me and stepped out into the cool night air, that strange sensation crept back in. The weight of being watched. And for the briefest moment, just before I reached Brad's Mustang pulling up to the curb, I could have sworn I saw movement again at the edge of the woods.

A dark silhouette. Still. And Watching.

Chapter Six

Thalon

I perched in the shadowed alley across from her apartment, the night air heavy with rain-soaked earth and the faint hum of mortal electricity. The city pulsed faintly around me, a thousand mortal hearts beating too fast, too loud. None of it mattered.

I could hear only one.

Hers.

Leyla's heartbeat was a rhythm I shouldn't have known but couldn't forget. It thudded softly against the hum of this realm, steady and bright like a beacon calling me closer. I could feel her warmth even through walls and distance; every step, every shift in breath tugging at something buried deep inside me. I told myself I was only watching. Only assessing.

That was a lie I had already stopped believing.

When she moved through her home, the lights kissed her skin. When she stilled, the air bent around her like it recognized its master. The first time I saw her, my father's command had flared inside me – *eliminate the magical disturbance*. But, the sigil that bound me to his will had burned without taking hold.

It was the first time in thirty-nine years that I had been able to disobey him.

The sigil obeys the King's blood, not mine.

And yet, for her, it faltered. That terrified me more than I'd like to admit.

She stepped out onto the porch, pausing like she'd heard something. My grip tightened on the dagger at my thigh, an instinct older than memory.

She didn't see me, but I knew she felt me. Her shoulders tensed; her lips parted. And then she laughed softly, dismissing the instinct that might have saved her life. Like all mortals do.

A car pulled to the curb. The human male leaned out the window, grinning like a fool. She smiled back, small and practiced, the kind meant to hide unease. The sound of her voice when she greeted him, light and almost shy, hit harder than any blade. He was courting her.

My heart began to race.

They drove away.

The taillights vanished into the mist. The urge to follow clawed through me, feral and consuming. The shadows beneath my feet stirred as if awaiting my command. But something in the air shifted first.

"Still stalking the mortal, I see." Elias's voice cut through the quiet, smooth and edged with amusement. My oldest friend, my fiercest irritation.

"You shouldn't be here, you are supposed to be keeping watch back at the house," I said.

He arched a brow. "Neither should you."

I turned my gaze back to the road. "This isn't your concern."

He laughed softly. "When it involves you disobeying your father's direct command, I'd say it's very much my concern. He'll start to suspect something is amiss soon. The King doesn't tolerate ghosts in his bloodline."

A muscle in my jaw ticked. "He would know if I were dead. The sigil would tell him."

Elias's smile faltered. The night itself shifted. The air warped, feeling wrong and heavy. Shadows twisted, splitting apart like flesh.

Elias's tone dropped. "You feel that?"

"Obviously."

The distortion tore open a breath later, and a Rift Wraith crawled through. Pale and skeletal, its eyes glowed molten silver, its limbs moving with a jerky hunger. The stench of decay and old magic filled the air.

"Damn," Elias muttered. "How did that slip through?"

"Because she exists," I said, drawing my blade. "The realm can feel her awakening. The disturbance has a pulse now, and it's hers."

The Wraith lunged. We moved together, a seamless violence honed by decades of training side by side. I slipped beneath the creature's claws, dagger flashing upward in a clean, brutal arc. The Wraith screamed, high and metallic, before collapsing into dust that shimmered once and was gone. Silence returned like a held breath.

Elias exhaled, running a hand through his hair. "So, it's her."

"Yes."

His gaze hardened. "Then you know what must happen."

I met his eyes, saying nothing.

"You have to bring her to Orrynne," he pressed. "To your father. You can't protect her from what she is."

I sheathed my dagger slowly. "No."

"No?" He frowned. "Thalon, you can't just…"

"She is mine to find. Mine to understand. My father will not touch her."

Elias studied me, "How are you going against his orders? You have never been able to… The sigil…"

"I do not have the answer. This planet? The weakening of magic in Orrynne? Her? Who is to say?" I looked over to him. "But, my body is now my own. And I want to see what the little mortal is about."

He followed my gaze toward the road where her scent lingered. Sweet, strange, and lightly threaded with magic. "Where's she going?"

"A gathering of sorts."

He gave me that insufferable grin. "Then let's go watch, shall we? Wouldn't want your little mortal to get eaten before you decide what she is."

I glared at him, but didn't stop him when he slipped back into the shadows. The air folded around us as we moved, silent and unseen. The city blurred into streaks of light, the mortal world nothing more than an echo beneath our feet.

Her scent pulled me onward, steady and bright; a tether I couldn't sever even if I wanted to.

I didn't know what would happen when I reached her.

Only that every step toward her felt like defiance. And destiny.

And desire I could no longer name without burning for it.

Chapter Seven

Leyla

Tonight, I was going to be normal. Go on a date. Watch a game. Pretend that my pulse wasn't still tuned to the echo of gray eyes and rain. Brad was dressed up in his clean-cut way. A button-up shirt and easy smile... Just the kind of man who belonged in daylight.

The opposite of everything Thalon represented. And maybe that was exactly why I said yes.

The arena pulsed with noise, the sharp tang of popcorn and sweat heavy in the air. People laughed, shouted, moved like a living tide. But sitting next to Brad felt like trying to breathe through glass. My attention kept drifting, and the back of my neck was in a constant state of prickling, as though eyes were tracing me from the shadows.

"You okay?" Brad leaned closer, voice half-swallowed by the roar of the crowd.

"Yeah," I lied, forcing a smile. "Just thought I saw someone."

But it wasn't someone... It was something. That same hum in the air, that static energy that followed me since my apartment.

I leaned forward as the woman behind me got up for snacks, not wanting to get hit by her purse.

A few moments later, I felt him. Felt his presence.

Thalon.

I didn't have to look to know. The air seemed to change when he was near…. thicker, charged, like the split-second before lightning strikes. When I finally dared to glance over my shoulder, my eyes went wide. He sat right behind Brad and I. Taking the couple's seats that were behind us. A smirk ghosted across his mouth. Lazy, knowing, and dangerous. The man beside him, all gold hair and wolfish amusement, met my stare with a silent, good luck stare.

My breath caught. I turned back too fast, heart hammering.

The crowd roared, but I barely heard them.

Why was he here?

Brad leaned closer again, shouting something about the score. I nodded like I cared, but all I could think about was the way Thalon's presence filled the space behind me, impossible to ignore.

Brad was talking about some play, but I couldn't focus. Every time Thalon moved, I felt it, like the tremor of thunder you don't see but sense in your bones.

The lights dimmed slightly, the announcer's voice booming over the speakers: "Alright, folks! You know what time it is… KISS CAM!"

The giant screen flickered to life, flashing laughing couples, exaggerated smooches and mock boos. Until it landed… On us. My blood froze.

I wanted to scream.

Brad chuckled, rubbing the back of his neck. "Do you… want to? I guess that's our cue."

"Oh… no, you don't have to—" I started, but he waved to the camera instead, earning a chorus of playful boos. I laughed awkwardly, heat creeping up my neck. But the camera man was insistent, and the crowds continue to roar. I tried to wave with Brad as well, signaling that we had no interest in kissing. Or I didn't, at the very least.

And then… A hand.

Warm. Sure. Possessive.

Fingers slid up the back of my neck, tracing the line of my throat, coaxing my head to turn. Every nerve lit up, my body recognizing him before my mind caught up.

"Play your mortal games properly, little light." The voice was a caress against my ear. Smooth. Commanding.

Thalon.

Before I could breathe, he tilted my chin and his mouth was on mine.

The world vanished. No crowd, no light, no air. Just him. The taste of storm and shadow and something ancient that burned against my skin. His kiss was both sin and sanctuary; devouring and deliberate. The kind of kiss that rewrote the rules of gravity.

When he pulled away, my lips tingled. My pulse refused to steady and the noise of the arena slammed back into me all at once.

Loud cheers, whistles, and laughter rang through the arena at what everyone had just witnessed.

I stared at Thalon in panic. Fascination. Something. Everything.

My mind was no longer working. And he looked like he wanted to possess me.

I glanced at his friend, who was looking at Thalon like he had lost his mind. And then my eyes landed on Brad…. The man practically had steam blowing out of his ears. He was standing now, jaw tight, face pale.

His voice came sharp and hurt. "What the hell was that?"

"Brad—" I started, but he was already on his feet, eyes flashing.

"You're kidding me, right?" His voice cracked. "You just… what, let some guy—?"

"It's not what you think." I tried to explain, but the words were hard to find.

"Really? Because it looks exactly like what I think." He gestured wildly toward Thalon, who was watching with unnerving calm, silver eyes faintly glinting under the arena lights. "Who the hell is he?"

Thalon's gaze hardened, his tone quiet but edged. "You should walk away."

"Excuse me?" Brad barked a laugh. "You think you can just—"

He didn't finish. Something in the air shifted. Something wrong. I could feel it pressing in around us. Thalon rose slowly from his seat, every movement deliberate.

"I said walk away." Brad's face twisted with anger.

He turned on his heel and stormed toward the tunnel exit, shoulders tense. The crowd barely noticed, now too caught up in the game. But I did. I saw the way Thalon followed him a few seconds later, silent as a shadow. My heart dropped.

"Thalon… Wait!" I pushed through the aisle, ignoring the curses and shoves, his friend keeping pace beside me with an exasperated sigh. The hallway lights flickered as we stepped into the corridor. Brad stood halfway down the hall, back turned, his breathing harsh and uneven.

Thalon's voice cut through the quiet. "You need to stop."

Brad turned. His pupils had swallowed his irises. His skin shimmered like oil, distorting, and when he spoke, his voice fractured.

The thing wearing his face smiled, too wide, too wrong.

And then his voice fractured into a guttural snarl. His pupils bled into black. His skin shimmered, distorting like water over fire.

"Brad?" I whispered, my throat tight. "Oh my God—" The thing that wore his face hissed, the sound layered, inhuman.

"You shouldn't have touched her," the being that used to be Brad rasped, voice vibrating like broken glass. Thalon stepped forward, his expression cold, a blade of shadowed metal materializing in his hand.

"Leyla, behind me."

"No!" I stumbled forward, panic and adrenaline tangling in my chest. "Don't hurt him… please."

He took a moment to look down at me in my panic.

"He's gone," Thalon snapped, eyes silver-bright.

The creature lunged.

I barely registered his friend pulling me back, shielding me as the lights shattered above. And then I saw them. Wings. Unfolding from Thalon's back like night itself.

Vast, dark, and edged in a violet flame. The air rippled around him, alive with power. For one suspended moment, he looked carved from the stars themselves, terrifying and magnificent all at once.

The creature slammed Thalon into the wall. I moved before I could think. I grabbed the metal railing beside me and swung with everything I had. The crack resounded like thunder. Light exploded from the point of impact, searing white and violet.

The thing screamed, its body convulsing before collapsing to the floor.

Silence.

My hands shook. The railing fell from my grip with a hollow clang.

"Brad?" I whispered. His face flickered. Now, human again. His chest rising in shallow breaths. He was alive.

Thalon's blade and wings dissolved into nothing. He stared at me, shock breaking through the mask of control.

"You shouldn't have been able to do that."

"I didn't... I wasn't..." My voice shook.

His friend strolled closer, hands in his pockets, grin sharp. "Well, that could have gone worse."

"Not helping, Elias," Thalon muttered.

Elias shrugged. "She handled herself. Better than most mortals who faint at the first sign of screaming wraiths."

I backed into the wall, my pulse unsteady. "What the hell was that? What did I just do?"

Thalon turned to me, eyes still lit from within. "He wasn't human. He was a wraith shell; something that slipped through the Rift."

"He wasn't human." It came from Elias.

"That's insane." My words came out hoarse. "That's insane." I began to back away… hearing the same words continuously come out of my mouth. But all I could see was Brad, laying there. He was breathing. That's what mattered.

Elias muttered under his breath, "You said she'd take it well." Thalon ignored him.

His attention stayed on me, steady and unnervingly gentle. "You're not safe, Leyla. You're part of something bigger than you know. The world, the universe, is far bigger than you can imagine. And people, wraith shells like Brad, will keep coming until you understand what you are." I shook my head, pressing my palms to my temples.

"Stop—please—just stop. You sound crazy." Thalon took a slow step closer, voice low.

"You have power, Leyla. It's waking whether you want it to or not." The hum in the air deepened again… an echo of something in me responding. I didn't want to believe it. Couldn't. But part of me already knew that something was changing in me.

Elias cleared his throat. "We should move before anyone sees this mess."

Thalon nodded, his expression tightening. Then, to me: "I'm not leaving you alone. Not tonight."

"What?" My voice shook. "You can't just… I don't even know you."

"On the couch," he promised, hands raised. "Until I'm sure nothing else followed you from the Rift." He looked to Elias. "What is the mortal expression? None of my business will be funny."

I hesitated. The image of Brad's flickering, twisted face seared into my mind. Whatever this was, I wasn't ready to face it alone.

"Fine," I whispered. "But you stay on the couch."

A ghost of a smile curved his mouth. That infuriating, dangerous almost-smile. "As you wish."

Chapter Eight

Leyla

The car ride was silent. Too silent. The kind of silence that pressed against my ears and made every shallow breath sound like a confession.

It wasn't peace. And it was far from comfort.

The hum of the city outside blurred into streaks of light through the rain-specked window, neon signs warping into long ribbons of color. My hands twisted in my lap, still trembling faintly, the faint metallic scent of the arena hallway refusing to leave my skin. The sound of the windshield wipers filled the air in rhythmic intervals… *thunk, shhh, thunk, shhh.* It became hypnotic, almost soothing.

Thalon drove, eyes forward. The dim glow from the dash carved his features into shadow—every inch of him restrained. Elias sat beside him, unnervingly calm for someone who'd just seen a man unravel into a monster.

No one spoke.

Until Elias broke the quiet.

"You shouldn't have revealed yourself like that," he said, tone smooth but edged. "There could have been more witnesses. And in front of her no less."

Thalon didn't turn his head. "She was already a target. This is the second being that has tried to attack her."

"She's also human," Elias replied sharply. "Or she was. And mortals don't handle this kind of truth well." I blinked, the words landing heavy in my stomach.

Target. Truth. Mortal. None of it made sense, but it was enough to make my pulse quicken.

Thalon's jaw flexed. "You saw what happened back there. The thing wearing her…" he paused, swallowing the words as if it made him ill. "…Date's… face wasn't some random wraith."

Elias scoffed. "And you think that justifies dragging her into this?"

"I didn't drag her in," Thalon snapped, finally turning toward him. His voice dropped, low and dangerous. "Something was already tracking her long before tonight." My heart stopped.

"What are you talking about? What is a wraith? Why was it in Brad?" I demanded, my voice sounding too small in the enclosed car.

Both men went still.

As if they forgot I was in the back seat entirely.

It was subtle, but I saw the way Thalon's hands grip the wheel tighter.

"She can hear us? You did not think to put up a barrier? Thalon, truthfully… where is your head at?"

The car slowed. He pulled over to the shoulder with frightening calm. The rain hissed against the windshield.

Then, Thalon turned in his seat, facing me. His expression softened; and that was somehow more terrifying than his anger. "Are you hurt?"

The question caught me off guard. "No," I whispered, shaking my head.

"Good." His gaze lingered on me for a moment, steady and deliberate, before sliding to Elias.

"You've been my brother in everything that mattered," he said quietly. "And because of that, I'll forgive your words. But if you ever question me again about my mate, I will end you faster than I would a Wraith." The words sank in before my brain could process them.

Mate.

Elias froze. So did I.

Thalon nodded and began to drive again. Elias managed to get the words I was thinking out.

"Mate?" he questioned. "That is impossible?" Sounding more like a question, than a statement.

"With her, I do not believe anything is impossible. My mission is no longer relevant, she is my mate… Our kiss sealed it tonight. Our connection… I have no doubt she is mine."

"Unbelievable." Elias shook his head. "It is unheard of for over six hundred years. There has only been chosen mates for centuries."

"I will protect her from all that is to come. All danger. ALL danger, Elias. Do you understand what I am saying?"

Elias shook his head in disbelief. "I will follow you. Until the end."

Elias managed to come over his disbelief rather quickly, although I certainly had more questions. Whatever this conversation was, it seemed intense. He thought I was his… Mate? Maybe they both escaped a nearby psych ward.

Elias looked at me over his shoulder, lips curling into something that wasn't quite a smile. "So, what does this mean for you, little mortal? It means you've got a lot more going on under that mortal skin than you think, sweetheart."

"Elias," Thalon warned.

"No," I cut him off. "Someone needs to start explaining."

We reached my building, the car rolling to a stop in eerie synchronization. I hadn't given him my address. That realization chilled me more than anything he'd said. Goosebumps spread along my arms. I needed to get out of here. Now.

Thalon exhaled through his nose, the sound more frustration than surrender. "You've felt it, haven't you? The way the air changes around you. The way things… notice you." I swallowed hard. Turning towards him, pausing just before my escape.

"That doesn't mean—"

"It does," he cut in gently, though there was a strange, tired gravity in his tone. "The world you know… the streets, the skyline, the noise… that's only a fraction of what exists. There are realms layered over this one, forgotten by design. Some ancient, and magical. And lately—" His eyes met mine, storm-gray and unflinching. "They are slowly dying. Life is dying, magic is dying. Darkness is awakening. Death is coming. Life will be no more, eventually. To all worlds, including this one. It has already begun in ours."

Thalon continued. "You were found. Marked."

"Marked?" My voice cracked. "By what? By who?"

"By me."

"Oh, brilliant," Elias muttered. "You want to maybe explain that before she jumps out of the car?"

Thalon's voice stayed even. "That morning at the store. When you touched me. It wasn't meant to happen, but I left part of my energy, part of my signature, on you. I believe it is what has started to draw the creatures of the dark out. And when I kissed you tonight. They can smell what you are now. Your magic is awakening."

The words hit me like cold water.

"So, this happened… Because I touched you?" His expression flickered—pain, maybe… or guilt—but he didn't deny it.

"Yes." For a long moment, I couldn't look at him.

I just stared out the window; the street lights a hard contrast to the black surrounding us. I didn't know what was real anymore. I couldn't focus anymore. I needed warmth, I needed comfort. I needed out. I let myself out of the back seat and headed towards my apartment door.

I heard Elias mutter something about "warding the place" and disappeared toward the back, leaving the two of us in the soft, humming light of the hallway, right in front of my door.

I crossed my arms, though it did nothing to stop the trembling. "You're really staying?"

Thalon's mouth curved faintly. "On the couch. I keep my word."

"Good," I murmured. "Because I'm locking my door." He smiled at that... small, fleeting, and almost human.

"I'd expect nothing less." The quiet stretched between us again and I turned to open my door. Knowing in my bones that my life would change from here forward, whether I let him in or not.

Rain pattered against my living room windows. I sat down my keys and slipped off my shoes. He stood near the couch, every inch of him coiled restraint and impossible stillness, like he didn't quite belong in rooms built for humans. I wanted to ask a thousand questions, but the exhaustion hit all at once, heavy and disorienting.

"I'm going to bed," I said softly. Making my way to the pantry and grabbing him a mound of blankets and pillows. I laid them out on the couch and waved my arms, "Here is your bed. We talk tomorrow."

And with that, I went to my bedroom. Laid in bed and covered my eyes. I could no longer do today. I was done.

I heard him from my room.

"Get rest, little light. I'll keep watch."

Something about the way he said it, steady and certain, made me almost believe him.

Chapter Nine

Leyla

I locked my bedroom door, for my own peace of mind I assumed more than anything. I had no doubt he could easily get in if he wanted to. Sleep came fast and easy for the first time in a week. The city sounds faded into a distant hum, replaced by something older, wilder, and far more insistent. My sleeping mind carried me to a place I hadn't consciously known existed, though I knew in my soul that it was intimately familiar.

THE DREAM

I found myself in a forest of impossible scale. Trees stretched so high I couldn't see their tops, their silver leaves shimmering as if dusted with starlight.

Mist coiled around gnarled roots like smoke caught midair, weaving itself into shapes that almost seemed alive. The air smelled of rain-soaked earth and something faintly metallic, tangling with the scent of my own fear. Every step pressed softly into mossy ground, yet each sound, each whisper of shifting leaves, echoed like it belonged to some secret audience. And then I saw him.

He stood in a clearing, calm and immovable, the shadows bending around him as though the forest itself deferred to his presence. His coat… dark and perfectly tailored, caught the faint silver light. His eyes, those same storm-gray depths, locked onto mine, and I felt it: recognition, longing, and a warning that hummed like a heartbeat through the air.

"You shouldn't be here," his voice was low, urgent.

"Where is here, Thalon?" I asked, though my voice barely carried.

"Not a place for mortals," he said softly. "Not yet."

The ground trembled. The mist thickened, curling higher, rising like ghostly fingers around my legs. Movement flickered at the edge of the clearing—dark shapes, jagged and crawling, shadows that weren't quite solid but weren't empty either. My heart hammered.

"Thalon?" I whispered. But he was gone.

The forest pulsed once… alive, aware. And then, everything shattered into darkness.

My room was filled with the night, heavy and silent. The sheets clung to me, damp with sweat. For a second, I couldn't tell if I was still dreaming. The air carried the faint scent of rain and smoke. And then something shifted. A cold wind swept through the room, though the window was closed. The shadows in the corner seemed to move, not with the rhythm of passing headlights, but with intent. My pulse thundered.

"Thalon?" I whispered. No answer. Then, suddenly—the door crashed open. Thalon burst into the room, hair crazed from deep sleep and energy rippling off him like heat.

"Leyla," he breathed, scanning the space as if expecting to find something lurking in the dark. "You're not safe."

My breath caught. "It was just a dream—"

"No." The word cut through the dark. "Something crossed over."

And before I could even ask what he meant, the lights flickered—and the shadows in the corner lunged.

The room exploded in motion.

I barely had time to scream before Thalon was between us, light crackling off his skin like lightning caged too long. The air hummed, every atom vibrating under invisible pressure. The creature screamed, a sound so sick that I knew it didn't belong in this world, and Thalon struck. It wasn't a fight, not really.

It was annihilation.

The creature twisted, its form dissolving into ash and smoke, until all that was left was the faint scent of burned earth. And then, silence.

Thalon stumbled back, chest heaving, one hand pressed to the wall as if it were the only thing keeping him upright.

"It's gone," he murmured. "For now."

I couldn't speak. Couldn't move. That thing was in here with me. In the corner. Waiting. My throat burned with words I didn't understand how to say. When he finally looked at me, there was something raw in his expression, a rare vulnerability cracking through all that otherworldly calm.

"I'll explain in the morning, my powers are weaker here in this realm," his voice slurred with exhaustion. "Just… let me stay close tonight."

He dragged the chair from my desk and sat near my bed, one arm draped lazily across the armrest, his eyes half-lidded but still scanning the shadows. I watched him fight sleep for as long as he could, until his chin finally dipped and his breathing evened.

And for the first time in what seemed like days, I felt safe enough to close my eyes.

Chapter Ten

Thalon

Morning came softly, spilling gold across the floorboards. I hadn't meant to fall asleep, but the weight of exhaustion won. The bed was empty.

For one wild heartbeat, old instincts screamed. They took her.

Power surged to my hands, shadows clawing at the edges of control. Then, I heard the sound of something clatter. A small *"shit"* came from the kitchen.

"Leyla?" She turned, barefoot and sleepy, spatula in hand.

"I made breakfast." The smell of coffee and sugar hit me before her words did. For a moment, I could only stare, at the way sunlight touched her hair, the tiny crease between her brows, the warmth that had no place in my world. "No monsters," she said softly. "Just pancakes."

Something in my chest unclenched. "Sit," she said. "And start explaining."

I obeyed. She met my gaze evenly.

"Start with the thing in my room."

"It wasn't a thing," I said. "It was a wraith. Drawn to your resonance."

"Resonance," she repeated, brow furrowing.

"The energy that vibrates between realms. Mortals can't feel it. But you… your magic hums with life itself."

Her lips parted. "When I touched you. That's when it started."

"Yes."

"And now they're hunting me."

"Yes."

Her voice trembled, but she held my gaze. "You could've warned me."

"I didn't realize it then. Your dream last night… I felt you cross over."

Her head tilted. "Cross over?"

"I followed your resonance," I admitted. "That wasn't a dream, Leyla. That was a crossing. Your power bridges what was never meant to touch again. You belong to both worlds."

She stared at me, a mixture of half-believing and half-thinking she was speaking with a mad man. "So, I'm what? I'm some kind of… link?"

"Likely the last *'link'* to exist, yes," I said. I pulled my shoulders back, knowing that this was far too much at once… But also knowing how little time we have for her to come to terms with her new reality. "Once, there was a Bridge that kept the realms alive. It fell when my father took the throne. Since then, our world has been dying. And not only ours, the other realms will start to see decay soon. Travel between realms is nearly nonexistent anymore. But when I found you… I felt a similar magic to what the bridge used to be."

"Your father?"

I nodded, voice low. "King Vaeris. He murdered the old royals and shattered the Bridge of Realms. My mother, his queen, was their friend. And when he bound me with his magic, I became his weapon."

Her eyes softened, pity glinting where fear might have been. I loathed it. Loathed him.

She began cutting fruit, likely sensing that I did not want or need her pity. Thank the Gods.

"You hate him." She stated as though it was obvious.

"Yes," I said simply. "And he fears you. Or rather, fears what he sensed in Orrynne—a magical disturbance. He is as paranoid of a King as they come. He wanted you dead."

The silence after that felt sacred. Heavy.

"You said you were his weapon," she whispered.

"Yes," I answered. Understanding crossing between us. Silence. The grip on her knife tightened.

"You came here to kill me, didn't you?" My gaze met the ground. Ashamed. I had no words for my mate. My beautiful mate who had a target on her head.

"I did."

"Past tense?" She questions. I look up at her eyes, fear that I placed there.

"Yes. Our kiss. Our connection. We are mates. Fated. It has stopped the hold that my father had over me. You have freed me, Leyla. Without even trying. His orders are no longer my will. That I can swear to you."

She nods her head and stares back at her fruit. Her hold on her knife, lightening just so. "You have saved me. More than once apparently. I have no reason to not believe you." She says more to herself out loud, but looks to me. "I would be lying if I said I could not feel something inside me changing. Waiting. Everything around me feels fragile. My senses are more heightened. There have been small…" She looked for the word. "Instances."

"It will only get worse. Unless you can control your powers."

"How?"

"Train. Learn to anchor what's waking inside you. Before it consumes you. Before he finds you."

"And you'll teach me?"

"If you'll let me." Her gaze lingered on me, afraid but unflinching.

"Then start now." And just like that, between the smell of coffee and fruit, the fate of the dying realms shifted course.

Interlude

Thalon — The Binding Sigil

I knelt in the center of Orrynne's throne room, the marble cold beneath my knees, but that was the least of my discomfort. The room gleamed with crystal pillars that refracted the light into fragile rainbows across the polished floor, each reflection perfect and cruel. They made everything beautiful, and yet I felt nothing but fear.

Father stood at the head of the hall, armor glinting like a blade of silver in the light. His presence filled the room, sharp and unyielding, and every subject watching from the balconies seemed to shrink beneath his gaze. I wanted to shrink, too, curl into myself and disappear. But I could not.

"Obey." His voice was smooth, deliberate.

He did not raise his hand. He did not need to. One word, and the room trembled. One word, and my stomach twisted with dread. I swallowed hard and tried to meet his gaze. I couldn't. Not fully. My eyes flicked to Mother. Cerys. She was bound, wrists chained, the silver from her cuffs still smoldering faintly, her hands trembling as she reached toward me. Her lips moved in a silent plea. I wanted to run to her, throw myself between her and him, but the silver sigil branded into my chest was already alive, writhing beneath my skin, pulling tight on my will like iron chains. Pain exploded through me, sharper than any fist, hotter than any fire. I gasped and tried to pull away, but the sigil clung, a living thing seeking to twist me into obedience.

Every breath burned, every heartbeat felt like it might rip me apart. Father's hand came down anyway, striking my side. The pain flared anew, and I fell forward, scraping my knees against the marble. I tasted blood, coppery and bitter. I hated that he could do this. I hated that he could strip me of my will and my dignity in a single motion. I despised that I was helpless.

Mother's scream cut through the room like ice. She was straining against her chains, her wrists raw and bleeding where the silver bit. I could see the panic in her eyes, the desperation that mirrored my own. And still, I could not reach her. The sigil's magic held me in place. I could only watch as Father's shadow passed over her, twisting the room with its authority, bending our lives into his design.

I clenched my fists and bit down on my lip until the blood mingled with my tears. The pain was unbearable, but beneath it, something flickered. Anger. Defiance. A promise.

I will free her. I will free us both.

I repeated it in my head like a prayer, a mantra.

I was small, but I could endure. I could survive. I could wait. Every detail of that day burned into my memory. The crystalline pillars, sharp and beautiful. The echo of Father's boots on marble. The sharp tang of burned silver. The way Mother's hair fell in waves around her pale, bruised face.

Every reflection, every whisper, every shard of pain was cataloged, stored for the future. Then came the silence after the ritual ended. The court, still and awed, whispered among themselves. I was left kneeling alone, my chest still burning,

Mother's cries fading into muffled sobs behind the guards. I dared a glance at her, and our eyes met. In hers, I saw everything I wanted to protect, everything I had failed to shield. But I also saw trust, fragile but unbroken.

She believed in me, even as I had no power. I curled my fingers into the floor and forced myself to stand, despite the lingering heat of the sigil. I would not let this define me. I would not let the chains of magic and fear hold me forever. I would learn every secret, every weakness, every hidden fear, and I would strike with precision. That night, when the guards finally dragged me to my chambers and I collapsed onto the cold bed, I did not cry. I did not scream.

I thought of Mother, of the boy I was, of the man I would become. And in the dark, I whispered to myself: 'I will not be broken. I will not be bound. And one day, he will learn what it means to fear.'

The sigil burned beneath my skin, but I welcomed it now, not as a chain, but as a reminder. Every mark of pain was a lesson. Every scar of magic was a promise. Every moment of helplessness was a spark waiting to ignite.

And I would wait.

I could wait.

I had to wait.

Chapter Eleven

Leyla

The drive to the bookstore was silent, except for the steady hum of tires against the road. Thalon sat beside me, seemingly deep in thought about something. His presence filling the small space like static before a storm. I tried not to glance at him too often. The inhuman stillness, the way his eyes scanned every passing car as if expecting one to sprout claws. It was unnerving.

"You really have to come?" I asked, my voice barely above the buzz of the heater.

"I'm not leaving you alone," he said. His tone was final, not unkind, but edged with something protective that made my chest tighten.

"Fine," I muttered. "But no scaring Mick. She's practically a sister to me and the only family I have."

When we pulled up to the shop, Mick was already inside, flipping the Open sign. She smiled when she saw me. And then she saw him trailing behind. Her brows furrowed instantly.

"Uh... morning?" She turned to Thalon as we stepped inside. "Are we doing the walk of shame this morning?" She wiggled her eyebrows in anticipation. I brushed past her and locked the door.

"We're closed today. It's an emergency."

"Excuse me?" Mick blinked, half laughing. "What kind of emergency closes our shop for the day? We have bills…"

"Mick. Please. Just… trust me," I pleaded with her quietly. There must've been something in my tone, because her smirk faded. She came around the counter, eyes darting between us.

"Alright," she said slowly, and turned the closed sign towards our sidewalk. "Start talking."

We sat in the little break room at the back — the one that always smelled like paper, cinnamon, and leaking espresso. I perched on the edge of the table while Thalon leaned against the wall, arms crossed. Even doing nothing, he radiated command. Mick watched him, half-expecting him to pull out a knife.

"So," I began, my voice unsteady. "Remember Brad?"

Her nose wrinkled. "Yeah. Hard to forget. What a douche-"

"I like her already." Thalon's voice interrupts and his face is lined with a knowing smirk. I ignore them both.

"He wasn't… he wasn't just Brad."

"Oh no," she said slowly. "Please don't say he's a serial killer."

"Worse," I whispered. "He wasn't human." Thalon's body tensed.

Mick barked a laugh. "Oh, for God's sake, Leyla. Did you not sleep? Because this…"

Thalon moved. Just a fraction.

But the lights flickered.

Mick froze.

"What the hell was that?"

"I'm learning this all at almost the same time as you, Mick. But I need your mind to be open. I need you to know that this is real. And that I am a part of it." She looked at me like she wanted to cry. I hated that. Hated seeing her worried. She rolled her shoulders back and took a deep breath. Bracing for whatever it was that was to come.

"Watch," Thalon said simply. The air thickened, like gravity itself leaned closer.

The shadows at his feet stretched, alive, curling around his boots.

The smell of earth filled the room, lightning and rain before a storm. Mick's chair creaked as she instinctively pushed it back.

"That's enough," I said, my voice trembling. "She believes you."

He ignored me, lifting one hand. The air shimmered. And then, with a sound that wasn't quite real, the shadows peeled away from him like smoke dissolving into light. Wings.

They unfurled slowly, impossibly wide, each feather edged in black with a violet light at their ends that caught the bookstore's fluorescent glare and turned it holy. The shelves seemed to shudder with the sudden wind that rushed through the room, pages fluttering open, the chime above the door singing like it knew a god had entered.

Mick's mouth fell open. "Holy. Actual. Shit."

I couldn't breathe. Couldn't move. He was… Magnificent. Terrifying. Beautiful. All in the same breath.

Every feather seemed alive, pulsing faintly with the same energy I'd felt when his hand brushed mine. The smell of ink and coffee tangled with the scent of rain and something ancient.

He met my gaze, voice low. "You wanted proof."

The world shrank to the space between us. I felt the pull in my chest again. The same one that had started this.

"They're real," I whispered.

"They are part of me," he said simply.

Mick stumbled back, knocking into the table. "Leyla, he… He has wings."

"I see that," I murmured.

"You're calm about this," she snapped. "Why are you calm?"

Because I couldn't look away. Thalon's wings folded slowly, shadows wrapping around him again until they were gone. The light dimmed; the air steadied. He looked less celestial now, but somehow more dangerous for it.

"So, what? He's a magician? An alien? Jesus, Ley, you're scaring me."

"I'm scared too," I looked to her. "But I don't get to pretend it's not real. People… Creatures, hunters, they're after me. I've been having these strange dreams. Something is happening. There are things that are now attacking me, targeting me. I can't avoid it, Mick." Silence hung heavy between us.

"Something woke in her," Thalon said, cutting gently across my words. "She's connected to the bridge between worlds. That's why she's being hunted. Why I'm here." Mick stared at him like she was waiting for the illusion to crack. It didn't.

Mick swallowed, jaw tight. "You're telling me monsters are real, and my best friend's mixed up in it? No. That's not…"

Elias appeared from the doorway like a conjured thought, golden-haired and lazy-smiled. "He prefers Fae, darling. And I'm the sane one."

Mick jumped. "Who the hell… where did you come from?"

He grinned. "Long story. We're working on our mortal manners."

"More like your mortal boundaries," I muttered.

Elias winked. "We don't have those where we're from."

Thalon shot him a glare that could have burned stone. "Enough."

I turned back to Mick. "I told you something's happening. He saved me. He's… teaching me."

She pressed a hand to her chest, still pale. "Teaching you what? How to sprout demon wings?"

Thalon's lips curved slightly. "If only it were that simple."

Finally, she turned to me, voice trembling. "Leyla… what does that even mean?"

"It means," I said softly, "that I'm not just in danger, I am danger. To myself, to you, maybe everyone." Thalon stepped forward then, careful, controlled.

"She needs training. If she doesn't learn to manage what's inside her, others will come for her—and they won't stop."

Mick's hands were shaking, but she lifted her chin. "So, what? You're her… what? Monster mentor now?"

He didn't flinch. "If that's what it takes."

Her lips parted like she wanted to argue, but the memory of his wings silenced her.

After a long, tense pause, she exhaled shakily. "Fine. I'll help. But if either of them pull any freaky dark-magic crap near me, I'm out."

"That's fair," I said, trying to smile.

Mick managed a weak laugh. "You owe me so much wine for this, Ley."

Thalon gave her a small nod, the faintest hint of respect in his gaze. "You're stronger than you think, too," he said.

"More like I need something strong," Mick muttered under her breath.

The four of us stood there in the quiet of the shop, between the hum of the old cooler and the coffee stained table. And for the first time, I realized something: this was the start of whatever came next.

Chapter Twelve

Leyla

We stayed closed the rest of the day. The storm outside rolled in quietly, dark clouds smearing across the windows. The shop felt suspended between worlds. Books breathing, light flickering, the air laced with rain and something ancient. Mick made coffee. Elias flipped through a poetry book, muttering sarcastic commentary under his breath. And Thalon… Watching me. Training me.

Always watching, though. It wasn't creepy.

Maybe a little.

But I found I quite liked it. I probably needed a therapist.

His gaze felt like heat; patient, deliberate, and searching for something I didn't know I had.

"Try again," he said softly. We were standing in the aisle between mythology and astronomy, the smell of paper and static sharp in the air. I held my hands out the way he'd shown me, palms open.

"It's not working."

"It is," he said. "You're listening with fear instead of focus."

I exhaled sharply. "I'm not afraid."

"Little light," he murmured, stepping closer, "your heartbeat disagrees."

I glared up at him, ready to retort, but the moment I did, the air changed. That same hum vibrating between us. He was close enough that the faint shimmer of his power brushed my skin like static. I thought back to last night… when he kissed me. Those lips. I wanted more.

The shadows around his shoulders stirred, whispering. His eyes flickered with recognition, and then, lust. I felt my cheeks go pink as the heat in the shop rose.

Mick appeared at the end of the aisle, coffee in hand, frozen mid-step. "Am I interrupting something?"

Elias leaned around the other end of the aisle, amused. "Only the impending apocalypse."

Thalon ignored them both. "You're fighting it," his voice low. "You keep trying to control something meant to flow through you."

"And how exactly do I do that?"

"Stop pretending you're human," he said simply.

The words hit harder than they should have. The lights flickered again, a pulse that matched the rhythm in my chest. Something deep inside me answered, a resonance that wasn't entirely my own. I felt it in my bones; the bridge he spoke of, the living thread connecting realms. And then… the shelves shuddered.

Books began to lift, pages fluttering open like wings. The air around us thickened with energy, bright and alive.

Mick yelped. "Leyla—"

"I'm not doing it!" I said, voice shaking.

Thalon stepped behind me, his presence a wall of heat and command. "Yes, you are. Don't fight it."

I couldn't breathe. "It's too much."

His hand found my wrist… firm, grounding. "Breathe, little light. Anchor it."

The energy coiled, wild, but his voice cut through it. Low, steady, certain. I focused on it.

On him and his darkness… His shadows. And the chaos softened.

The books floated down. The air stilled.

When I turned, his eyes burned in to me. For a heartbeat, everything in the room; the storm, the flickering lights, the entire trembling universe just disappeared beneath the weight of that gaze.

"You did it," soft pride ringing through.

Mick let out a shaky breath. "Well," she muttered, "that was terrifyingly cool."

Elias clapped lazily. "That's progress, Bridge. Not too shabby."

Thalon ignored him, his attention still on me. "You see now? You are not powerless."

I nodded slowly, still shaking. "But I can't control it."

"No," he said. "Not yet."

The tension broke with a soft crack of thunder outside. Rain tapped against the windows, steady and cleansing. Mick turned the Closed sign to Open, just for comfort; like pretending we were normal again might make it true.

"Elias will stay with you both," he said, his voice a low rumble that made the air itself seem to lean closer. "I have a matter to attend to. Leyla, if it's okay with you… I think Elias and I should stay with you, at least until we have your powers under control."

I nodded automatically. My pulse was still uneven from the weight of everything that had happened… The wings, the air, the strange hum in my bones that hadn't gone quiet since.

Mick elbowed me sharply.

"Right. No," I corrected myself. "I just met you. Mick, can you stay with us too? We can both sleep in my bed. They can take the living room."

She nodded instantly, folding her arms. "Damn right. You think I'm letting you stay alone with two immortal men in your apartment alone? Not a chance. You'll thank me later."

Her tone was light, but her eyes weren't. For once, the reckless one was the cautious one.

Seems the tables had turned.

Thalon's jaw tightened; whether from amusement or restraint, I couldn't tell. His gaze lingered on me a heartbeat longer than it should have.

"And Leyla, the world won't wait for you to accept what you are," he said quietly.

"And what am I?" I asked.

He looked over his shoulder, that shadow-soft smile curving his mouth.

"Mine."

And then he was gone. Mick's eyebrows shot to her hairline. In no way was she prepared for the amount of intensity this man…. This *Fae'*… brought to the table.

Truthfully, neither was I.

Chapter Thirteen

Leyla

The week blurred together. Wings, shadows, electricity, near-breakthroughs, and failure. Every night after closing, we drove past the last gas station in town and into the fields where the land opened into nothing. Far from eyes that might notice a girl bending the light wrong. It was quiet there, safe enough for Thalon to teach without worrying about who, or what, might be watching. By the fourth night, my hands ached from holding energy that refused to stay.

The air shimmered when he guided me through focus drills, but the light would sputter and fade, leaving only the sound of my ragged breathing.

"Again," Thalon said, his voice even. I glared at him through the dark.

"You say that like it's working."

"It is working," he replied calmly. "Just not how you expect, little light." I rolled my eyes at his little name for me.

"Feels like failure."

He stepped closer, the dead grass crumbling under his boots. "Power isn't forced into obedience. It's invited. You're still fighting it. I wish I could assist more, my power is at insignificant levels in this world."

I turned away, staring out toward the tree line. The night air felt heavy, humming faintly against my skin, the same resonance he kept talking about. "Maybe it's fighting me."

Behind me, Thalon exhaled softly, and when he spoke again, it was quieter. "That's because it remembers what it was. What you were."

I frowned. "What does that mean?"

He hesitated before answering. "In the Borderlands, where I suspect your lineage to derive from, the bridge acted as life and possibility between realms. Your lineage, they were born of life magic… pure creation. When my father shattered the bridge, he betrayed that magic. Betrayed life itself. What you feel inside you isn't chaos. It's grief."

"A bridge can grieve?" I ask. Not to be offensive, it seems important to his people. But needing clarity all the same.

"Essentially. The bridge is physical, yes. But, it was created by life magic. The bridge is accessible to all Fae no matter their location. It is linked to the fae's emotions and being. The bridge is an accessible magic instilled in all fae from birth, thanks to the life magic created by your lineage. The bridge has emotions. And it is hurt that it was betrayed."

"By your people," I said, the accusation slipping out before I could stop it.

Thalon didn't deny it. "By my father."

The silence that followed was sharp enough to cut. I looked at him then, really looked, and saw something like regret behind the calm mask he always wore. After that, the training went quiet. He corrected my stance, adjusted my breathing, but neither of us said much more.

By the seventh night, I was unraveling. My body ached. My dreams bled into waking. The shadows that once whispered now spoke full sentences, their voices curling around my name.

Sometimes, I woke up tangled in my sheets, the faint scent of smoke lingering as though something had followed me back.

Everyone had practically moved in. The space was tight. We were all walking on top of each other.

It made my nervous system go into overdrive. Thalon learned to make what he called, "human pancakes." He and Elias took a break from their intensity to make us breakfast. It was nice. But crowded.

The looks Thalon gave me ignited a fire in my soul. I wanted space. I wanted space with him.

Mick noticed my burnout first. "You look like you've been living on black coffee and stress," she said as I flipped the sign to Closed one evening.

She was perched on the counter, twirling her keys. "You two need a break."

"I can't just stop," I muttered. "If I don't get control of this—"

"You won't," she interrupted, hopping down. "Not if you burn yourself out first."

Thalon leaned in the doorway, silent as ever. His expression said he disagreed, but not strongly enough to argue with her. Mick grinned, sensing her advantage. "There's the fall festival in town this weekend… Halloween Town, remember? The corn maze, the bonfire, all that stuff. We could use some normal human fun."

"I don't really do… crowds," Thalon said, crossing his arms.

"Yeah, and I don't do apocalyptic fae princes, but here we are," she shot back. "Come on, all of us can go. I'll drive."

Thalon glanced at me, uncertainty flickering across his face, then nodded reluctantly. "If she insists."

"Good, because I do." Mick said, clapping her hands. "Tomorrow night. And you…" she pointed at me with her mischievous grin, "are wearing something cute."

I rolled my eyes, but the idea of a night away from training my nearly non-existent magic didn't sound so bad.

Chapter Fourteen

Leyla

The next night came faster than I was ready for. Rain had washed the city clean, and the air carried that crisp bite of late October. Bonfires, fallen leaves, and the faint sweetness of caramel from the festival downtown. The apartment was chaos.

Mick had music blaring from the bedroom while she hunted for her other boot, and Elias was leaning against the kitchen counter with the kind of amused smirk that said he'd been watching us all night like some form of entertainment.

"Mortals," he murmured to Thalon, who was sitting stiffly on the couch. "They take longer to prepare for war than we do."

"War doesn't involve eyeliner," Mick shot back from down the hall.

Thalon didn't respond.

He hadn't said much all evening, but the tension rolling off him was enough to fill the room. I could feel him watching the hallway, even before I stepped out.

Mick emerged first, her short black dress and witch hat somehow both ridiculous and perfect, her confidence blazing.

"Ready to haunt some hearts?" she said, spinning once.

Elias gave a low whistle. "If hearts don't stop first."

Her grin widened as I stepped out behind her. My outfit wasn't my idea, it had been hers. A deep green velvet corset that clung a little too perfectly, a slit skirt brushing my thighs, and boots that had no business being as tall as they were. A delicate gold chain looped around my arm like a charm. I felt exposed and powerful all at once, like someone I didn't quite know yet.

Mick smirked. "See? Worth the suffering."

But I didn't see Mick. Not really.

Because Thalon had stopped breathing.

He stood slowly from the couch, shadows curling around his boots like mist. His eyes, those storm-gray depths, swept over me once, lingering where they shouldn't. His throat worked like he'd swallowed a word too dangerous to speak aloud. The silence stretched, electric.

Elias elbowed him lightly. "You're staring again, Prince."

Thalon blinked, tearing his gaze away with effort. "She's… overdressed for mortal festivities," he said, voice too even to be real.

Mick snorted. "That's code for you look incredible, by the way." Heat rose to my cheeks.

"We're going to be late," I said, grabbing my coat before either of them could make it worse.

Elias offered Mick his arm with a mock bow. "Shall we, little witch?"

She rolled her eyes but took it, laughing as they stepped into the hall ahead of us. That left Thalon and me. I started toward the door, but the air shifted. Heavy. Charged.

He didn't follow. Not right away.

When I turned, he was still standing in the dim light of the apartment, his gaze fixed on me like I was the only thing tethering him to this realm.

"Thalon," I said softly. "They're waiting."

He took a slow step forward. "Let them."

The words brushed over my skin like a touch. Before I could think, before I could breathe, he closed the space between us. His hand slid to the back of my neck, and the world tilted. My spine hit the wall; gently, but firm enough that I felt the strength he was holding back.

"Thalon—" I started, but his voice cut through the air, low and dangerous.

"Do you have any idea what you do to me?" My breath caught.

The hallway light flickered; his magic leaking through control. He didn't wait for an answer. His lips found mine in one smooth, devastating motion. It wasn't gentle. It wasn't patient.

It was fire, all restraint finally breaking.

His hand tangled my curls, his mouth demanding, claiming, tasting like rain and dark wine. My knees nearly gave out, but he caught me, pressing closer until there was no space left to hide. The faint hum I'd felt since meeting him roared to life, flooding through me.

That connection, the bond he swore existed between us, it sang. Light and dark twisting together, sparking in every nerve. When he finally pulled back, his forehead rested against mine, breath uneven.

"You shouldn't let me do that," he murmured.

"You shouldn't want to," I whispered back.

He smiled… that slow, dangerous thing that stole every coherent thought from my head.

"Too late for that."

Outside, a sharp honk shattered the moment. Mick, of course. "Come on!" she shouted through the car window. "We're going to miss the haunted corn and the cider!"

Thalon exhaled through his nose, pulling back just enough to meet my gaze. His thumb traced the edge of my jaw, deliberate, lingering. "This isn't over."

I swallowed, trying to find words that didn't exist. "Didn't think it was."

He smirked… the smallest hint of mischief. "After you, little light."

The drive to the festival was a blur of neon and laughter. Mick and Elias bickered like they had known each other for years, the air thick with teasing and flirtation.

I sat quietly in the backseat, next to Thalon. My heart still trying to catch up with what had happened. Every time I glanced up, Thalon's reflection met mine in the window. His gaze was steady, unreadable. But beneath it, I could feel it… that same tether pulling tight between us.

When the festival lights came into view, glowing like distant fireflies, he reached over and brushed his fingers against my thigh, a whisper of touch.

Just enough to remind me.

That no matter how far the night carried us, I was already his.

Chapter Fifteen

Leyla

The festival glowed like something out of a dream. Strings of orange lights stretched between food trucks, laughter carried on the cool air, and the smell of caramel and bonfire smoke tangled together like memory.

I tried not to stare, but it was impossible. He moved through the crowd with a kind of quiet authority that made everything else fade. Even surrounded by laughter and flickering lights, he looked otherworldly. Too composed, too dangerous, too him.

When his gaze found mine, it was like the entire fair fell away.

The noise. The crowd. The music.

Gone.

Only that sharp gray heat, pinning me where I stood.

"Your mortal traditions," his voice low enough to make my pulse stutter. "They're… loud."

Elias chuckled. "Translation: he hates fun."

Thalon ignored him completely, his eyes still on me.

"You look…" He trailed off, searching for the right word. Then his voice dropped, almost reverent. "…unreal."

Heat shot up my neck. "You mean ridiculous."

"I do not."

Before I could respond, Mick hooked her arm through mine. "Alright, brooding prince, let the witch have her fun. Corn maze awaits!"

Elias offered her a mock bow. "Lead the way, enchantress."

We headed off toward the maze entrance. Thalon stayed close behind me, silent, his presence a steady thrum at my back.

The maze swallowed us, sunlight dwindling as the stalks grew taller around us. Laughter echoed from distant paths, the smell of earth and dried corn filling the air. For a while, Mick and I walked side by side, her whispering about *"losing the boys"* and chatting lightly through the maze while *'the boys'* were no longer behind us. But soon the path split, and she darted ahead. I stayed behind, trying not to let my thoughts spiral.

And then I felt it. Presence.

I didn't see him at first. Just felt him near.

I turned a corner and collided with a wall. A hard chest, actually. My breath caught. My hands went up instinctively, brushing against the front of the coat I recognized before I even looked up.

"Thalon," I breathed, my voice barely audible over the rustle of corn, the distant screams.

He didn't say anything at first. His gray eyes capturing mine, storm-laden and unrelenting. Electricity raced across my skin at the mere brush of our hands.

My fingers tingled. My heart hammered.

Every rational thought scattered.

"You're not safe out here by yourself, mate." There's that word again. The one that seems to pull me closer. The one that scares me… But also sends a small thrill through my chest.

His hand hovered just inches from mine, a teasing promise of touch… The little touches, the whispers of promises over the past week. It was all building far too fast, and yet far… Far too slowly.

His lips curved faintly, almost imperceptibly, like he was testing the gravity of the moment.

"I…" I started, but the words faltered under the pull of him.

The world around us disappeared. The rustling corn, the distant laughter, the chaos of the fair… All of it dissolved into nothing but the static electricity of being near him. Every brush of fabric, every subtle motion sent shivers down my spine. My senses were screaming, and I couldn't tell if it was fear, desire, or both. I dared a step closer. He mirrored me.

The space between us shrank to a whisper. His hand rose slowly, hovering near my jaw, and I leaned into the sensation, breath catching, heat pooling deep in my chest. A silence stretched between us, heavy and electric. The distant sounds of the fair faded to a murmur. My stomach fluttered, nerves alight with anticipation, and for a brief, suspended moment, I forgot everything… Mick, the crowd, even myself—except for him.

And then, suddenly, a rustling ahead had us both in our fighting stance and ready for whoever dared to interrupt our moment. A person in a ridiculous scarecrow costume jumped out, arms flailing, trying to startle us.

My heart lurched in surprise, but Thalon moved faster than I could react. He stepped forward, his presence instantly dominating the cornfield. And I swear the figure practically shrieked and stumbled backward, eyes wide, flailing like a puppet.

"Get lost," Thalon commanded, his voice low and dangerous.

The scarecrow froze for a moment, then bolted down a side path without another word. I blinked, heart still racing, when he turned back to me, the storm in his eyes softening just slightly.

Without a word, we began walking side by side into the deeper twists of the corn maze, our steps slow and deliberate, the tension between us crackling like the last sparks of a fire that refused to die. And somehow, in that charged quiet, I felt… safe.

Chapter Sixteen

Leyla

We moved cautiously through the maze, the cornstalks brushing against our arms, rustling in the wind like whispers just out of reach. My pulse thudded in my ears, my heart racing not entirely from fear of what may be around the corner.

Every step I took, I could feel the heat of his body near mine, the steady strength in his stride. The earlier scare still hummed under my skin, leaving me both exhilarated and unnervingly aware of him.

"You're not scared anymore," he murmured, his voice low, teasing, almost playful.

"I'm… cautious," I replied, trying to sound composed, though my stomach twisted and my hands itched to touch him. I felt ridiculous next to him in this costume. We caught up with Mick, and Elias found his way to our small group as well, saying goodbye to a group of girls who had trailed behind him.

Ahead of us, Mick's laughter cut through the dark. She was a beacon of light and chaos, swinging her flashlight back and forth, skipping like the world had never known fear. Elias trailed after her, pretending to be annoyed, though I caught the small tilt of his grin.

Thalon and I stayed behind, a quiet shadow to their noise. His hand brushed mine once, twice, deliberately accidental. The simple contact made the air hum.

My stomach twisted, heat and nerves tangled until I couldn't tell which was which.

We were halfway through when it happened.

A sound… Sharp and wrong. A rustle that didn't belong to wind.

Then came the growl. Low. Animal. Too close. A scream shattered the air.

Mick.

"Go!" Thalon's command tore through the silence like thunder. Elias was already sprinting, flashlight beam slicing wild arcs through the rows. Thalon grabbed my wrist, pulling me after them, and the world blurred. Corn, dirt, sky, all flashing by too fast. We burst into a clearing, the ground torn up, stalks flattened in violent spirals.

Mick lay sprawled on the ground, her leg slick with blood. Elias knelt beside her, his face pale, eyes burning with the kind of fury that came from fear.

"Oh my God! Mick!" I dropped to my knees, reaching for her. "It's okay, it's okay, just…."

She gasped, trembling, voice fractured. "It came out of nowhere."

Thalon's head snapped up, his body going still. The air changed.

A shadow moved behind her.

Something long, lean, and wrong. A creature… Its skeletal body crawling with pale tattered skin. Its eyes burned faintly silver.

It wasn't human. A wraith.

Elias lifted a knife, ready, but the thing lunged before he could react. Thalon shoved him aside, summoning a flicker of shadowed light from his palm, magic that sparked and fizzled before it reached the creature.

It wasn't fear this time. Or anger. It was deeper, ancient, something that didn't feel entirely my own. My chest burned, my pulse turned molten, and I couldn't breathe. The air around me began to vibrate.

"Leyla—" Thalon's voice reached me, distant, drowned out by the ringing in my ears. I wasn't thinking. I wasn't even me anymore. I was every heartbeat of the world.

The pressure built until I thought I would shatter. And then… I did.

Light erupted. Not gold. Not white. Something between, like dawn breaking through storm clouds. It poured from my hands in rivers, twisting with shadow, alive and wild.

The creature shrieked, its body disintegrating into ash and smoke, the sound splitting the air like metal screaming. I couldn't stop it. I didn't want to stop it.

The light kept coming.

Mick was saying my name. Elias was shouting something I couldn't hear. Thalon's power clashed against mine, trying to contain it, but it was too much. Too vast.

The ground trembled. The maze bent.

Every cornstalk leaned toward me. The light began to change, threads of it bleeding into the dirt, running across the field like molten glass veins. The earth cracked open in thin fractures that pulsed with color.

"Leyla!" Thalon's voice boomed through the chaos. "Stop! You have to stop!"

But I couldn't. The magic wasn't leaving me, it was becoming me. The light inside my chest clawed toward the sky, desperate, hungry. The air split with a sound like thunder turned inside out.

"The Bridge!" Elias shouted. "Thalon, it's opening!"

A rift tore through the night above us, a fissure of light and shadow, infinite and alive. It pulsed like a heartbeat, and I felt it answer mine.

Thalon's arms were around me in the next instant, solid and fierce. "Leyla, listen to me. Breathe. Let it go. You are not ready yet!"

"I can't—"

"You must!"

He pressed his forehead against mine, his voice breaking like he could force calm into my veins. "Leyla, look at me— look at me!" But the magic had already claimed me. The bridge roared its grief.

The earth beneath us dissolved into blinding radiance. I saw Mick clutching Elias's arm, saw Thalon's hands on my face, his eyes blazing silver and full of something I had never seen before. Fear.

And then the sky tore open. The light seemed to consume everything.

We fell upward, into the crack of creation, into the nothing between worlds.

Thalon's shout echoed through the blinding white: "Hold on to me!"

I reached for him. But then there was only light. And falling.

Chapter Seventeen

Leyla

Falling didn't feel like falling.

It felt like being unmade.

The air tore away from my lungs, and sound vanished altogether. For a heartbeat, or maybe forever, there was only light. Blinding, endless light. Then the light fractured, and darkness poured in to devour it.

I couldn't tell which way was up. Couldn't tell if I was moving at all or simply suspended in nothing. My fingers reached for something, anything, but only found the texture of air that felt alive.

"Leyla!" Mick's voice echoed from somewhere far away, muffled by a thousand voices, a thousand shadows. I reached for it, my hand brushing something. Her hand. Warm and trembling and human. That small connection was enough to keep me anchored.

The rest of me was weightless, drifting through what looked like smoke and stars all at once. Threads of light twisted through the void, each one pulsing like a heartbeat. Some were warm gold, some deep violet, and some—some looked alive.

They moved like veins through the darkness, carrying whispers.

Whispers that knew my name.

You've been found.

The words rippled through the air, the same as the letter that had started all of this. Only now, they sounded older. Deeper. Like the voice belonged to something that had been waiting for centuries.

"What are you?" I tried to shout, but my voice came out soundless, absorbed by the shifting mist.

You are the Bridge.

Mick's touch was gone. The light around me flared, threads twisting toward my chest until they sank into me, glowing through my skin. Images flashed before my eyes. A woman with silver hair wearing a crown of thorns. A city made entirely of glass. A boy with wings made of night, huddled and hurt. A forest burning with fire and smoke. And a throne carved from mirrored glass dripping in blood.

Each vision struck like lightening, gone before I could understand it.

Thalon's voice, sharp and raw, cut through the haze. "Leyla!"

The void cracked. Light fractured around me, and suddenly he was there.

Thalon.

His hand reaching through the chaos, the edges of his form flickering like static. Behind him, Elias was a blur of motion, fighting to hold open a rip that twisted the air itself.

"Take my hand!" It was a plea, raw and frayed.

I reached. The distance stretched and collapsed all at once, as if the space between us didn't obey the same laws anymore. The moment our fingers touched, the universe convulsed. Power surged through the connection. Searing, divine, and just… Impossible. It felt like the world itself recognized us and tried to rewrite its shape around that truth. The darkness screamed.

Light collapsed inward, pulling us with it, and everything folded into a single, blinding point, and then burst.

I hit the ground hard enough to knock the air from my lungs. For a long moment, all I could hear was the pounding of my heart.

Then, slowly, the world began to rebuild itself around me. I was lying on cool dead grass. The air shimmered faintly, carrying the scent of rain and something sweet, like wild honey. Above me, stretched a sky that looked nothing like Earth's. The stars were moving, tracing patterns in slow, deliberate arcs, and two moons hung low on the horizon, one a pale gold, one a soft blue.

Mick was sprawled beside me, groaning, her blonde hair tangled with bits of glowing twigs. "Please tell me that was a bad acid trip."

Elias stood a few feet away, brushing dust from his coat with infuriating calm. "Welcome to Orrynne," he said dryly.

I blinked at him, then turned to Thalon. He was kneeling next to me, breathing hard, a faint shimmer of silver veins still pulsing under his skin from whatever he'd done to pull us through. His eyes met mine, full of exhaustion and something deeper.

"You're hurt," I whispered.

He shook his head. "Not badly. The crossing burns."

"Crossing?"

"The space between realms," Elias answered. "You ripped a hole through it. Congratulations."

Mick groaned again. "Oh, good. So, we're not dead?"

"Not yet," Elias replied cheerfully.

I pushed myself upright, every muscle trembling. I glanced down at Mick's leg, satisfied that even though I may have caused some sort of an explosion… Her leg was healed. She was no longer bleeding out. She saw my eyes and looked down at her legs, searching for her gashes. Now, just stained red skin remained.

The world tilted slightly, too vivid, too real. Even the wind seemed to hum, brushing against my skin like it recognized me.

"Thalon…" I said softly. "Where are we exactly?"

He glanced toward the horizon. The forest glowed faintly where the light of the twin moons touched the branches, turning them silver-blue. The air felt thick with power. Older and heavier than Earth.

"The Borderlands," he said at last. "Where your ancestors were born."

Elias snorted. "A fine place to crash, really. A place with no rules, and creatures that like the taste of mortal fear. Oh, and can't forget the witches and vampires."

Mick shot him a glare. "You're really bad at comforting people, you know that?"

He smirked. "I wasn't trying to comfort you."

I stood slowly, my legs unsteady. When I looked down, I saw faint light still threaded beneath my skin, pulsing in rhythm with the world around me. Thalon's gaze followed it, unreadable.

"It's begun," he murmured.

"What has?"

He met my eyes. "The bond between you and the bridge. It recognized you when you crossed. You're marked now, Leyla. You can't go back. At least not yet." Mick stumbled to her feet beside me, gripping my arm for balance.

"Excuse me? Not yet? As in… we're stuck here?"

Elias sighed, looking to Thalon. "You want to tell her or should I?"

Thalon hesitated, his jaw tightening. "The bridge hasn't revealed any sort of power in over twenty years. We all thought it was destroyed. The amount of power you just displayed, it wasn't just power—It was resurrection. You need to learn to control it to bring it back. That could take days, maybe weeks. Until then…" His eyes softened. "We will survive here."

Mick blinked, staring between them. "Survive? No. No, I didn't sign up for surviving. I came for caramel apples and corn mazes, not otherworldly exile!"

Despite the fear curling through me, a laugh bubbled up. It came out broken, but real. Thalon's expression eased at the sound. Just slightly.

Elias turned toward the shimmering treeline, his tone shifting from amused to wary. "We should move. If we landed here, others felt it too."

"Others?" Mick asked, her voice barely a whisper.

"Things that hunt the border," Thalon said quietly. "Drawn to your type of magic."

The wind shifted, and somewhere in the distance, something howled. Not a wolf. Not anything from our world.

Thalon extended a hand to me. "Stay close." I took it.

The warmth of his skin grounded me as the air around us seemed to hold its breath. The path ahead glowed faintly, winding deeper into the drained silver forest. And as we stepped into it, the sky above us shifted, stars rearranging into the shape of a crown. I didn't know what it meant. But I knew, deep down, that Orrynne had been waiting for me all along.

Chapter Eighteen

Thalon

The landing was brutal. The crossing left a residue on me, a low hum beneath my skin. This time it was stronger. She was the source. Her presence had torn the veil open, and even after guiding her through, she carried the shock in her very bones. I watched her rise slowly, trembling, her wide eyes drinking in the glow of the Borderlands. She did not know how dangerous this place was, how easy it was to lose herself here.

The air itself was alive, heavy with magic that whispered secrets we weren't meant to understand.

"Stay close," I murmured, even though my hand had already found hers.

Her fingers curled around mine, small and warm, grounding me more than she could ever know. Mick groaned somewhere behind us, stumbling over dried shimmering roots, and Elias moved ahead with that infuriatingly calm stride of his, brushing at the air as though he could smooth out the chaos. I knew the moment we arrived, others had felt it too. Shadows twisted between the trees, shifting with intent. Not all who watched were creatures of malice, but in this place, intent could cut as deep as any blade.

The magic here was feral, unbound and ancient. While the rest of the courts in Orrynne struggled to maintain their magic, the Borderlands did not. The magic coiled around the soul, whispered to the weak-minded, tempted the desperate. Even now, I could feel it pressing against Leyla's skin, curious. Drawn to her.

I scanned the edges of the tree line, muscles coiled, senses straining. How different this had become from her world. Once a world with the most beautiful creatures and vast colors, now covered in death and destruction.

"They will be here soon," I said quietly, more to myself than to anyone else.

Elias glanced at me, expression unreadable. "I expected nothing less."

Leyla's voice broke the tension, soft, almost reverent.

"It's beautiful."

I looked at her in confusion. Her gaze landed on the horizon with quiet wonder, twin moons reflected in her eyes. The land pulsed faintly beneath our feet, something it hadn't done in decades. Rivers of silver light winding through the dark. A stag stood in the distance, antlers tipped in gold, its eyes bright as stars. The creature bowed once, slow and deliberate, before vanishing into the mist. And she smiled.

How could she smile here… In a place that devoured beauty as easily as it created it?

"Beautiful can kill," I said, voice low. "Never let your awe make you careless."

She flinched slightly but didn't let go of my hand. I felt the pulse of her bond with the veil, still fragile, still screaming with energy she couldn't yet understand. My chest tightened at the thought. Every choice I made now could push her further into danger, or protect her. We moved forward slowly. The Borderlands reacted to us, the wind twisting, the air thickening, whispers threading through our minds. I kept a steady grip on her, alert for the first sign of movement in the shadows.

"Tell me about this place," she asked quietly.

I hesitated, then sighed. "The Borderlands exist between all realms. Part of Orrynne, yes. But untamed by any court. It is the marrow between worlds, a bridge of its own. Most fae avoid it. Magic here is wild… unpredictable. And it demands a toll from those who cross."

She glanced at me. "A toll?"

"Life," I said simply. "Magic. Sanity. Futures. The Borderlands take what they choose. Elias and I barely survived the last crossing."

Elias made a sound that might have been a scoff. "Barely survived? I'm insulted. We were mostly dead."

Mick shot him a glare. "That's supposed to be reassuring?"

He shrugged, smirking. "You're still breathing, aren't you?"

Leyla ignored them, her brow furrowed as she tried to piece it together. "And the Bridge?"

My chest tightened. "Once, the Bridge made travel between realms effortless. Fae, mortals, spirits, all connected by its life magic. My father sought to destroy that unity. He wanted control, isolation. When the King and Queen of the Borderlands were murdered, the Bridge shattered. What remains is this… dying land, fading magic, a single fragile portal; practically pointless in itself due to its danger, and death to our kind. Not a single fae has been born since he has taken the throne. The Bridge was created by life-magic, with it destroyed, the land has punished us. And soon, other realms will see the same effects."

Elias' voice turned grim. "A realm slowly bleeding out while the King rots on his throne."

I didn't look at him. I couldn't.

Mick's voice peaked out through our conversation. I forgot she was even here. "What is out there?"

Elias chuckled, dark and dry. "You've already survived the crossing; the rest will test you differently. There are too many unknowns out here in the wild."

I didn't correct him. There was no reason to pretend. The Borderlands didn't allow half-truths. A flicker at the edge of the woods caught my eye, movement too quick for a human to track. I froze, listening. The air tasted of iron and smoke, and instinct prickled along my spine. Vampires.

"They're here," I said softly, sliding a protective arm around my mate's shoulders. "But they're watching, not attacking. Yet." Leyla's pulse thrummed against my side. I felt it, raw and unrefined, and a strange surge of protectiveness flared in me. Here, in the Borderlands, the connection between us mattered more than any rule or court.

"Thalon," she whispered, voice trembling, "what happens now?"

I let out a slow breath and tightened my grip just slightly. "Now. We survive the night. We learn. And we keep moving.

The Borderlands are patient, and depending on if the vampires have had a good meal, they can be reasoned with. I do not believe the vampires are the ones that pose the highest threat at the moment. The witches are… let's say a little more unpredictable. Less refined."

"Echoes are what we need to keep an eye out for." Elias chimed in.

The wind shifted again, carrying a low, melodic hum. Somewhere in the distance, a shadow moved with deliberate purpose, its shape inhuman. I didn't flinch, but my eyes narrowed. Leyla drew closer, and I felt the bond pulse again, stronger, brighter.

This world recognized her. It knew her.

And that recognition had painted a target across her back.

I would protect her. Whatever came next.

"They're drawn to her," I said, mostly to myself.

Leyla's pulse hammered against my side.

I felt it, quick and chaotic.

Her magic called to them, whether she wanted it or not. She was a beacon, the bridge flowed through her veins, and they knew it. A rustling sound came from our right, concealed by the silver trees.

The creature stepped forward, silent, smooth, each motion predatory. The forest seemed to bend around it, shadows stretching and swallowing the light.

"Leyla. Focus," I ordered, my hand tightening over hers. "We cannot not let them touch you. At least, not yet."

Her eyes widened, but fear didn't win. She nodded once, her jaw tightening, that spark of defiance blazing through the terror. I could feel her magic bristling beneath her skin; chaotic, radiant, and dangerous.

The Echo lunged.

Instinct took over.

I shoved her behind me, shadows erupting as I drew a line of silver fire and shadows across the ground. The barrier hissed like water on flame, buying me a breath before the creature twisted and struck again. Leyla cried out… not in pain, but a warning.

Another Echo had broken through, its elongated hand gripping Mick's temple, feeding from her memories. Mick's scream cut through the clearing. Leyla moved before I could stop her, pure instinct and heart. She tore the creature's hand away, power flaring from her palms in frantic bursts of light. Elias appeared behind the Echo in a blink, his dagger at the ready.

The blade cut through smoke and flesh alike, and the creature dissolved into ash with a shriek.

And then… the world answered her.

Threads of light erupted from the earth, racing up Leyla's arms and coiling around her wrists. The air trembled as her magic intertwined with the land itself, forming a single pulse. The remaining Echo screeched, writhing as those threads wrapped around it and burned it into nothing.

Silence followed. The forest began to press in around us.

Leyla collapsed beside Mick, shaking, her chest heaving. Her hands fluttered helplessly over her friend's face.

"Help her," she whispered, voice breaking. "Please."

Elias knelt, gently lifting Mick from her arms. He carried her up a slope of dead grass, settling her beneath the soft glow of moonlight. I followed, keeping close to Leyla, ready for anything else the night might conjure. Mick's body jerked once.

Her breathing steadied.

Slowly, she stirred, eyes glassy but alive.

Her voice was hard to hear, barely audible. "I… Leyla, I can't remember. I know you, I know mom. I know why we are here… I can't remember anything before this. I…" she cried into my mate's hair. "What happened to me?"

Leyla looked up to me, searching for answers. Searching for something.

"They are Echoes." I look to Leyla. Elias's fists clenched at his sides. "They take memories, they can become you in a sense. That is how they live. They must have started from the beginning with Michaela. Her earlier memories can be restored, but it will take some time."

The tension radiating from Elias was palpable. "We are lucky she still remembers anything at all."

Leyla looked down to Mick, tears streaming down her face. "I am so sorry you are in this, Mick. We will find a way back home. I swear it." They cried with each other. For hours. For minutes. It was hard to tell. Elias and I looked away, letting them have this moment together.

Mick's voice was rough. "I don't think home is an option anymore, Ley. This is it for us, isn't it?" How likely those words are, she has no idea.

Leyla opened her mouth, but Mick continued. Her hand gripping Leyla's wrist with fierce determination. "No matter where we are, we have each other. Always. Don't you dare try to send me back alone, do you hear me? I'm staying. I'm not leaving you here."

"Mick…"

"Mick, nothing." She managed. "I'm staying, and I'm okay."

But hearing those words, the conviction behind them, shifted something in me. Even in the face of terror, Mick remained unbroken. Loyal to the bone. That kind of courage deserved respect. And from this moment on, she would have my protection; not only because she was tied to my mate, but because she had proven herself worthy of it.

Leyla clung to her friend, her sobs muffled against Mick's shoulder. Every sound still reached our ears; the quiet promises, the grief, the exhaustion.

Our bond hummed between us, a soft ache I couldn't ignore.

All I wanted was to ease my mate's worry. I could feel the sorrow in her bones. I could feel the worry for her sister.

We have barely spoken of what we were. What we are destined to be. I hadn't dared tell her the depth of what being my mate entailed. She was new to this world, still finding her footing. But the truth couldn't stay buried forever. Our fates had already entangled; her kiss had sealed it. Whether she knew the full depth of it or not, she was mine, bound not by possession, but by the inexorable pull of our bond.

And I would protect her until the end.

The forest shifted again, and I felt it. The weight of unseen eyes, the watchers gathering beyond the trees. Whatever had come for her wasn't done. The air smelled of blood and starlight, a promise of violence waiting to break.

"We are not safe here," I murmured. "Not yet. We need to find camp. Elias and I will take shifts."

Leyla's eyes looked to me, small and unsteady, but I felt something else too… A flicker of trust. The Borderlands were patient. And so was I. But whatever hunted us would not wait.

And I would not let it take her.

We made camp miles from where we'd fallen, near the Waystone, a monument of black stone etched with faintly glowing runes. As the sun bled into the horizon, Elias and I gathered what we could: branches, brush, a few unlucky forest creatures.

The fire crackled low, throwing shadows across the forest floor. Neither Mick nor Leyla commented on what was roasting, though their faces betrayed a quiet discomfort. Still, they ate. Hunger always won over hesitation.

Elias, ever the showman, produced a hidden vial of seasonings from his vest. Mick laughed, the sound thin but genuine, and called him a "walking spice rack." He looked smug for the rest of the meal. I could feel the tension on Leyla ease.

Once the fire dimmed, Elias and I agreed to take shifts. He volunteered first, settling near Mick, his posture relaxed but his eyes sharp. She murmured in her sleep, half-formed words spilling into the air, fragments of the memories she'd lost. I caught Elias glancing at her more than once, though he tried to pretend otherwise.

When it was my turn, Leyla didn't argue when I lay beside her. I half expected her to fight me on it, the same fiery defiance she'd thrown at me every time I insisted on sleeping in her room on Earth, instead of guarding her living area. But this time, she only nodded, exhaustion softening the edges of her fear. I threw my cloak over her as she slept, covering that "costume" that made me lose every train of thought. She didn't know it, but the moment she rested her head near mine, the bond pulsed steady and strong. It was more than magic. It was recognition.

I vowed silently as I watched her breathe, the faint rise and fall of her chest reflected in the firelight.

Until my dying breath, I would keep her safe.

Chapter Nineteen

Leyla

When I woke, the world was singing. It wasn't music in any normal sense. No melody or words. Just a low hum that pulsed through the ground and up into my bones, like the earth itself was alive and dreaming. A hymn full of melancholy. For a moment, I lay still, afraid that if I moved, I'd wake from it.

But when I opened my eyes, it was still there. The faint melody present. And I was in another world entirely. Orrynne.

The light was unreal, threads of gold and blue weaving through the brittle branches overhead, painting the world in color that didn't exist on Earth. The air smelled faintly of rain and honey, thick and heavy with chaotic magic.

I sat up slowly, the weeping grass brushing against my palms.

It was breathtaking.

And lifeless.

All around us, the clearing glowed faintly, yet the trees were dead, skeletal, their bark cracked and silvered. It was as if the realm itself had once been alive and was now only pretending. Across from me, Mick slept curled in Elias's cloak he loaned her, hair tangled and catching the strange light. The lines of exhaustion had eased from her face, though unease still lingered even in her rest.

"Morning little light," Thalon's voice came from beyond the campfire, smooth as shadow. I turned, my cheeks instantly warmer at the sight of him. And yet... I remembered the weight of him beside me all night, the slow rise and fall of his breathing, the solid large heat pressed against my back. My mind wandered without permission... lower, darker.

When my gaze flicked downward, he smiled. Slowly. Knowingly.

He'd felt it too. I cleared my throat, desperate for composure. "Is it... morning here?"

He stood near the Waystone, a towering slab of gray-green crystal, etched with symbols that glowed faintly in rhythm with his touch. The runes reflected in his eyes, giving them a silver sheen. Elias was further off, kneeling near a pool of sunken water that looked like liquid glass. I rubbed at my eyes.

"Close enough. The Borderlands follow their own time."

I pushed to my feet, still dizzy from sleep and from everything else.

"How long was I out?"

"Only a few hours," he said. "You needed the rest."

I glanced at Mick. "Is she... she's okay?"

Thalon nodded, though his expression darkened slightly. "The Echoes took pieces of her, your connection pulled her back. That connection matters. Keep reminding her who she is." Something in the way he said it made me uneasy, like he was talking about more than Mick.

I moved to the edge of the clearing, taking it all in. In the distance, the forest faded into mist, and beyond it, something vast glimmered, a mountain made of light or crystal, I couldn't tell. The air itself buzzed faintly, full of power. It felt like standing at the edge of something infinite.

Thalon came up beside me, his steps silent. "You're hearing it, aren't you?"

I nodded slowly. "The hum?"

He tilted his head, eyes scanning the horizon. "The song of the realm. It recognizes you now. The veil marked you when you crossed, and in doing so, tied you to this realm."

My stomach twisted. "Tied me?"

"Yes," he said simply. "It doesn't let go easily."

I wanted to argue, to demand he tell me how to undo it, but the way his voice softened stopped me. He wasn't warning to scare me. He was warning me because he understood what it cost.

After a moment, I asked, "And you? You're tied too, aren't you?" He hesitated, then nodded once.

"But differently. I was born of it. You were chosen by it."

Chosen.

The word sat uneasily in my chest.

Mick woke and glared at Thalon. Then, looked at me with that sisterly recognition. "Leyla," she yawned, stretching her arms, "you okay?"

I managed a faint smile. "That's supposed to be my line."

Thalon knelt again at the Waystone, pressing his palm against its surface. The runes flared briefly beneath his touch. "We'll stay here until the mist shifts. Then we move west."

"West?" I asked.

"To the crossing point," Elias answered, standing and shaking droplets from his fingers. "There's a mage there. If anyone can help you understand this… it'll be him."

At the word *'mage'*, something unreadable flickered in Thalon's expression; tension, maybe even dread. His eyes kept drifting to the tree line as though something watched us from beyond.

"What happens if the mage can't help?" I asked. Thalon's voice was quiet.

"Then we adapt. And you learn to live here."

He said *you*, not *we*.

It shouldn't have hurt, but it did.

I turned away, letting my eyes wander back to the horizon; where the twin suns climbed higher, one gold, one pale blue, casting shadows that shimmered like molten glass. The hum beneath my feet pulsed in rhythm with my heart. But for the first time since the maze, I didn't feel like I was falling anymore.

I was standing, somewhere between worlds… Yes.

But, the worlds were now watching to see what I would do next.

Chapter Twenty

Leyla

The farther we walked from the Waystone, the louder the world became. Not in sound exactly, but in presence. The forest began to breathe with us. Light rippled through the dead leaves and silver branches like music without notes. Even the ground seemed to become more alive, pulsing faintly beneath my boots as if it had a heartbeat of its own. The song hadn't stopped since I woke. It just changed, and deepened, the closer we moved west.

Mick trudged beside me, muttering under her breath. "If this forest starts talking, I change my mind. I'm out. Like, gone. First chance I get. Find yourself a new sidekick."

I smiled. "You'd leave me here alone?"

She gave me a look. "Depends. Do trees eat people?"

Elias's dry voice floated from up ahead. "Only if they like you."

"Great. Love that." Mick pulled Elias's cloak tighter.

It was around then that the absurdity of it all hit me. Mick and I, still wandering through a strange glowing forest in matching sexy witch costumes. Torn skirts, corset tops, fishnet tights… We looked like a couple of lost Halloween decorations that had wandered into a fairytale.

Mick sighed, glancing down at her ripped stockings. "You know, if I die in this outfit, I'm haunting everyone."

"Agreed," I said. "I'm not exactly dressed for a bloodline revelation."

Thalon's low chuckle drifted from behind us. "You both look… memorable."

Mick groaned. "That's one word for it."

But his gaze lingered a little too long on me; the faintest trace of warmth beneath those storm colored eyes. I tried not to think about how that look alone made my pulse stutter.

The forest thickened, mist curling between the trees. Golden dust floated through the air, catching on Thalon. His hair, his lashes; and for a moment, he looked carved from light and shadow both.

After a while, his voice cut through the silence. "We're close."

"To what?" Mick asked.

"An old sanctuary," he said. "The ruins of the Borderlands."

Elias's tone hardened. "You're taking us there?"

Thalon didn't glance back. "It's hidden from the courts. The King's wards can't reach that far. And it's on the way to the Mage."

That shut everyone up. Even Mick didn't argue after that.

The walk stretched for hours, the air growing thicker with every step. The feeling of being watched never left, but it wasn't hostile, not yet. More… curious. When we finally reached the ruins, I understood why Thalon had chosen this place. They weren't ruins in the way I expected.

The towers still stood, half broken but shimmering faintly under the twin suns. The vines that crawled over the pale stone glowed at their edges, and pools of sunken water reflected the light like stained glass. It was hauntingly beautiful, a graveyard that refused to die. A pulse thrummed low in my chest as soon as I stepped past the threshold. My heartbeat matched the faint hum in the air. When my fingers brushed one of the archways, warmth sparked under my skin… Alive.

"Leyla." Thalon's voice cut through sharply. He was beside me before I even realized he'd moved.

He caught my hand just as a soft glow flared under my wrist. Lines of light spread beneath the surface; faint, silver, forming a curling pattern that pulsed once and faded.

"What is that?" Mick whispered. Thalon didn't let go.

"Your bond to the Bridge is deepening." His eyes met mine, bright with wonder. "You're part of the realm now, body and magic both."

"I don't want this."

"I know." His voice lowered to that sweet sound, the one he seemed to use just for me. He shook his head slightly. "We will figure this out together."

Elias stepped into one of the half-collapsed chambers. His fingers brushed the wall, clearing moss away from ancient carvings. "Look at these."

The symbols looked almost alive, curling patterns that mirrored the mark under my skin. Beneath them, faint figures were carved in stone: a fae crowned in light, a human beside her, their hands joined.

Mick squinted. "So, what? Ancient royal couple goals?"

Elias smiled faintly. "Something like that. This temple belonged to the House of the Borderlands, the last royal family left standing after Thalon's father's coup." He hesitated, glancing at Thalon. "...Before your father took the throne and unified the courts; or conquered them, depending who is telling the story."

I stared at him. "And what does that have to do with me?"

Thalon's voice was soft. "Everything."

My pulse stumbled. "You're saying I'm—"

"An official descendant," Elias finished quietly. "You carry their blood. We thought as much back in your world, but this confirms Thalon's theory."

I took a step back, shaking my head. "That's impossible...."

Thalon's gaze held mine, steady and unflinching. "You grew up not knowing who your birth parents are, Leyla... It is becoming more likely by the minute." The words hit like a physical thing. For a heartbeat, the world swayed, and then the mark on my wrist flared brighter, responding to my denial.

Mick cleared her throat after a long, tense silence. "Okay, so Leyla is related to royalty, and now has magic. Cool. Do I at least get a cool title for moral support?"

Elias's mouth twitched despite himself. "Perhaps, 'Human Disaster Ambassador'?"

"Rude," she said, bumping his shoulder. I barely heard them. My fingers brushed one of the carvings. Two figures etched into stone, one fae, one mortal, their hands joined beneath a burning arch. The same symbol on their palms glowed faintly through centuries of dust. A hum filled the air. My skin prickled.

"Leyla—" Thalon's warning came too late. Light spilled from the carving, sweeping across the wall in intricate shapes. The ancient sigils flared alive, weaving into words none of us had seen before.

Elias's voice dropped to a whisper. "It's an invocation. An old one."

"What does it say?" I asked.

He read slowly, translating as he went. "When the blood divides the realms, the Bridge will awaken. They alone will restore the World." The word *Bridge* vibrated through me like a note struck in my bones. I backed away, breath catching.

"That's what the shadows called me. Back at the maze." Thalon's expression was unreadable.

"Then it's not coincidence. The realm was calling its heir home. Our suspicions were correct." The air pulsed once and everything went still. The forest outside quieted. Even the wind stopped moving. Then, slowly, every shadow in the ruins shifted, bending toward a single point in the trees. Something was watching.

Mick gripped my arm. "Leyla… What was that?"

Elias's hand went to his blade. "Spy."

Thalon's eyes flashed. "The King's."

At the edge of the trees, something glimmered… a figure cloaked in darkness, its form thin as smoke. Red eyes caught the light for half a heartbeat before it dissolved into mist. The air broke its silence all at once. The ruins groaned, like the realm itself was waking.

Thalon's hand found the small of my back. "We move. Now."

Elias nodded, already moving. "The King will know soon."

Mick stumbled after us, muttering under her breath, "Great. Royal blood, creepy monsters, and a prophecy. Next time I'm picking the field trip." Despite the terror clawing at me, a laugh escaped.

As the ruins faded behind us, one truth echoed louder than all the rest: Orrynne hadn't just recognized me.

It had claimed me.

We didn't stop moving until the twin suns sank behind the horizon and the sky turned violet. By then, every muscle in my legs burned, and Mick had long since started muttering that she was going to haunt Thalon if she died in this "enchanted hellscape."

Elias only laughed, but Thalon didn't even bother to look back. His focus never faltered.

We studied Mick's memories along our journey, it seemed she couldn't remember her childhood other than just pieces. It seemed her teenage and adult years were still intact, Thalon was hopeful that her earlier memories would return eventually.

We wound through a grove of glass-barked trees that caught the dying light, scattering it like shards across the ground. The air buzzed faintly with magic.

It felt like the whole forest was listening. When we finally stopped, Thalon swept his hand along a low ridge, and the rock shimmered, revealing a hollowed alcove beneath. A safe haven of sorts—quiet and glowing faintly with soft blue veins of quartz.

"This will do," he said, voice low, almost a growl. "The King's spies won't scent us through quartz. We will camp here tonight."

Mick groaned. "Fantastic. Maybe I can finally feel my legs again." She flopped down dramatically.

I stayed standing, watching Thalon work. His movements were precise, almost ritualistic, as he traced a sigil across the ground, sealing the space. The faint silver pulse beneath his skin glowed brighter with every line he drew. When he looked up, our eyes met. For a moment, the air felt thicker.

The light from the sigil bathed his face in pale silver, highlighting the sharp lines of his jaw and the shadow under his cheekbones. He looked otherworldly, dangerous, but when his gaze dropped briefly to my lips before looking away, something fluttered low in my stomach.

"Sit," he insisted. "You need to rest."

"I'm fine."

"You're shaking."

He stepped closer, close enough that I could see the faint pulse of shadows at his wrist. He reached out and brushed his fingers against my arm. His touch was cooler than I expected, and it sent a spark racing straight through me.

I swallowed hard. "Are you always this bossy?"

The corner of his mouth twitched. "Only when I need to be."

I sat before I could think of it. He didn't gloat, but the slight twitch of his mouth betrayed him.

Elias came back to our camp with a few… rodents. I didn't want to know what they were. I was just thankful to eat something. The meal itself wasn't half bad. Mick and I looked at each other in shock as Thalon demanded to feed me. Something about insisting I was his mate. When I declined, his shadows began to stir. I decided it wasn't worth it to argue. Maybe it was a part of their culture.

The faint blue flame of Thalon's conjured fire continued to crackle.

Mick was already half-asleep, curled in Elias's cloak. Elias leaned back against the stone a few feet further, eyes half-open, always watchful. Thalon settled across from me, elbows resting on his knees, gaze trained on the flickering light.

The silence that followed wasn't empty, it thrummed with something electric. Every breath felt charged. He didn't look away this time. And I didn't either. When a gust of wind slipped through the alcove, carrying the faint scent of rain, I felt the pull again. That invisible thread between us tightening. I wanted to lean into it. I wanted—The air changed.

The forest, which had been humming faintly all evening, went still. Deathly still.

The kind of stillness that means something is watching.

Elias straightened instantly. "Do you feel that?"

Thalon was already on his feet, blades drawn. "Something's coming."

Mick sat up groggily. "What… What's happening?"

Before any of us could answer, the shadows near the edge of the clearing rippled. And then it split open. The creature that stepped through wasn't like the others. Too thin. Too fluid. Its wings gleamed like oil-slick glass, and its face was smooth, wrong, carved from shadow and polished bone. It's eyes, red…. A demon.

"The King sends his regards," it hissed, voice echoing inside my skull rather than in the air. My body froze.

Elias moved fast, a blur of steel and light. Thalon followed, the silver glow in his veins blazing brighter as he struck. The creature met his blade with a sound like breaking glass and laughed.

"You hide her well," it crooned, its burning red eyes locking on me. "But not from His Majesty."

Thalon's sword sliced through its chest in a flash of silver. "Tell the King he will get nothing from me."

The creature only smiled wider, even as cracks of light spiderwebbed across its body. "You are your father's son," it whispered, voice stretching like silk. "You will betray her too."

Then it shattered—not into blood, but into light— dissolving into the night. The forest went silent again. I stood frozen, heart hammering. Thalon's chest rose and fell sharply, his blade still slick with starlight. He turned toward me, eyes dark and wild.

"Are you hurt?" I shook my head, though my voice barely worked.

He took a step closer. I could still feel the heat, or whatever passed for it, radiating from his magic. His hand hovered near my arm, like he wanted to touch me again but didn't dare.

"Leyla," he said quietly, "what it said—"

"Don't," I cut him off. "Just... don't."

His expression flickered, confusion—maybe, hurt. But he said nothing. Mick came to my side, slipping her arm through mine.

"We need to try to rest while we can," she said with faint breath. "We'll figure it out tomorrow."

I nodded, even though sleep felt impossible. As I lay beside her later, I could still feel Thalon's gaze from across the fire.

Heavy. Searching. Unreadable.

And underneath the lingering echo of fear, one thought burned steady and unshakable: If the King wanted me, it wasn't just because of what I was.

It was because of what I was to him.

Chapter Twenty-One

Leyla

By dawn, the clearing felt hollow. The fire had died to cold ash, and even the air seemed to hold its breath. None of us spoke about what the messenger had said. But the words still clawed at the back of my mind.

His father's son. He will betray you too.

Thalon moved ahead of us, silent as a shadow, cutting through the fog. Mick and Elias followed a few paces behind, talking quietly. Or pretending to. Everyone was pretending. I couldn't shake the image of the creature's grin, or the look on Thalon's face after it vanished. He'd looked… afraid. Not for himself. For me.

The forest shifted as we walked. The skeletal trees gave way to towering spires of pale stone, their branches moving without wind. The ground glimmered faintly beneath our steps, as though the realm itself wanted to remember where we'd been. After a while, Thalon stopped before a half-collapsed archway carved into the hillside. Strange glyphs pulsed faintly across the stone.

He pressed his hand to them, and the air rippled, parting like a curtain. Two horses stepped through. Or what passed for horses here.

They were enormous, their coats a deep metallic silver that shimmered in the half-light. Their manes flowed like smoke, and their eyes burned with soft, luminescent fire.

Mick gawked. "Okay, that's… terrifying."

Elias smiled. "Fae steeds. Bound to shadow. They don't tire. They don't spook."

"Perfect," she muttered. "Death-proof horses for the apocalypse. Love that. That would have been great two day ago."

Thalon's hand brushed the neck of one, and the creature bowed its head obediently. He spoke to it in a low, melodic tongue I didn't know, words that sounded like wind over glass. When he turned toward me, his expression was different again. Softer, but unreadable.

"I ordered the steeds to our location when we entered Orrynne. It takes time to travel with my shadows." He answered Mick and then looked to me. "You'll ride with me," not a question. A command.

"Why? I can—"

He arched a brow. "You can't. Fae steeds sense imbalance. You'd be thrown before we left the clearing." Dismissing my objection entirely.

I opened my mouth to argue, but he was already reaching for my hand. His fingers brushed mine… so steady and sure. The world seemed to tilt slightly. The hum of the realm deepened in my chest. He helped me up easily, settling behind me with one arm braced around my waist. His magic still pulsed faintly under his skin and I could feel it through the thin space between us.

"Relax," he murmured near my ear.

"That's not exactly comforting," I muttered.

His breath heat against my neck, and the faintest smile touched his voice.

"Then I suggest you trust mine. His name is Lokarious." The horse shifted, muscles coiling like water under us, and then we were moving, fast. The ground blurred into streaks of silver and brown. The wind whipped through my hair, and I felt Thalon's chest rise and fall against my back, steady and sure. For a heartbeat, I forgot to be afraid.

We rode until the forest melted into rolling plains of tanned grass. Every blade shimmered like glass in the light of the twin suns. Mick's laughter echoed behind us and even Elias somehow looked younger, more carefree. But the moment of peace didn't last. As we slowed to rest, a shadow passed overhead, not a cloud, but something alive. Massive wings stretched across the horizon, vanishing into mist before any of us could track them. Elias swore softly.

"Hunters. The King has already sent them." Thalon's jaw tightened. "We ride until dusk. No stops. If we come by the vampires… Pray to your Gods that they've fed."

Mick's eyes went wide. Both of us went silent, out of fear. There was nothing to say. We were out of our league and likely to be killed… Soon.

We rode for hours, the light shifting from gold to violet to the faint silver of night. When we finally stopped by a river, the silence between Thalon and me felt heavier than before. He dismounted first, turning to help me down. I hesitated, suddenly aware of how close we'd been all day, how often I'd felt his breath, the press of his arm, the steady rhythm of his heartbeat against mine.

He reached up, hands at my waist, and lowered me slowly. Too slowly. My pulse faltered. His eyes met mine, dark and unreadable in the fading light. When my feet touched the ground, I didn't step back.

Neither did he.

For a long moment, the only sound was the rush of the river and the steady thrum of power in the air, the realm itself whispering just under the surface.

Finally, his hand brushed my check. "You should rest."

I wanted to. I didn't move. "Thalon," I said, my voice barely above a whisper. "What that thing said, about you being like your father—" His expression hardened.

"It lies."

"Does it?" He looked away, jaw tight.

"It doesn't matter what I am. What matters is what I'll do to keep you alive." There was a heat in his words that made it hard to breathe.

"Cold?" he asked quietly. His concern only for me. His attention solely mine. Since that day at my bookstore, now weeks ago. It feels like a lifetime ago but also like I still stood next to a stranger. A stranger that I wanted a lifetime with. I knew in my heart that Thalon would be it for me. Whether that was a long, beautiful life together, or the death of me... I wasn't sure.

"A little," I said. The lie came easily. It wasn't the cold. It was the way the air here listened. The way his presence made every nerve in my body stand on edge.

Chapter Twenty-Two

Leyla

We rode again after a long stretch. Slower now. Mick and Elias were a few paces behind, arguing quietly; her sarcasm, his dry patient humor, their strange rhythm a small comfort in a world that felt like it was unraveling.

"How far to the Mage?" I asked.

"Half a day if the mist doesn't shift," Thalon said. His voice was steady, but I could hear the weight under it.

"He lives in the Wastes beyond The Borderlands. If anyone can unbind you from the Bridge, it's him."

"Unbind me," I echoed. "You make it sound like a curse."

His jaw tightened. "It is."

The silence that followed pressed heavy on my chest. The dying land stretched endless around us, its magic fading like breath. I could feel it… the way the realm reached for me, brushing invisible tendrils against my senses. Like it knew me.

I wanted to tell him. I wanted to say that I could feel it calling to me. But I didn't.

Not yet.

The world narrowed to the rhythm of hooves and breath. The wind caught at my hair, carrying with it the scent of iron. Thalon rode behind me, solid and silent, his chest pressed against my back. I could feel his heartbeat through the layers between us—steady, deliberate, and far too close. Neither of us spoke. Words would have ruined the fragile, trembling thing building in the quiet.

His hand rested lightly on the reins at first, but as the path grew rougher, his arm came around me, steadying me. The smallest shift of his fingers against my waist sent a shock through me that had nothing to do with fear.

He leaned closer, voice low against my ear. "You're shaking, little light."

"I'm fine," I lied.

The truth was, I wasn't sure if it was fear or something else entirely. His breath brushed my skin; warm, careful, and devastating. His fingers lowered to my thigh, a barely-there touch that made it hard to think. The air between us thickened until even breathing felt dangerous. With every rock of the steed, his fingers etched closer to my middle, making my insides tighten in anticipation.

"Leyla…" he whispered, and my pulse stumbled.

I turned slightly, enough to see his eyes in the fading light. The storm-gray of them had softened—no armor, no mask. Just him. And pure lust. For me. The space between us vanished until the world was only his breath and mine.

And then, all at once, the forest went still.

No wind. No birds.

Nothing.

Thalon tensed behind me, every muscle in his body coiling like a drawn bow. "Do you hear that?"

I frowned. "Hear what?"

He didn't answer, already leaping off of the fae steed, his hand on the hilt of his dagger.

A man with blonde hair and form fitting clothing stood, yards away from Thalon with his hands folded before him.

"Gyor." Thalon greeted the lone man.

"Thalon." The man said in greeting and was suddenly in front of our group, I did not see his legs move—it was as if he teleported. Both Thalon and the man folded their arm in front of their chests and pounded once. "A pleasure to see you, my friend. My apologies for the surprise introduction."

"You certainly seem to be in better spirits since the last time we spoke."

Gyor winced uncomfortably but shook his head in understanding. "Yes, again you have my sincerest apologies, Prince. We as a species were quite hungry then, after the fall. Please, forgive my past transgression. We now have a solution that works for us all. The hunger is sated."

Thalon nodded his head in a hesitant approval.

"Good." He gestured towards Elias. "Elias and I are passing through, I hope we have not trespassed on your lands or caused any issues."

"Well, it's technically all of your father's land now isn't it?" He questioned Thalon, but began to laugh at his own words. "But I appreciate the sentiment, Thalon. Yes, you have caused quite a few questions, indeed. The vampires ask why you and your pack head West towards The Wastes. Is this a mission of the King?"

"No mission of the King." Thalon hesitates but looks toward me in question. "Gyor, this is Leyla and her acquaintance, Mick."

Mick muttered something about '*meeting someone in this damned costume,*' but I cannot hear her over the sudden pounding in my ears. This man. I feel a connection to him. Not one similar to Thalon and I's, but familiar. He puts out his hand to meet mine.

"Humans shake in your world, do they not? It is a pleasure to meet you, Leyla." I reach for his hand and when our fingers connect, my feet are suddenly deadened weight to the ground beneath me. I feel settled, assured.

He drops down to his knees. "It is her."

Thalon's snarl was immediate. The air crackled. "Explain now. I give you this grace to you alone due to our history, Gyor." He would kill him, of that I have no doubt. "Now."

Gyor remained on his knees, with my hand now in both of his, as he looks to Thalon. "She is your mate, that much is clear. I apologize, Prince. But understand me…"

I take my hands away from this stranger and move to Thalon instinctively. Gyor gets to his feet at impeccable speed.

Gyor remained perfectly still, his eyes reflecting the moonlight like shards of polished crystal. When he finally spoke, his voice carried the kind of quiet power that could still a storm.

"You are the Bridge of Realms," he said softly, reverently. "The Heir. The one my kind has waited for since the darkening of the courts. You will bring peace to what remains of our kind… And perhaps to the realms beyond."

The night seemed to hold its breath.

And in that silence, I knew that fate herself called our paths to meet.

The weight of his words sank into the silence that followed. I didn't know what to say—what to be in that moment. This was the third time someone had called me that, and yet I still didn't understand what it meant. Only that every time I heard it, something inside me seemed to recognize it before my mind could catch up.

"I…" My voice trembled. "Thank you, Gyor. My name is Leyla. It's… a pleasure to meet you as well."

He inclined his head, the faintest smile touching his lips. "The pleasure is mine, Bridge of Realms."

Thalon stepped forward, placing himself just slightly between us. His voice was low, wary. "Your presence here, Gyor, is unexpected. What business brings you so close to the Wastes?"

Gyor's expression shifted. "I might ask the same of you. My vampires dwell nearby, in the Hollow Vale. We have… changed since your last visit, Thalon." My body froze. Vampires.

I knew in my bones the fear that presented itself in front of me. The vampiric books I read and cried over on Earth were not the reality that stood before me. Elegant, yes. Still, deathly. But the undercurrent of a predator was obvious from where I stood. Mick looked like she was going faint.

His gaze flickered to me again before settling on Thalon.

"My apologies again for the bite, it seems you have had a full recovery."

Thalon's jaw tightened. His fingers brushed his chest as if remembering a lingering pain. "I have."

"Then come!" Gyor clapped, and spread his hands in welcome. "You and your companions may rest within our walls. It has been long since we offered hospitality to travelers— longer still since we had cause to."

Mick raised an eyebrow. "You mean… Vampires have a village? Is that safe?"

That drew a low, amused laugh from Gyor. "A city, once. Though time has stripped it of its crown. What remains, we keep—order, civility, and restraint."

Thalon's eyes narrowed. "Restraint?"

Gyor inclined his head solemnly. "We no longer hunt the living. The blood of beasts sustains us now. The animals that remain suffice. The taste is duller, yes, but it keeps us whole. We choose life over hunger."

Something softened in Thalon's face. He gave a slow nod. The history between him and Gyor is one I am dying to know. Perhaps literally soon. "Then you have my respect."

"Good," Gyor clapped his hands, and for a heartbeat his smile revealed the faintest flash of his fangs; not threatening, only ancient.

"Come. The night grows deep, and the Hollow Vale welcomes you."

The Hollow Vale rose from the cliffs like a dream carved from shadow and starlight. Pale towers coiled upward, their surfaces threaded with veins of glowing silver. Bridges of glass arched over dark rivers that pulsed faintly, alive with hidden magic. As we entered, the vampires stopped what they were doing. Each turning, silently, to watch us. Their eyes gleamed like liquid gold. Not hostile, not curious exactly… But assessing. Questioning.

None approached.

None spoke.

They simply watched, and the air around us felt thick with unspoken questions.

Gyor leaned close enough for only Thalon and I to hear. "They wonder who you are. But I will not tell them. Not yet. You will have peace tonight. After you depart, I will speak of it—no sooner."

Thalon gave a small nod, but his hand intertwined with mine, his fingers lacing through my own, laying a silent claim. Even with the uncertainty surrounding us, the electricity from our touch remained. I leaned into his touch while the comfort of his shadows surrounded our intertwined fingers.

"There is, however," Gyor continued, "one among us who may be worth meeting. She is ancient. Older than the Hollow Vale itself. A vampiric witch of my kind. I ask to tell her of your presence, only with your permission. She has… seen things others have only dreamed of. If you wish it, she may offer guidance."

Elias lifted his head at that, a flicker of recognition in his eyes. "The witch. You mean Serika?"

Gyor looked pleasantly surprised. "Ah. So, you know of her?"

Elias nodded. "She's trusted. Her magic is older than the Courts, and she's never once betrayed a guest."

Mick crossed her arms. "Yeah, sure, visit a vampire witch in the middle of the night. Sounds totally safe."

Elias gave her a dry look. "Safer than not knowing what's coming for us."

Thalon's jaw tightened. "We're not going in unarmed."

Gyor smiled faintly. "You won't need to be. She keeps no guards, only her wards. Come, then—if the Bridge of Realms wills it."

I swallowed, glancing at Thalon.

His expression said everything: *I don't like this, but I'll follow you anywhere.*

"Let's go," I said quietly. "If she can tell me what all of this means—I want to know."

Chapter Twenty-Three

Leyla

Serika's home was carved into the side of a cliff, a curved dome of black crystal that shimmered faintly in the dark. Inside, silver veins pulsed through the stone like they were almost alive, lighting the chamber in soft, ghostly hues. The witch was waiting for us.

She looked almost human—save for the agelessness in her face and the faint red tint in her irises. Her hair was the color of fire, her skin translucent, and her voice, when she spoke, was like silk over stone.

"Gyor," she said with a nod, "you've brought the scent of change into my home." Her eyes drifted toward me. They widened just slightly. "Ah. So, it is true. The Bridge walks again."

Thalon stiffened beside me, his hand ghosting near his weapon. "You will speak respectfully."

The witch smiled faintly. "I always do, fae prince. Do not mistake my knowledge for threat."

I could only imagine what we looked like to these vampires... To this witch. Two damsels in torn witch costumes, a brooding prince, and a sunshine haired playboy. It would be hysterical if my life wasn't quite literally being turned upside down.

Elias made his way up in front of our group. "Serika. It's been decades. I hope you've been well." The hint of his charm peaked through and Serika's shoulders noticeably deflated just so.

Mick's brows shot up at that, her jaw tightening faintly. I caught it, that flash of something complicated in her eyes, and made a note to ask her about it later.

Elias continued, his tone even. "We've come seeking truth. You've seen the prophecy, haven't you?"

Serika tilted her head. "Let's get to it then."

She clapped her hands and motioned for us to join in her living area. Stone couches with covered cotton surrounding a small indoor campfire. Only the campfire was made of crystals. And how the fire remained aflame was beyond my understanding of this world. We sat on the cotton cushions.

I felt the ease in my bones leaning against something so soft after days of surviving in the woods. My comfort was cut short when Thalon picked me up by my middle and sat me on his lap.

I no longer had the energy to resist. Instead, I leaned back into him. I could almost feel his heart rate slow, as if he was at ease when I was this close.

Her gaze studied Thalon and I, but she continued. Bracing herself for a tale I wasn't quite sure I was ready to hear.

"I've seen what remains of the prophecy. The threads are tangled, but fate never hides from me." She turned back to me, her gaze sharp and impossibly kind all at once. "You wish to know who you are. And to see if there is a way out. The fix you seek cannot lie with the Mage. And I am certain that he would be…. Less than helpful. Even with his powers, he himself cannot change fate." She took a moment to let this sink in, hey eyes all too knowing. "I despise other witches who speak in riddles. Hear it plain, child, here and now. Before the Bridge there was a Kingdom. And before the Kingdom, there was balance."

The silver veins in the walls brightened, responding to her words.

"Your parents," she said, "were the King and Queen of the Borderlands, the last rulers remaining of the courts before the fall. Before the never ending suffering, the endless lifelessness. Their union bound light and shadow, life and death. When they ruled, Orrynne thrived. There was no one ruler above all; the courts thrived on their own. The land was alive. The Bridge brought life, peace, and prosperity among the land."

My breath caught. "My parents—they were truly the King and Queen?"

"Yes. And they were betrayed," Serika finished gently. "By the former Borderlands King, your grandfather. Your mother's father—who could not bear to see peace shared among the realms. He partnered with Thalon's father to take over the Courts." She took a moment to let that sink in. "Your mother was betrayed by her own father, yes. He coveted your mother's power, the power of creation, and when she refused to yield it and married a mortal, he destroyed them both through King Vaeris. The Borderlands burned. The Bridge collapsed."

Thalon's jaw clenched, his voice low. "Because of my father."

Serika nodded. "He broke the Bridge, scattering its remnants through the realms. But not all things can be undone. Your mother's final act was to hide you, her only child, beyond his reach. Born of two worlds, mortal and fae, bound by the magic of both." The words fell over me like cold water.

"So, I'm…"

"The one and only Heir of the Borderlands," Serika said simply. "The living bridge between realms. And with your awakening, the prophecy stirs again."

The chamber seemed to darken, as if the world itself was listening. "When you come into your full power," her voice quiet but resonant. "The realms will heal. The earth will breathe again. Rivers will run. Children will be born. Life to the realms will be restored once more. The veil between life and death will open, and close, as it was meant to. Balance will return."

Mick let out a shaky laugh. "Well… that doesn't sound terrible."

Serika's eyes softened as she looked toward Mick, but her tone stayed grave. "All life demands balance, child. Restoration requires exchange." She looked to me, regret shining in her red-tinged eyes. "To awaken what was lost, something must be given."

The temperature in the room dropped.

"What kind of exchange?" I asked, though I already knew.

Serika stepped closer, her presence overwhelming in its stillness. "The Bridge restores what is broken. But when its purpose is fulfilled, the Bridge must fall. When your task is complete, Bridge of Realms… your heart will cease, and the realms will live."

The words hit like a blade.

Thalon's magic snapped.

He picked me up from his lap and sat me gently down on the cotton. The air around him rippled, the light in the room dimming under the weight of his shadows.

"Enough," he growled, voice low and dangerous. "You will not speak her death into existence."

Serika didn't flinch. "It is not I who chooses, Prince. It is written in the marrow of what she is."

Thalon stepped forward, eyes burning. "Then I'll rewrite it."

The silence that followed was thick enough to drown in. Even Gyor looked away, as if unwilling to stand between them. Finally, I reached out, resting my hand on Thalon.

"Thalon." His gaze snapped to mine, still fierce, but I saw the fear beneath it. The fear one has when their loved one was just given an expiration date. He was scared of losing me. My fingers drew rough circles around his arm. "It's fine," I said softly. "We came here for truth. Now we have it."

He didn't answer. But when his hand closed over mine, his grip was trembling.

Mick broke the silence first, her tone small but firm. "Then we make sure that prophecy never comes true. Right? There has to be another way."

Elias nodded. "Prophecies are warnings, not sentences. We'll find a way."

Gyor inclined his head, eyes shadowed with thought.

It was he whose voice broke the silence. "There is more you must know, Leyla." He gestured toward the window of black glass that overlooked the glowing valley below. "Our kind once served your bloodline, your parents specifically, Queen Arya and King Marlon. Long before the fall, before the corruption spread across the Courts, the vampires were bound to protect your mother and father in the Borderlands, when they still ruled in peace. Your lineage was sacred to us."

Thalon's expression hardened. His anger was growing by the minute. Not at us. At his parent. At the fae who raised him.

Gyor's gaze was steady, unreadable. "The vow of protection was never broken, only forgotten." His attention returned to me. "If you are to fulfill what was foretold, you must learn to wield what you carry. It is not just light or life… it is the balance of all things. We can teach you, if you'll stay." The room fell silent again.

Thalon turned sharply, tension flaring in every line of him. "You want her to stay here? In a den of vampires?"

Gyor's tone remained calm, patient. "Not a den. A sanctuary. We no longer hunt the living. We have learned to master hunger… To rule it, not be ruled by it. That control is the foundation of power. It is something Leyla will require on her journey."

Serika, still standing by the window, nodded once. "Your power is awakening, Leyla. Wild, raw, and dangerous. The fae can teach you control of magic, but not balance. That is ours to give."

I looked at Thalon. He didn't meet my eyes. His jaw was tight, his shoulders tense. Like he was bracing for a blow.

Elias stepped forward then, quiet but certain. "They're right, Thalon. I've seen what she's capable of already. If she doesn't learn to contain it, it'll consume her before it saves anyone."

Thalon's head snapped toward him. "You would have her train under them? The same bloodline that nearly destroyed…"

"… The same bloodline that tried to save your realm," Gyor interrupted softly. "Your father made sure no one remembered that part."

The words hung between them, sharp and heavy. Thalon looked away first. I could see it in him. The war between pride and reason.

Gyor inclined his head toward me again. "You need not decide now. Rest. Leave with the sunrise if that's your will. But know this. The Vampires will fight for your existence. We fight for life. We fight for the future. And that is you, Bridge of Realms."

Elias and Mick had their own rooms across the corridor, though "rooms" hardly seemed the right word for what awaited us. Thalon had insisted—no, demanded—that I share his. "For protection," he'd said. I hadn't argued. Not after everything.

I walked Mick to her door first. She caught sight of the marble tub, the folded linens, and the clean clothes laid neatly on a stone bench and nearly burst into tears.

"I'm not leaving," she said, half laughing, half sobbing. "Go. Before I change my mind."

I hesitated. This place was beautiful but strange, carved into the bones of the mountain itself. Still, I understood. She needed quiet. Safety. Solitude. So, I left her to it.

When Thalon and I entered our chambers, I stopped dead in the doorway. The room was unlike anything I'd ever seen—cut directly into the cliffside, yet somehow warm, lit by veins of soft crystal embedded in the stone. A wide archway opened to a balcony that overlooked the glowing lake far below, its light reflecting in shifting waves against the dark ceiling above. The bed dominated the space, large and imposing, carved from obsidian and polished until it gleamed. Silver silk sheets spilled across it like liquid moonlight.

Nearby, a table held an assortment of small luxuries I hadn't seen in what felt like weeks: clean clothing, soft towels, a pitcher of water, even jars of scented oils and lotions. In the far corner, steam curled from a sunken bath carved right into the stone floor, its water faintly shimmering with traces of magic. For a moment, I couldn't speak. After so many nights on damp earth and cold ground, this felt almost unreal. A sanctuary carved from the chaos outside.

Thalon watched me quietly, amusement flickering at the corner of his mouth. "You can take the bath first," he said, though there was a teasing undertone that made my stomach twist. "Or," he added softly, "we could share it."

My breath caught.

His eyes were unreadable, but there was a warmth there… An invitation I wasn't sure I was ready for.

I managed a shaky laugh and shook my head. "I think I'll manage on my own, but thanks for the offer big guy."

He held up his hands in surrender, though a faint smirk tugged at his lips. "As you wish, princess." He paused for just a moment before heading to the bed. "Though, for the record…

Big doesn't quite cover it." My face went hot instantly, and his quiet chuckle followed him outside of the room.

When I finally slipped into the bath, the heat stole the ache from my limbs. The scent of lavender and something faintly metallic filled the air. For the first time in what felt like forever, I exhaled without fear. When I emerged, the exhaustion returned like a tide, but softer this time, almost peaceful.

Thalon was already stretched out on the bed, one arm behind his head, his sword within reach even in rest. I slid under the silk beside him, leaving a respectful distance, though the warmth of him still reached me. Neither of us spoke. Only the slow, steady rhythm of his breathing filled the space between us. For the first time in days, the silence didn't feel dangerous. It felt like safety.

I laid awake beneath the silver ceiling of the Hollow Vale, the witch's words echoing in my mind.

When your task is complete, your heart will cease.

Beside me, Thalon kept watch again, silent and unmoving—except when I turned toward him. His eyes caught the faint blue light, and he reached out, brushing his thumb over my wrist, where my pulse beat fast.

"As long as I draw breath," he promised, "you will too."

Chapter Twenty-Four

Leyla

Dawn bled pale and silver over the Hallow Vale. Thalon and Elias readied the fae steeds in silence while the morning mist curled low over the ground. The air smelled faintly of ash and iron. I stood by the edge of the cliff, the wind tugging at my hair. My thoughts were too loud—the witch's prophecy, Gyor's offer, Thalon's silence. Mick's footsteps crunched softly behind me.

"You're really thinking about it," she said quietly. I didn't answer. She came to stand beside me, her arms folded.

"Whatever you choose—leaving, staying, whatever—I'm with you. Got it? You burn kingdoms down, I'll bring the matches." That made me smile, even through the heaviness in my chest.

"You're sure? This isn't your fight. You were attacked once already, I do not want to put you in danger any longer," she just shrugged. As if what she was offering wouldn't probably cost her life.

"Besides mom, you are now the only thing in my life worth fighting for. We're sisters." She shrugged as if it was never even a question.

The simple truth of it broke something open in me. I turned toward Thalon, who was tightening the reins on Lokarious. He looked up at me, eyes shadowed and unreadable.

"I'm staying," I said. The words hit the air like a spark. Elias froze. Mick just nodded once, solid and steady at my side.

Thalon's jaw clenched. "You don't understand what you're agreeing to. These vampires—"

"—are the only ones who can teach me what I need to know. I can feel it." I stepped closer, voice steady now. "You said yourself the King is hunting us. If I can't control this… then I'm not just a target. I can feel my power growing every day. I cannot be a weapon in the wrong hands."

Thalon's eyes burned into mine. For a long moment, he didn't speak.

Then, he stood in front of me, his hand coming up to brush my hair behind my ear, almost reverently. "You trust too easily."

"Maybe," I whispered. "But I trust you too. And you're still here."

He exhaled sharply, something between a sigh and surrender, and turned toward Gyor, who had been waiting silently in the courtyard.

"If she stays, we all stay," Thalon said. "I will be by her side every second, she will not go unprotected. I won't leave her to you alone."

Gyor bowed his head. "Then we have an accord. The Fae Prince, the Bridge of Realms, and the remainder of your party will be welcome in the Vale."

Serika appeared in the courtyard, her silver hair gleaming in the light. "Good. We begin tonight. The blood remembers— and so will she."

I looked once more at Thalon, at the faint flicker of conflict still in his eyes. Then I turned back toward the heart of the Vale, where the first of the training halls shimmered with pale light. For the first time, I wasn't running anymore.

I was choosing.

The days in Hollow Vale passed differently than they did above ground.

Here, time seemed to flow like shadow. Unhurried, fluid, and eternal. The air was always cool, the light soft and silver, pulsing faintly from the veins of crystal that laced every wall. Even the silence had a heartbeat. For the first time since leaving the mortal lands, I wasn't running. The vampires kept their distance at first. Always curious, but polite. They brought dinner to our rooms and ensured we were comfortable. Overall, the vampires seemed to be very accommodating hosts, especially considering they never hosted the living.

They spoke in hushed tones, their voices melodic and strange, their movements graceful as mist. Some watched us from balconies carved into the black stone, their gold eyes glowing faintly in the dimness. I could feel their curiosity pressing at the edges of my mind—not hostile, just ancient. But none dared to approach until Gyor made it known that I was under his protection.

After that, they bowed their heads when I passed.

It was unsettling.

Thalon hated every second of it.

He stood at the edge of every hall we entered, one hand always resting near the shadowed blade at his side. Even when he wasn't speaking, his presence felt like a storm held barely in check. Elias, on the other hand, seemed to adapt easily — asking questions, studying the vampires' rituals, their architecture, their strange way of life. Mick was somewhere in between, wary but fascinated, especially after one of the vampires offered to teach her how to walk silently through shadow. It turned out to be less about stealth and more about confidence.

On the second night, Serika led me deeper into the Hollow Vale, through halls that glowed with veins of living silver, into a chamber that opened onto an underground lake. The surface shimmered like glass, reflecting the light of the crystals above.

"This," she said, "is the Mirror of Blood."

It wasn't red, as you would expect—it was colorless, like starlight trapped beneath ice.

"Step in," Serika said. "Let it read you."

I hesitated, glancing back at Thalon, who stood just beyond the threshold. He looked like he wanted to drag me out by sheer will and murder Serika all at once.

"She'll be okay," Elias murmured. Thalon didn't move. But he didn't stop me either.

The water was cool against my skin, then cold enough to burn. I gasped, and in that breath, something shifted. The world around me blurred.

I saw flashes—not visions exactly, but memories that weren't mine.

My birth mother, the former Queen, her hands covered in soil that glowed faintly gold. A man beside her—tall, dark-haired, his eyes kind. Their laughter echoed through a valley of green. Then the same valley, burned to ash. A crown of glass. A sword dripping red. A cry, a newborn's wail, and then, silence. Death.

When I stumbled back onto the stone, it was Thalon who caught me.

"What did you see?" Serika asked as if she already knew what the strange, watered mirror would show me.

"My parents," I whispered. "And the fall."

Serika nodded. "The Mirror remembers all who share your blood. It has shown you truth—not to torment you, but to remind you of what was lost. The Hollow Vale was built to protect that memory." I looked around… Really looked. The carvings along the walls, the faint sigils etched into the crystal—all of them bore the same insignia that had been on the medallion my mother wore in the vision The Mirror had shown me.

"This place…" I said slowly. "It was theirs."

"It was," Serika said. "And now, it is yours."

That night, Gyor joined us in the great hall—a cavern of black stone and soft light, where the vampires gathered to speak, eat, or simply exist. Their "meals" consisted of crimson liquid poured into crystal goblets—animal blood, I realized, treated more like wine than sustenance. They didn't hide what they were. But they didn't revel in it either. There was dignity in their restraint—a strange, noble sadness that hung over everything.

"You're adapting quickly," Gyor said, settling across from me. "Few mortals can stomach our halls for long."

"I'm not mortal," I said, before I could stop myself. He smiled, slow and knowing.

"No. You are something far more unique." Thalon's chest rumbled quietly from my right.

"She's exhausted. You should let her rest."

"She is welcome to rest when she chooses," Gyor said, still looking at me.

"But her kind was not made for rest." Serika's voice floated from the shadows. "The Bridge must master her powers, or devastation among not only our world will continue, but all realms."

I rubbed at my temples. "You make it sound like I'm supposed to save everyone."

"Not everyone," Gyor said. "Just everything."

Mick muttered, "Oh, well, that's so much better."

Laughter, soft and unexpected, rippled through the hall. Even Thalon's mouth twitched, almost a smile.

Later, when the others slept, I found myself standing at the balcony that overlooked the sunken lake, hardly any water remained where I imagined it was once full.

The air shimmered faintly with the magic of the Vale, and for the first time, I felt… calm. Thalon joined me, silent as always.

"You're changing," he said finally.

"I'm learning."

"That's not what I mean." His eyes caught the light — storm-gray, unreadable. "They look at you like you're theirs. Like they've been waiting for you."

"Maybe they have."

He exhaled slowly, the sound weary. "Just don't forget who you are, Leyla."

I turned toward him, meeting his gaze. "Maybe that's exactly what I'm trying to find out."

The silence that followed was long, heavy but not uncomfortable. When he finally reached out and brushed his fingers against mine, the world seemed to steady around us. Below, the lake shimmered faintly, and for the first time, its reflection didn't look like a stranger.

Chapter Twenty-Five

Leyla

It was on the third morning that I met Auren, a girl my age, or what seemed to be my age, with hair as white as moonlight and eyes the color of melted copper. Her voice carried a lilt, like laughter kept secret. I was sitting near the Mirror of Blood, tracing circles across the water, when she appeared soundlessly at my side.

"You shouldn't stare too long," she said, crouching beside me. "The water remembers faces. Sometimes it keeps them."

I blinked, startled, and then smiled despite myself. "Good to know. I'll try not to give it mine for too long."

Her grin widened, sharp but playful. "You're the Bridge, aren't you? The one they whisper about in the halls."

"I suppose that depends on who's whispering."

"Everyone," she said simply. "You walk too loudly to be anything ordinary."

That made me laugh, a sound that felt strange in my own mouth after days of tension.

"I didn't realize I was being that noisy."

Auren tilted her head. "You're alive. That's enough to cause a stir down here." Then she extended her hand.

"I'm Auren. I used to serve under Queen Arya, your mother. Or… I did, at least before everything… changed."

The words pulled me upright. "You knew her?"

A shadow crossed her face, but her voice stayed gentle. "Not well. But I remember her kindness. She treated us as part of the Borderlands, not her curse. You have her eyes, you know." That lodged somewhere deep in my chest, where grief and gratitude tangled.

"Thank you," I said softly.

"Come," she stood. "If you're to survive Serika's lessons, you'll need to learn more than balance. You'll need to move like us."

The training chamber Auren led me to was smaller; intimate, candlelit, its walls etched with runes that pulsed faintly red. Auren moved across the floor like smoke, barefoot, her body bending with effortless grace.

"Your life magic is the ultimate power," she said. "But power is useless without intention. The body is a vessel, you must learn to move it as one with your energy. We call it the Thread."

I raised a brow. "You're going to teach me to dance?"

Her smirk returned. "Something like that."

The next hour passed in a blur of motion. She taught me how to feel the hum of the Hollow Vale beneath my feet. To draw its energy upward with each step, each breath. I stumbled often. Auren only laughed, correcting my stance with a nudge of her hand.

"Not so rigid, the Bridge will not obey those who force it." By the end, sweat glistened down my spine, my limbs thrummed, and when I looked around, faint trails of silver light followed every movement I made.

"You see?" Auren said, smiling proudly. "The realm is answering you."

Before I could answer, a familiar voice echoed from the doorway.

"She's glowing," Mick said, leaning lazily against the archway. "You forget to tell me you were learning vampire ballet?"

Auren laughed and ached a pale brow. "And you must be her sister."

Mick blinked. "You know about me?"

"Everyone knows about you. The mortal girl who fended off an Echo upon entering our world? Legendary." Mick grinned, cheeks faintly pink.

"Well, I don't know if I… You heard about that?"

"Of course. We have excellent gossip." She nudged her head towards Elias, who had his back turned to us in the hallway behind Mick.

The three of us dissolved into laughter, the kind that shook something loose and alive in my chest. For the first time in what felt like a long time, I felt normal; as if the prophecy, the danger, the burden of being the Bridge had momentarily lifted.

When Auren offered to show us the dining hall, we followed. The Great Hall of the Hollow Vale was a stoned cathedral carved from rock and glass. The vampires gathered at long tables of black marble, speaking in soft tones, their voices blending like a low hum. Crystal goblets gleamed red, filled with the thick, shimmering elixirs they called the crimson. Mick wrinkled her nose as she sat beside me.

"That's blood, right? Please tell me that's not dinner for everyone."

Auren smiled. "Only for us. You'll find your meals at the far table. Herbs and meat we retrieved from the upper valleys, considered sacred now in our dying world. We've learned to accommodate guests of the living variety for their occasional appearance."

Thalon arrived moments later, his dark hair damp from training, his sleeves rolled, his eyes like a storm threatening to break. The moment he entered, the room shifted. Conversations hushed. Vampires inclined their heads slightly…. Wary and respectful. The tension between fae and vampire was ancient and almost palpable.

"Still making friends, I see," he murmured, standing above my seat. His arm brushed mine, just barely, but it was enough to set my pulse skipping.

I gestured towards Auren. "She's dangerous. A good teacher so far."

"So are you, little light." His mouth curved, just slightly.

Elias joined Mick across the table, already deep in a quiet debate about vampire alchemy versus ancient fae spellcraft. Mick gestured animatedly with her hands, and Elias smiled in that patient way of his, which somehow made her more flustered than calm. Thalon noticed it too.

"Your sister and my friend seem… interested in one another."

"She'll deny it to her dying breath."

"So will he," Thalon said. "They're doomed."

That made me laugh—quiet, unguarded, the sound slipping out before I could stop it. For a heartbeat, he just looked at me, eyes softened by something that felt dangerous. The air shifted between us, thickening until it carried the faint scent of him— smoke and rain and something wilder underneath.

When I turned back toward the table, my hand brushed his leg. The contact was brief, accidental… but the spark that followed wasn't. Heat crawled up my neck, and I started to pull away. He caught my hand instead. Deliberately this time. His fingers curled around mine, rough and steady.

"Careful, mate," he murmured, his voice a low warning that didn't sound much like a warning at all.

The world seemed to shrink to that single point of touch. The laughter, the clatter of dishes, even the whisper of the lake outside, all of it fell away. It was just him. Just the weight of his gaze, the warmth of his skin against mine, and the dizzying awareness that neither of us moved.

Then, like a spell breaking, Auren's voice cut through the moment—bright, amused, and wholly unaware.

"Eat, before Serika comes to drag you to your next trial," she said, slipping gracefully into the seat beside Mick. "You'll need your strength."

I pulled my hand back, the ghost of his touch still tingling against my skin.

The next few days settled into a strange rhythm. Training with Auren in the mornings, lessons with Serika in the afternoons, and shared dinners in the Great Hall at night. The Hollow Vale had its own pulse, even if most of its tenants didn't. The air itself seemed to hum faintly, as though the cliffs remembered what it was to live, and slowly, I began to move in time with it. Auren proved an unrelenting teacher. Her patience was endless, but her standards were merciless.

She taught me to awaken dead roots with nothing more than a whisper, to coax brittle vines back to life until they curled around my wrist like living lace. She showed me how to weave shadow and light together through balance rather than force. To let them breathe through one another, forming something new and quietly powerful. They were small things, simple tricks perhaps, but each lesson felt like a door unlocking inside me, one after another.

Over and over, she made me repeat the same motions until my hands trembled and the edges of my vision swam.

"Again," she would say, her tone steady, the faintest smile at the corner of her mouth. And I did. Until I could feel the magic moving through me, soft and rhythmic, like breath in my veins. It wasn't so wild anymore, my magic was learning.

Mick joined us often, never able to sit still for long. Half helping, half complaining, she provided a kind of chaotic balance to Auren's calm precision. "You two make this look easy," she muttered one morning as Auren corrected the angle of her stance for what had to be the tenth time. "I'll stick to punching things."

"Sometimes punching is magic," Auren said, eyes sparkling. "It depends on the intent."

That earned her a laugh and a life-long friendship with Mick. The two of them grew close quickly—late-night conversations, shared stories, teasing Elias. Even Thalon seemed more relaxed here, caught in the strange balance of light and darkness the Hollow Vale offered. He spent all of his time with me, ensuring my safety. His gaze never lingered elsewhere, and I found I quite liked his gaze dedicated to solely me. The nights, however, those were the hardest.

Sometimes I thought he did it on purpose, brushing my arm as he reached for his dagger, leaning close enough that his shadows whispered across my skin. It wasn't cruel. It was torment of the sweetest kind. One night, after training, he leaned against the doorway, watching as I unwound my hair. The light caught his eyes, silver in the dark.

"You've changed," he said quietly. "You move differently now."

"I'm learning from the best," I teased, turning slightly toward him. "Guess a few vampires had what it takes to unleash my power."

"I meant your power," he said. "It feels… older."

"Older?"

He nodded. "Like it remembers."

I hesitated, heart twisting. "Maybe it remembers what was lost."

His gaze softened, the storm in his eyes dimming to something warmer. "Or maybe," he said quietly, "it remembers what's to come."

The words lingered between us like smoke—delicate, dangerous, impossible to ignore. I felt them more than heard them, settling somewhere deep beneath my ribs. For a heartbeat, neither of us moved. The faint glow of the crystals painted shifting light across his face, catching the sharp lines of his jaw and the soft curve of his mouth. The air itself seemed to hold its breath. He took a slow step closer.

The space between us vanished in an instant, and I could feel his breath against my skin, warm and steady. The dark hum of his magic stirred again, brushing against mine in a way that felt far too intimate to be accidental. It wasn't a touch, not exactly—but it felt like one, sliding over my senses like the whisper of a storm.

My pulse stuttered. Every inch of me was aware of him—the faint scent of steel and smoke clinging to his clothes, the way his presence filled the room, the quiet steadiness in his eyes that promised something I wasn't ready to name.

"Thalon…" I started, though I wasn't sure what I meant to say.

Before I could find the words, a soft knock broke through the tension, followed by Mick's familiar voice muffled through the door. "Leyla? Dinner's ready. And Elias says if you two don't show up soon, he's going to drink the vampire wine and regret it later."

The spell shattered. The air between us loosened.

Thalon exhaled, a hint of a sigh escaping him. "Saved by your sister."

"Again," I said, trying, and failing, to steady the flutter in my chest. But even as we turned toward the door, the air still hummed faintly between us, echoing with everything neither of us had said.

He offered me his hand. "Come, Bridge. Let's face the night."

The Great Hall glowed with a warmth that had nothing to do with fire. Light pulsed gently from the crystal veins running through the walls, painting everything in shifting shades of silver and violet. The long tables were lined with earthenware dishes and flickering candles that gave off faint tendrils of sweet-smelling smoke. The air was thick with the scent of roasted herbs, warm bread, and that faint metallic smell—the scent of the Vale itself, living and ancient.

Auren sat beside Mick, her gestures animated as she explained how the Hollow Vale sustained itself. Her voice carried easily over the quiet murmur of conversation, elegant and certain, as though she were reciting the heartbeat of the realm itself. "The crystals," she said, tapping her fingertips lightly against the table's polished stone surface, "are veins of pure magic. They pulse with the essence of the realm, life and death in perfect balance." The faint glow under her touch shimmered, as if the Vale responded to her words. "We draw from them only what we give back."

Thalon leaned forward, his elbows resting on the table, curiosity softening the edges of his usual composure. "And the blood you drink—?"

"It is all animal," Auren said simply. Confirming Gyor's previous testimony. Her tone carried reverence. "Taken with care. The life that sustains us must be honored, not stolen."

Mick tilted her head, her usual sarcasm fading for a moment. "You make immortality sound… ethical."

Auren smiled faintly, but there was something wistful in it. "Hardly. It's not about being good," she said, her eyes glancing toward the glowing ceiling as if searching for something unseen. "It's about surviving with grace."

The words lingered, soft and thoughtful, until Elias—never one for silence—raised his cup and broke the spell. "Grace or not, I'll take surviving over starving any day," he said, earning a hardy laugh from Gyor that echoed warmly across the table. His laughter was contagious. It spread like a ripple, drawing even the quiet ones into its rhythm.

For the first time since arriving, I felt the Hall come alive. Voices blending, glasses clinking, light spilling across polished stone. The shadows seemed to retreat for once, content to linger at the edges instead of swallowing the room whole. Auren leaned close to Mick, sketching shapes in the air with her hand as she spoke of the Vale's creation. How the crystals had once been rivers of pure light, how they'd hardened after the fall of the first realm, sealing the power that kept their world from crumbling entirely.

Mick listened wide-eyed, interrupting only to throw in a half-joking, half-serious, "So, basically, this place runs on blood and pretty rocks."

Serika laughed quietly from across the table, her usually sharp gaze softened by the candlelight. Even she looked almost human tonight.

The meal stretched long into the night. Dishes were cleared, replaced with sweet fruits and glasses of dark, spiced wine that shimmered faintly when poured. I caught Thalon watching the reflections dance across his cup before his gaze slid to mine. There was something thoughtful there. Quiet, heavy, and far too knowing.

When we finally left the hall, the Hollow Vale had fallen into its midnight hush. The corridors glowed faintly with silver light from the veins that ran through the walls, their pulse slow and steady like the heartbeat of something ancient. The laughter and clatter of the meal faded behind us, replaced by the whisper of our footsteps against polished stone.

Thalon lingered beside me as we walked. His hand brushed mine once, light as breath. Accidental, maybe, but neither of us moved away. The silence stretched between us, full but comfortable, like a secret neither of us needed to name.

And I knew that this fragile peace we had found—the rhythm of training, laughter, and the illusion of safety—was only a breath away before the world shifted again. Before the storm that waited just beyond the horizon found us.

Chapter Twenty-Six

Thalon

The Hollow Vale had grown too quiet. Even the air felt like it was listening. I stood at the edge of the training chamber, its walls carved from living crystals, silver veins pulsing faintly beneath the surface like the heartbeat of the realm itself.

The Mirror of Blood glimmered below us, reflecting Leyla's figure in fractured light. She stood barefoot in the center of the floor, her pulse quick and wild in my ears. Serika circled her slowly, silent.

"This isn't control," the witch murmured. "This is surrender. You must learn the difference."

Leyla's jaw tightened. "You said to trust the magic. I am feeling the magic here." She points to her chest.

"Yes," Serika said, "but you must go deeper. Magic trusts no one. To call life from death, you must understand the cost." I didn't like the way she said it.

"Serika," I warned, my hand resting on the hilt at my side. "You said this would be safe."

Her red-tinged eyes flicked toward me. "Do not mistake discomfort for danger, Fae Prince. You cannot coddle her into greatness."

Leyla looked back at me then, steady and defiant. "I can handle it."

Gods, she believed that.

I almost believed it too.

She had made so much progress here in Hallow Vale. So much more progress than the little time I had to teach her on Earth. Although I hate to admit it, the vampires were excellent in their approach with her. Her evolution since landing here has been extraordinary to see. She was magnificent in every way.

Serika's hand rose, pale and elegant, and the air in the chamber shifted. The silver veins on the walls brightened, their light bleeding into her palm until it glowed like molten glass. Then she pressed that light against Leyla's chest. Leyla gasped— the sound sharp, breathless.

The glow spread under her skin, racing down her arms, her throat, her veins. And then, just as suddenly, it dimmed. The light flickered and vanished, leaving her pale and trembling.

"Serika—" I started forward. The witch didn't stop me this time.

"To bring life, she must prepare herself for the inevitable. Balance, Prince. This is the most vital lesson."

Serika's words were calm, almost reverent, but something in the air shifted as she spoke. I felt it before I saw it—the pulse of magic rippling outward from where Leyla stood, delicate and wild all at once.

The light around her dimmed, the air thinning like it was being pulled from the room. Leyla swayed, the color draining from her face. For a heartbeat, she looked ethereal. Light itself bending toward her, drawn by some invisible gravity. Then her eyes fluttered. Her lips parted as though to speak, but no sound came. Her knees gave out.

I moved before I could think, crossing the distance in a breath. She was weightless in my arms, her body slack, her skin cool. Too cool. The pulse beneath my fingers was faint, barely there, but there.

"Leyla," I breathed, the word catching somewhere between a command and a plea. I brushed the hair from her face; it clung to her skin, damp with sweat.

Her lashes trembled, but she didn't wake.

The faint glow that had surrounded her moments ago flickered once, twice, and died.

Behind me, Mick's footsteps rang out against the stone—sharp, fast, panicked. She skidded to a halt beside us, eyes wide with fear and chest heaving. "What the hell was that?" she snapped at Serika, her voice cracking under the weight of fear. "You said this was safe!"

Her hands hovered over Leyla's shoulders, trembling, unsure whether to touch her or not. The air still hummed with the sweet magic of my mate and the echo of Serika's—a low, dissonant vibration that made my skin crawl.

I looked up, rage pressing hard against my ribs. Serika stood in the center of the circle she had drawn, the remnants of her spell glowing faintly at her feet. Her face was unreadable, eyes like glass. "It was safe," she said softly. "Until she reached too far."

Mick's voice rose, furious and frayed. "Too far? She's unconscious! She—she could've—"

"She's not gone," I interrupted, sharper than I meant to. My thumb brushed against Leyla's wrist, feeling that fragile flutter of life again. "Her heart's still beating."

Serika's expression didn't change, but something in her eyes softened. "Then she has already begun to understand," she murmured. "To bring life, one must first touch death. It is the oldest truth of our kind."

The words meant nothing to me.

Not when Leyla's body was limp in my arms, her head resting against my chest like something precious and breakable.

"Get out," I said, my voice low, dangerous. "All of you."

Serika bowed her head slightly, not in apology but acknowledgment, and turned away. Elias hesitated, eyes darting between us, but the look I gave him left no room for argument. Mick stood her ground, knowing I didn't mean her. When they were gone, the silence rushed in. Thick, heavy, pressing close.

I adjusted my grip, holding my mate closer. Her breath ghosted faintly against my collarbone, shallow but steady. "You can't save the world if you destroy yourself first." I whispered, though my voice trembled with something that wasn't anger.

The crystals embedded in the walls pulsed faintly, their light reflecting across her face, painting her in gold fires and shadow. For a moment, it looked as if the Bridge itself was watching; waiting to see whether she would wake.

And so, we would wait too, both I and her sister, unwilling to let her go.

Chapter Twenty-Seven

Leyla

At first, there was nothing. No sound. No light. No pain. Just silence—vast and endless. Then, slowly, a hum began. Soft at first, like a pulse deep within the earth. I knew that sound, I'd heard it before in dreams, in the Borderlands, when the world itself had sung to me.

I opened my eyes and found myself standing in a field of silver grass. The air shimmered faintly, every blade whispering as if alive. Ahead, a woman waited. Her hair was dark, long, and wild—just like mine. Her eyes were the color of storms before rain.

"Mother," I whispered. She smiled. It was gentle and sad, like she'd been waiting for me a very long time.

"You're learning."

"I don't understand," I said. "I couldn't control it. The witch—she—"

"I know," she said softly. "She showed you the cost, but not the truth."

"What truth?"

"That balance isn't about taking or giving." She stepped closer, her bare feet barely touching the ground. "It's about remembering that life and death are the same breath. You do not steal from one to feed the other. You become the bridge between them."

I swallowed, heart pounding. "It hurts."

Her smile deepened, almost bittersweet. "Creation always does. You cannot heal the realm without feeling its pain."

The wind picked up, swirling silver grass around us. "When you wake, you will want to stop," she said. "You must not. Every time you fall, the world will show you more. Trust it. Trust yourself. You need to be ready for what is coming, my daughter. And it is coming sooner than you think." She reached out, her fingers brushing against my forehead. The world blazed white.

"Remember the song," she whispered.

Then the light swallowed her, and I fell back into my body.

I woke to the feeling of someone holding me. Warmth, steady and real.

Thalon.

His shadows still curled faintly across my skin, feeding warmth back into me.

'Again." I managed to get out.

Mick's voice came from somewhere to my right, sharp and anxious. "Are you insane! You almost died!"

"I'm fine," I croaked. My throat felt raw, my limbs heavy, but I pushed myself upright.

"I saw something."

Thalon's eyes narrowed. He studied me for a long moment, staring into my eyes, assessing the damage. He then let out a sigh. "Gods damn it. Get Serika back in here."

Serika arrived swiftly with that strange grace she carried. As if she was waiting just outside and knowing Thalon would call for her. She gestured her head for me to continue. I did.

"My mother. She said balance isn't taking, it's becoming. She said I can't stop. I think she was telling me that something is coming. I think a lot sooner than any of us expect. We need to be prepared. I need to be ready. And I can't do that unless I keep going."

Mick sighed, rubbing her forehead. "You are actually insane."

Thalon's jaw clenched. He looked between the three of us, then finally down at me.

"Fine," he said. "But if we do this, we do it my way. No more draining. No more death. I train you." His eyes point murderously at Serika.

"Agreed," I said.

Serika's voice drifted from the doorway. "You may try, Fae Prince. But remember: To wield life, she must first understand death."

Thalon didn't even look at her. "Then she'll learn through mine."

The witch's eyes glinted, but she said nothing more, the remainder of the observers exiting with her. Mick included, although begrudgingly. Elias bribed her with some game she had become addicted to with the vampires.

Thalon now stood a few feet away, his sleeves rolled to his elbows, the air around him humming with dark energy.

"Your power feeds on emotion," he instructed. "You can't ignore it. You have to control it. Shadows answer to intention, not fear." He moved closer, his presence electric. "Reach for mine."

I hesitated. "Yours?"

He nodded once. "You felt it before. You can feel it again. Shadows are not just darkness, they are the memory of light. Find it."

I reached out with my magic, tentative, like touching the edge of a blade. His shadows stirred instantly, coiling toward me. They met my power halfway. The same strange balance we'd felt before, where neither consumed the other.

Thalon stepped in behind me, his voice low against my ear. "Breathe with it. Let it find your rhythm."

The shadows tightened around my arms, curling over my shoulders like living silk. His magic pulsed through mine. Steady, powerful, grounding. It wasn't gentle. It was consuming.

"Don't fight it," he murmured. "Match it."

I did. Releasing the tension from my body and focusing on the pull I felt. And suddenly, everything inside me aligned. Light and dark, push and pull, heartbeat and breath. I could feel the hum of life everywhere: in the walls, in the stones beneath my feet, in him. Power rippled outward, silver meeting black, and the air filled with the faint scent of rain and blood.

When I opened my eyes, the entire room glowed faintly, as if it was alive. The vines in the corners of the stones seemed to awaken from death, sprouting new life–majestic looking flowers. Thalon's shadows still surrounded me, holding me steady.

"You did it," he said quietly.

I turned toward him. His face was close, too close, his breath warm against my cheek. "It's a start."

His eyes darkened, unreadable. "You're dangerous when you look at me like that."

"Maybe that's the point," I whispered. He exhaled sharply, stepping back, but not far enough.

"Again," he said, voice rough. And we did.

Hours passed like minutes. The training became rhythm—him grounding me, me pushing him, our magic twining in dangerous harmony. Every surge of power pulled us closer until I couldn't tell where his shadow ended and my light began.

By the end, I was shaking. Breathless but alive. He reached out, brushing a lock of hair from my face, his fingers lingering a heartbeat too long.

"That's enough for tonight."

I met his gaze, hands rested on my hips and panting for breath. "You don't get to decide when I stop."

He almost smiled—almost. "No. But we must ensure that we have energy stored, just in case. We never want to be depleted."

"Can't keep up with me?" I teased, the words leaving my mouth softer than I'd intended, almost breathless. The look that crossed his face was instantaneous—sharp, hungry, entirely unguarded.

He stalked toward me with a deliberate slowness that sent heat curling low in my stomach. The air between us seemed to tremble, thick with something electric and ancient.

"Do you think…" his voice dropped low, rough. "…I truly can't keep up with you, my love?" I was dead. I had to be dreaming.

My pulse spiked. The title burned through me. My love. It sounded dangerous when he said it, reverent and possessive all at once.

I couldn't move. Couldn't breathe.

My body felt caught in some invisible gravity that pulled me toward him no matter how hard I tried to resist.

"Thalon," I whispered, though his name felt more like a plea than a warning. "You don't mean that."

His hands, which had been tracing lazy paths down my arms, stilled. Then, slowly, they rose.

One sliding beneath my chin, his thumb tilting my face upward until I had no choice but to meet his eyes.

They glowed faintly in the half-light, a storm raging, consuming.

"Perhaps," he murmured, "I have not been as forthcoming as I should have been, my little light."

His breath brushed across my lips, warm and steady. "I tried to give you time—to let you find your strength without drowning in everything else you've had to learn. But let me be direct, as you deserve. You are my mate. Mine." The words hit like a spell, sinking straight into my bones. I swallowed hard, every heartbeat echoing painfully loud in the silence that followed.

Suddenly, every inch of space between us felt too small, every flicker of candlelight too bright.

"What does that mean exactly?" I managed, my voice barely audible. "A fated mate?"

"It is everything you think it is," he said, eyes never leaving mine, "and more."

His thumb brushed along my jaw, and I swore my knees might give out. "Fate has bound us together. From birth… And long before then. You were always destined to be mine. Until my last breath, you will be mine. And I, yours. I will never so much as glance at another woman." His voice roughened, the edge of restraint fraying. "You are it for me. Forever."

"It sounds like… vows," I whispered.

He gave a low, knowing hum, tilting his head just enough that the movement drew my focus to his mouth. "Something I am certain you are referring to from the human world. But if it is vows you require, my sweet mate…" His hand slid to the back of my neck, his fingers threading through my hair. "Then hear them here and now."

The air around us seemed to pulse with his words. "I will protect you against any foe. I will lay my life down for you without question. I will learn every detail of you. Every flaw, every breath, every stubborn thought—and I will love all of it. From the moment I kissed you, that was it for me. There is no other life I wish to live."

My breath caught, trembling. The weight of it, the certainty in his voice, it felt like something eternal. He leaned closer, the shadows shifting with him, brushing my cheek with his. "And when your power comes in fully," he whispered, "you will feel it too. The bond. How it grows stronger with every heartbeat. How it burns when we're apart."

His mouth hovered inches from mine. His voice dropped, quiet enough that it felt meant only for the space between us. "And all I have yet to experience," he said, his lips ghosting against my skin, "is a…" His breath shivered down my neck.

"Little…" His lips brushed the corner of my mouth.

"Tiny…" His teeth grazed my bottom lip, slow, deliberate, sinful.

"Kiss." My body was molten. Every thought scattered.

"Thalon—" I could barely form his name.

The heat rolling off him was unbearable, his magic humming in tune with mine, like our hearts had forgotten how to beat separately. My fingers curled into his shirt, pulling him closer without meaning to.

He smiled against my skin, voice a low promise. "Leyla—"

The sound that cut through his words was deafening. A deep, distant boom shook the walls, followed by the sharp crack of splintering stone.

The light from the crystals flickered violently. Screams echoed from above… Dozens, maybe hundreds. Thalon's expression hardened instantly.

The warmth in his eyes was gone, replaced by cold, deadly focus.

And then, almost to himself, barely more than a whisper. "The King has come."

Chapter Twenty-Eight

Leyla

The world fractured with the sound of thunder. Not from the sky, no. This thunder came from within the stone itself. The ground trembled, a deep, bone-shaking rumble that made my teeth ache.

The stones screamed.

The sound was unearthly. Splintering, cracking, crying out as if the mountain itself had come alive and was tearing itself apart. Before I could even draw breath, the walls of the training hall split open. The silver veins that ran through the stone burst outward, shattering into a thousand burning fragments. For a heartbeat, they hung suspended in the air like molten stars. Then, fell around us in a storm of light and dust. The force hit me before the sound did.

The shockwave slammed into my chest, stealing the air from my lungs, sending me stumbling backward. The floor pitched violently beneath me, and I might've hit the ground if Thalon hadn't moved faster than thought itself. His arms wrapping around me, shadows coiling like a living thing to shield us from the blast. The world dimmed, wrapped in a cocoon of moving darkness.

His magic rippled through the air, cold and alive, pressing against my skin like mist. I could feel his heartbeat against my back—steady, anchored—while everything else fell to chaos.

"Stay behind me," he ordered, voice low and sharp, vibrating through my bones.

I tried to speak, to ask what had happened, but the noise drowned everything. The clash of steel followed, ringing through the shattered hall. Sparks flared somewhere beyond the veil of dust. Fae and vampire magic hissed, sharp and bright, colliding with something darker—something that didn't belong here.

Through the haze, Elias appeared, sprinting down the corridor, his sword drawn and blood streaking his temple. His expression was grim, wild. "The hunters are here!" he shouted, his voice echoing through the ruins. "They've breached the upper gates. There's a mage with them!"

Thalon's hand tightened around mine. The air between us changed. Charged, dangerous, and certain. The war we'd been trying to outrun had finally found us.

Thalon's expression hardened into something cold and deadly. "The Hollow Vale is hidden. How did they find us?"

"They didn't," came Serika's voice from behind the rising smoke. She moved into view, her red hair singed and tangled, her crimson-tinged eyes glowing faintly. "They were led."

The words hung between us like poison. A second blast shook the floor beneath our feet, cracks racing through the marble, glowing red from the inside out. Magic, dark and tainted, pulsed through the walls, eating away at the Vale's heart.

"Go," Gyor appeared in the chaos. "Now."

We ran. Shadows and smoke and screams blurring together as we rounded corners and climbed the spiraling stairs. Every hall was chaos. Vampires fought in clusters, their movements quick and fluid — claws flashing, blades gleaming, fangs bared. They moved like a single heartbeat, protecting their sanctuary. My sanctuary. Through the haze, I caught sight of Gyor, his sword cleaving through one of the King's hunters. When he turned, his golden hair was matted, his face now bloodied, but his voice still carried like thunder.

"To the Heart Chamber!" he roared. "Protect the Bridge!"

The words sent a jolt through me. The vampires rallied instantly, forming a line between us and the hunters.

"Come!" Thalon barked, dragging me toward a corridor I barely recognized. His shadows escaped him, protecting and killing all at once. The silver veins on the walls had gone dim, pulsing faintly like a dying heartbeat. The Hollow Vale was still alive, but barely. Auren appeared through the smoke, her eyes blazing copper fire.

"The outer wards have fallen," she shouted. "We can hold the inner sanctum if we get to the crystal! It'll shield the survivors!"

"Then let's go," Thalon said. But before we could take another step, a scream split the air, sharp and familiar. Mick. My heart stopped.

I turned, just in time to see her down the hall, two of the King's hunters dragging her through a breach in the wall, her body thrashing against their grip. I thought that Elias has already gotten her to safety. One of the hunters had his arm wrapped around her throat; the other held a dagger at her ribs.

"Mick!" I screamed, breaking from Thalon's grasp. Her eyes found mine—wide and terrified. For one heartbeat, she reached out her hand toward me. And then, in a shimmer of black smoke, they were gone.

"No!" I lunged forward, but a band of shadow whipped around my waist, yanking me back. Thalon's arms locked around me, his strength unyielding as steel.

"Let me go!" I struggled, my magic sparking violently. The air crackled between us, light and shadow colliding. "Thalon, they have her! They have her—"

"I know," he hissed, voice breaking, "but if you run now, they'll have you too."

I slammed my fists against his chest, shaking, screaming. "Then have them take me!"

"Leyla, listen to me!" His grip tightened as another explosion tore through the upper vaults. The ceiling cracked, raining shards of crystal. His shadows coiled above us, holding the debris at bay. "If you die, this was all for nothing. We'll find her—I swear it—but not if we get buried in here!"

Tears burned my eyes. Every part of me wanted to tear away, to chase her until my lungs gave out. But the walls were collapsing around us. The heat, the screams, the crackle of breaking wards—it was all too much. My knees gave out, and Thalon caught me again, pressing his forehead to mine.

"We'll find her," he whispered, fierce and raw. "I promise you. But we have to move."

Auren appeared again, blood now staining her lips, her blade glowing faintly red.

"The heart crystal, now!" She ordered. "Go! I'll cover you."

Thalon looked at her, really looked, and something passed between them. Respect. Resignation.

"The Bridge must live," she said. Then she turned and ran toward the oncoming wave of hunters, light gathering at her palms. She was radiant, silver and red and unstoppable, before the blast consumed her. The shockwave threw us both back. The air went white… And then complete darkness. When I could see again, the corridor behind us was gone. Only dust and flame remained. Thalon dragged me to my feet. Elias was already waiting ahead, hauling a wounded vampire by the arm.

"Gyor's alive!" he shouted. "He's calling the retreat! There's another passage—East!"

We ran. The lower halls were chaos. Vampires guided the wounded through hidden tunnels that pulsed faintly with wardlight. Their elders and guards all retreated toward the shimmering heart of the Hollow Vale. Gyor met us with Elias at the end of the corridor, his armor scorched, a deep cut across his cheek.

"You must go," he commanded. "The King's mage is dead, but more will come. The eastern caverns lead beyond the cliffs. We'll seal the rest and rebuild from what remains."

Thalon clasped his arm. "The Vale stands?"

Gyor nodded once. "Barely. But it stands. The heart still beats."

His gaze softened as he turned to me. "Your friend—"

I shook my head, swallowing the ache that threatened to break me.

"We'll find her." It came from Thalon.

Gyor reached up, placing a bloodied hand against my temple — a strange, old gesture of blessing. "May your path be shadowed by strength and lit by purpose, Bridge of Realms."

I nodded, unable to speak. Then, Thalon was running again, with me in his arms and Elias by our side. Behind us, the Hollow Vale shuddered, wounded but alive. Its heart crystal pulsed faintly, like the rhythm of a dying world refusing to fade. At the tunnel's mouth, I turned one last time—to the faint light, to the smoke curling upward from the ruins.

"Mick," I whispered. "Hold on."

The King's hunters had taken my sister.

Little did they know what they awakened in the process.

Soon, they would all be dead.

Chapter Twenty-Nine

Thalon

The forest closed in around us, branches clawing at our clothes, roots threatening to trip us with every step. I could feel it before my eyes confirmed it—something was following.

"Thalon," Leyla whispered, tight with unease. "We're not alone."

I didn't answer. Elias, ever vigilant, scanned the shadows ahead. Then I saw her—a figure gliding between the trees with unnerving silence.

"*Serika,*" I muttered under my breath. Recognition sharpened my instincts. The witch had followed us.

She stepped into a clearing, and the moonlight revealed her fully: tall, cloaked in black with silver runes tracing the edges, eyes glowing faintly red. She didn't flinch under my gaze.

"Why are you following us?" I demanded, voice hard.

"Because you will need me," she said calmly. "Mick's spell—what she carried—led them to you. She didn't know what she was doing. It is essential I am with you if she is to return safely. I have seen it." Leyla gasped.

I clenched my jaw. "We're running, not taking advice from a witch."

Her gaze met mine, unwavering. "Without me, she will remain lost… or worse. And there's more, you need to know why she led them here. Mick was marked with a tracker spell."

I froze, the words sharp and heavy. "A tracker spell?"

Serika nodded. "Yes. I realized it as soon as the King's hunters arrived. I could smell their presence on her… lingering, twisted into her own aura. It was subtle, almost invisible, but enough to trace. She didn't know it, of course. She thought she was protecting you, hiding from them. But every step she took led them closer."

Leyla's hand tightened on mine. "Mick… she didn't mean to…"

"I know," I said, jaw tight. "We're going to fix it."

Serika's red-tinged eyes locked on mine. "I am the only one who can safely remove the tracker. And I can shield her from being followed again. But you need me with you now."

I let out a low growl, irritation flaring. I didn't like being commanded, didn't like anyone telling me how to protect the people I swore to keep safe. But this was Michaela. Leyla's sister. Her blood in all but name. I couldn't ignore it.

"Fine," I said, voice low, reluctant. "We're moving, but I lead. You follow. No arguments."

Serika inclined her head, a faint smile brushing her lips, as if she accepted the arrangement for now.

We pushed deeper into the forest, shadows thickening, the air growing heavier with danger. My senses screamed again— movement ahead, deliberate and dangerous.

"Up ahead," Elias hissed. Two figures emerged from the underbrush, eyes glinting. Kidnappers.

I shifted instinctively in front of Leyla, placing her safely behind me. "Stay close."

Serika lifted her hand, silver runes glowing along her fingers. A hum filled the clearing. The attackers froze mid-step, rooted to the ground as if bound by invisible chains. I scowled, unwilling to admit it, but she had just cleared a path that no blade or brute force could have achieved so quickly.

"Move," she said.

And we did, slipping past the frozen figures. I cast her a glare, my distrust simmering beneath the surface. But she had proven—temporarily, at least—that she was necessary.

Eventually, the forest thinned, revealing a long-forgotten property nestled among rolling hills. My eyes flicked to Leyla.

"We are going to the former King and Queen's summer estate, it is not known by many. It is closer to the border, easier to extract Mick, but the King will likely never expect us to be. It is our safest option to strategize our next move, without compromising your safety."

Serika nodded. "I will put up wards, we will be safe."

I exhaled slowly, letting my tension ease just a little. Finally, a place to regroup, plan, and protect my mate. Serika would be with us, for now—but the silent promise I had made to Leyla, and her sister, remained mine alone.

And I would keep Leyla safe, no matter the cost.

Chapter Thirty

Thalon

The forest finally thinned, revealing a clearing bathed in pale moonlight. Nestled in its center stood a sprawling house, neither fully castle nor purely cottage—its walls warm with the memory of a home, yet built with the quiet grandeur of royalty. Brown vines crept along stone and wood alike, softening its edges, while tall windows reflected the moon like watchful eyes. Leyla stopped mid-step, her breath catching. She didn't speak, only let her fingers brush over the rough stone of a pillar as if feeling the history itself. Her eyes were wide, almost dazed.

"This… this is your family's home," I said carefully, keeping my voice low. "I believe that this may have been where you were born, before my father; well, before he took over the rest of the realm."

She ran her hand along the carved edges of the doorway, tracing shapes she had never known consciously but seemed to recognize instinctively.

"I believe that is why I was sent to Earth by my father. The magical resonance here matches what I sensed when I found you. He wanted to see if there was truth to the tale, if you perhaps were the magical disturbance that was detected. He didn't want a threat to his throne going unchecked."

Leyla's fingers moved to a carved window frame, the wood worn smooth with age. She leaned against it lightly, her gaze drifting over the rolling hills beyond. "I wish I could have met them. My life on Earth… It was just not what I would have chosen for myself. Mick and her mom took me in when I was older. She became… the sister I needed. She grounded me when I couldn't keep myself steady."

She lingered there, almost in a daze, hands tracing the stone and wood around her. Her lips moved as if speaking to herself as much as to me. "I should be able to find her. I should be able to bring her back…"

I kept my hand lightly on her shoulder, steadying her even as her thoughts seemed to drift.

"We will," I said. "And this place… It can help us. You're safe here, for now. We can regroup, make a plan to extract Mick."

Serika had already begun moving along the perimeter, hands raised as silver runes glimmered faintly in the moonlight. A hum filled the air as she whispered wards into being, a lattice of protection forming invisibly around the house.

"Those wards will alert us if anyone tries to cross the boundary," she said quietly, almost to herself. "No one will find us tonight."

Elias moved around the house methodically, scanning the perimeter. Even in the calm of the clearing, his vigilance reminded me how dangerous the situation remained.

"No signs of pursuit yet," he reported. "But we shouldn't linger too long."

Leyla stood near the doorway, now running her palm along the edge of the carved wooden railing on the porch. The house had a cottage feel—warm, welcoming—but there were subtle reminders of its former royalty: gilded emblems, tall arched windows, and the faint scent of old incense lingering in corners. Her fingers paused at a small engraved emblem she didn't recognize, and her lips moved softly.

Her eyes glistened in the moonlight. She pressed her forehead lightly to the railing, leaning on it as if it could anchor her thoughts. "I just… I need Mick." She whispered. "We are the only family that either of us have left. She keeps me grounded. I keep her from losing herself. I can't do this without her."

I tightened my grip on her shoulder, letting her lean on me for a moment. The house was a refuge, yes, but it was also a reminder of all the things she had never known, the life she could barely grasp, and the family that had disappeared before she could even remember them.

"We can stay here for as long as you need to regroup," Serika cut in. "But the tracker spell on your friend is still active. We move fast, and we move wisely." Leyla exhaled slowly, tracing her fingers along the banister one last time before straightening.

"We will find her," Leyla said, voice steadying. "We have to bring her back."

I didn't need to say anything. I had already vowed to protect her, as I had vowed to protect Leyla and keep her safe.

No words were needed.

Chapter Thirty-One

Leyla

I carried the bundle of letters to a small writing desk near the window, laying them out carefully as I tried to focus. But my mind kept drifting, imagining Mick trapped somewhere, the fear in her eyes, the panic that must be coursing through her. I pressed my palm against the desk, letting it ground me. She needed me—and I needed her. I barely slept last night. I allowed my body rest for the energy I knew this journey would require. But nothing more. Mick was taken. And I would refuse sleep entirely if my body allowed.

"We don't have the luxury of time, we need a plan and now," Elias demanded.

I leaned against the desk, my fingers tracing the letters again. "I just want her back…" My voice trembled, and I clenched the paper, as if squeezing it harder could pull her out of danger.

Serika turned, her expression gentle but firm. "I have heard of how she encountered an Echo upon entering Orrynne and survived. I suspect that is when the tracker spell took its effect. The King has been experimenting more. He likely had the Echo implant the tracker when it would come in contact with your group. The moment the King's hunters arrived, I could sense it. A similar magical scent that flowed through their battalion." I swallowed hard. My chest tightened, relief and guilt mingling. Mick had always tried to protect me, and I knew she wouldn't have led them to us on purpose.

"No," Serika said. "It was placed on her without her knowledge. That's why we need to move quickly—and carefully. I can still feel the magical remnants of the spell, long enough for you to reach her, but only for a small window of time." Thalon's jaw clenched again, but he nodded.

"Fine," he said tersely. "But this is on me. We get her back, and no one else interferes. Agreed?"

Serika inclined her head. "Agreed. But we need precision." I looked out the window at the clearing outside, the moonlight spilling over the vines and stone.

"I'll do whatever it takes," I whispered. Thalon stepped closer, his hand brushing mine lightly as he looked at me.

"We'll get her. And you'll stay close. No distractions, no mistakes." I nodded, gripping the edge of the desk. My thoughts went back to my childhood, the empty spaces in my early foster homes, the absence of family... and now Mick. The bond we shared wasn't just friendship—she was my sister. And I would do anything to keep her alive. Serika began to trace runes along the floor, her voice rising and falling in a quiet chant. The air shimmered faintly, and I felt the tension in the house thicken.

Outside, the world waited.

Somewhere out there, Mick was waiting for us, and time was slipping through our fingers.

The hum of Serika's wards filled the room like a faint heartbeat, low and constant against the quiet. Then, without warning, it broke.

A single sound shattered the calm.

Boots crunching over the gravel outside. Slow, deliberate, unhurried. I froze. My pulse spiked, thudding in my ears. The air changed, tightening, heavy with magic I didn't recognize.

Thalon's hand went to the hilt of his sword instinctively, his entire body shifting in one fluid, protective motion. Elias mirrored him, his stance low and ready.

Then, the front door opened. Not flung, not forced, but pushed with such composure that even the walls seemed to acknowledge her arrival. The wards dimmed, the light of their runes flickering submissively. She stepped inside, and the room itself seemed to draw breath. Tall, regal, and impossibly composed. The fae woman stepped into the threshold like she'd been carved from moonlight and power.

Her gown shimmered like spilled silver, each movement catching the light in soft ripples. The fabric clung to her figure before spilling in a waterfall of silk around her boots. At her throat gleamed a choker of black diamond, and from her shoulders flowed a mantle of delicate threads so pale it looked like captured starlight. But it was her presence that silenced us.

Her eyes—ice blue and sharp as cut glass—swept across the room with predatory precision, missing nothing. Every motion was deliberate, graceful, but carried a weight that made the air hum in her wake. She was beauty and danger perfectly entwined.

"Mother," Thalon breathed. The word barely carried, but it trembled with disbelief. His jaw clenched, the faintest muscle twitch betraying what he felt beneath that unshakable façade.

I'd seen Thalon fight monsters and face death without flinching, but in that moment… he hesitated. Cerys didn't look at him. Not yet.

She moved deeper into the room with unhurried confidence, the soft whisper of her gown brushing against the stone. Her fingers trailed lightly across the back of a chair, then along the edge of the desk. A silent act of possession, as if she were reacquainting herself with something she'd long ago forgotten. Her gaze found me. The intensity of it stopped me cold.

Calm. Measured. Searching.

It wasn't curiosity—it was recognition. As though she'd spent years trying to remember a dream and had finally woken inside it.

"You," she said softly, almost reverently. Her voice was mesmerizing. But also, edged with something sharp enough to cut. "You are the daughter of my dearest friend."

Her words struck like the pull of a tide, dragging something deep inside me forward. Her expression shifted—her regal composure flickered, revealing sorrow buried beneath decades of restraint.

"I am Cerys," she said, her tone carrying the weight of both crown and grief. "And I have waited over twenty years for this moment. To see her bloodline alive before me."

I stumbled back a step, unable to find words. The letters I'd been holding crumpled slightly in my hand, the paper softening under the tremor of my grip. Thalon's eyes darted to me, then back to her.

His voice came low, careful. "Mother," he said, the word edged in warning. "This isn't—" She silenced him with the faintest lift of her hand.

"Your mother," she said, turning back to me, "was my closest friend. We dreamed of peace. A realm free of my husband's cruelty. We believed it could exist." Her voice softened, but beneath it lived something darker, simmering. "And she…" Her eyes darkened, sorrow curdling into steel. "…she was taken from me. Betrayed. Slain by the same man who I have been tied to for centuries."

The words hung in the air like smoke.

Thalon's voice was rough now, laced with disbelief. "Why are you here?" His eyes were searching hers; trying to understand.

Cerys's lips curved into a smile—faint, deliberate, and deadly.

It wasn't the warmth of a mother's joy, but the sharp, poised satisfaction of a predator finally scenting blood. Her voice, when she spoke, carried that same lethal grace. "Because finally," she murmured, each word drawn like the pull of a blade, "I have the chance for revenge. After centuries of silence, I can strike at him. Thalon. This is our time."

The air seemed to darken around her, charged with quiet fury. Even the candlelight on the walls flickered in response to her rising energy, their light bending toward her like loyal subjects awaiting command.

"I've heard the whispers," she continued, her tone trembling faintly with something between excitement and disbelief. "That the King's son has found his fated mate." Her gaze cut to Thalon, sharp and assessing. "Your sigil—it is broken, is it not?"

Thalon hesitated. I could see the war behind his eyes, the flicker of realization and dread. Finally, he gave a single, stiff nod.

Cerys's composure faltered for the briefest instant, panic and exhilaration tangled together in her voice. "Then it's true," she breathed. "After all this time."

Her shoulders straightened again, her expression hardening back into the marble calm of a queen.

"I have waited lifetimes to see my husband's ambitions undone. To see his cruelty returned to him tenfold. Nothing. No God, no magic, no creature of this realm or the next will stop me now."

The silence that followed pressed close, taut and suffocating. Thalon's hand raked through his hair as if he could steady himself with the motion. His lips parted, but no words came. He tried again, and still nothing. Just a hollow sound swallowed by the charged air between them.

Cerys let him flounder in that silence before she turned to me. Her movements were slow and deliberate, like a queen descending from her throne to address a chosen heir. When her gaze met mine fully, the weight of it was almost unbearable.

"And you, child," she said softly, her voice threaded with something that sounded like reverence. "You carry her blood. Your mother's blood. The same courage that defied a crown. The same resilience that refused to die even when everything else did." My breath caught.

"You will help me see this through," Cerys continued, stepping closer until the scent of her, jasmine and smoke and cold metal, overwhelmed my senses. "And together…" She paused, her eyes glinting with dangerous promise. "…we will bring them justice."

Her gaze flicked briefly to Thalon, then back to me. "And your friend," she added softly, almost as an afterthought—but her tone was too measured, too purposeful. "Your friend will be free."

I opened my mouth, ready to speak, but Thalon's sharp glance froze the words on my tongue. His warning was clear.

Not yet.

Cerys's expression softened, though the calculation in her eyes never faded.

When she spoke again, her voice dropped to something quieter, almost intimate. "I've been able to check on your friend… Mick, is it?"

The name struck me like lightning. My body went rigid.

"They've thrown her into the dungeons," Cerys went on, her tone low but steady. "Deep beneath the dungeon entrance. I managed to get food to her through a contact… a small mercy, I know. Though it was all I could do without drawing attention. She is alive." Her lips pressed together briefly, the faintest flicker of genuine sorrow breaking through. "But barely.

The spell they've used on her, the trackers, it will remove her strength. She won't last long."

The air left my lungs all at once. My chest tightened painfully, my heart thrumming against my ribs. The letters in my hands crumpled under my grip.

"She's alive," I whispered, my voice breaking on the word. Relief and terror tangled in my throat, indistinguishable from one another. "But—"

"Exactly," Cerys interrupted, her tone quickening, sharp with urgency. "Alive, but fading. Every hour she remains there, her body will eventually succumb to the dangers of the dungeon. Every moment we hesitate, he wins. That is why I am here now." Her voice rose, the queen returning to the surface. "Together, we will save her. And when we do…" Her expression hardened into something feral. "…My husband will finally pay for everything he has done."

Thalon's jaw tightened, a muscle feathering beneath his skin. Disbelief flashed in his eyes, quickly swallowed by something darker. He pushed back from the table so abruptly the chair scraped harshly against the stone, the sound slicing through the tension like a blade. Horror carved itself into his features, raw and unguarded. He wasn't just looking at his mother now. He was staring at the first strike of a war he wasn't certain we could survive.

Cerys merely smiled, the faintest curve of her lips betraying neither guilt nor hesitation. "All great victories begin with risk, my son," she said softly, the words falling like silk and steel all at once.

Before I could stop myself, I stepped forward. Toward her.

Toward the woman who had just walked out of her castle and into my life. The air around her shimmered faintly, heavy with power and memory, yet I felt no fear.

Only awe. To hold onto this and endure what she has for so long… It took my breath away.

I reached out a trembling hand to her. "I'm Leyla," I said quietly, my voice catching somewhere between reverence and disbelief.

Because in that moment, standing before her, I knew she wasn't just a queen or a stranger. She was a miracle—the living thread that had been waiting, all along, to pull my story into hers.

Chapter Thirty-Two

Thalon

My mother's presence filled the summer house like a storm tempered by quiet authority. Even as she laid out the urgency of rescuing Mick, I couldn't stop my mind from tracing the deeper threads of what we were really fighting for. Mick's safety was our focus, yes—but Leyla… My mate carried something far greater. Something that stretched beyond this moment, beyond even the wrath of my father.

"Leyla. She is the Bridge of the Realms. If she fails, if she is harmed," My voice faltered. "Life itself, the realms, and everything we have tried to protect could die with her."

Her expression softened, faintly, but only slightly. "Your mother understood that, you know," she said, now looking at Leyla, her voice tinged with nostalgia. "She and I… we were inseparable in our youth. Young, foolish, determined. We dreamed of a world where the realms could coexist, where children could run freely across fields and silver forests, laughing without fear." I could see it now, the fire that had driven her all these years, hidden under a carefully crafted mask of indifference. The rare times she showed any emotion were the beatings in my youth. That was long ago, now.

"She sounds wonderful." Leyla whispered, more to herself. "I wish I could have met her."

Cerys nodded, her eyes distant for a moment.

"Yes. And when she sent you to the mortal realm, it was to protect you. Not just from my husband, not just from the chaos of the Borderlands that erupted after their murders, but to give you a chance to grow strong enough to restore what was lost. To one day bring life back to the realms. She wanted children to laugh, to play, to live without the shadows of fear her world was steeped in." A tear sat on her cheek. "I wish she were only here to see it."

I swallowed, the weight of it settling heavy on my chest. Leyla's journey… My mate… She carried the hope of generations. The power to restore the world that had been stolen. A weight I vowed to help her carry.

"And now," Cerys continued, her eyes flashing with both grief and determination, "Finally, I have the chance to act in her stead. I owe her that much… and more." She paused, her gaze hardening. "There is more you should know. The King…" Her eyes darkened further. "…He is not just content with holding her. He wants her for experimentation. A mortal child, subjected to tests he claims will strengthen his power. That is why we must act tonight, at nightfall. There is no time to waste."

I clenched my fists, my anger simmering beneath my skin.

Visions of Mick trapped and threatened by my father's twisted ambitions ran across my vision. Years of seeing what he would do and being bound by the sigil to do nothing to stop him. Now, my mate's only family is just another one of his victims. I would kill him.

Chapter Thirty-Three

Leyla

The outskirts of the City of Glass unfolded before us like a dream carved from starlight and danger. Even from this distance, it shimmered. A living crystal sprawled across the horizon, its towers catching the dying light of dusk and scattering it into a thousand fractured rainbows. Every spire gleamed like a blade. Every bridge glowed faintly from within.

The summer house where we had been hiding must have been only a few miles from the outer wall, but it felt as though we were crossing a threshold into another world entirely. This one built of light, silence, and deafening fear. The air here was sharper, thinner, charged with static. The faint hum of wards thrummed underfoot, a reminder that the city did not merely exist, it watched. As we moved along the narrow glass path, my reflection flickered beside me, fractured across the mirrored walls. I pressed my fingers to the smooth surface of a low barrier, half expecting it to pulse back with life.

The glass was warm to the touch, vibrating faintly with trapped magic. Beyond it, the city stretched like a labyrinth of spires and walkways, bridges weaving impossibly through the sky. My stomach twisted. Thalon had tried to describe this place on our journey... How the King had built it as both marvel and prison, beauty layered over brutality. But nothing could have prepared me for its magnitude. The City of Glass wasn't just beautiful; it was alive. A masterpiece of power and paranoia. Every reflection felt like an eye. Every glint of light seemed to follow our movements.

Cerys led the way.

Her silhouette moved like a shadow of moonlight against the gleaming city. Her gown caught the wind like the wing of some great bird, and the faint click of her heels echoed in perfect rhythm with the hum of magic. She moved as though she owned the ground beneath her feet. And perhaps, she had.

She paused occasionally, brushing her hand across the smooth faces of the glass spires or tracing invisible sigils in the air. The faint glow of runes followed her fingertips before fading, like whispers swallowed by the city itself.

"The wards and patrols are heavier here than any place you will see," she said softly, her voice barely audible. "We must move quickly, and carefully. Follow my lead."

Behind us, Serika walked with her head bowed, her focus drawn entirely inward. The faint aura of her magic shimmered around her hands like smoke caught in moonlight. For most of the journey, she had been silent, her energy attuned to the faint pulse of Mick's spell — that cursed tracker that tied her to the King's reach.

Now, she slowed, her hands rising, the air thickening with power. She murmured a final incantation under her breath, the ancient syllables vibrating through the ground like distant thunder. Lines of gold light coiled and twisted around her wrists before unraveling into the air. A final rune blazed between her palms, bright enough to make the glass shimmer in response.

Then, with a sharp flick of her fingers, the rune burst into a shower of embers and vanished.

"The tracker spell is gone," she said at last, her voice steady, though her face had gone pale. "Mick's presence will no longer be felt by the King's hunters." Relief flickered through me, but it was short-lived. Serika's gaze lifted to Cerys's, and something grim passed between them. "But the King's reach is long. He may sense the magic's unraveling. Even from here."

Cerys nodded once, her eyes hardening as she turned back toward the city. The reflection of the towers burned silver in her gaze.

"Then we move before he does," she said. And with that, the Queen of Orrynne stepped forward, toward the glittering heart of her husband's kingdom, and toward the danger waiting within.

I let out a breath I hadn't realized I was holding. Relief mixed with fear. Mick was alive, but barely. Every step from here was dangerous.

Thalon stepped forward, letting the shadows coil around him like liquid silk. He gestured subtly, and the darkness spread across the roads and bridges ahead, folding over us, hiding us from every guard's sight. In his homeland, his power was unparalleled. The shadows responded to his thought, bending and twisting, swallowing our movement completely. I could feel the raw energy thrumming in the air. Protective, yet tense, as though the city itself tested him.

Cerys guided us with a quiet authority, pointing out patrol rotations, hidden walkways, and back paths. "This sector is lightly warded," she said, motioning to a narrow alley suspended between two spires. "We can cross here, but the moment you step out, the guards on the lower walkway will see you. Thalon's shadows will cover us, but move fast."

Elias fell into step beside me, his sword ready, eyes scanning every reflection and glimmer. I could sense the tension in him, the anger simmering beneath his calm. Hours passed, or perhaps minutes; time seemed to stretch unnaturally in the city. The glinting towers gave way to the darker stone of the dungeon district, the spires sharp and ominous, shadows pooling beneath the walls.

Cerys slowed, whispering instructions. "The entrance is hidden beneath this tower. Stay close, and do not make a sound. Every step is counted."

Torchlight guttered along wet walls, throwing the corridor into a wash of sickly gold and black. Cerys moved ahead like a shadow of her own, silent and certain, fingers trailing along the masonry as though reading the room for answers.

"Guards rotate every fifteen minutes. The deeper we go, the less they expect intruders." She pointed to a narrow passage that sloped downward; we followed, our steps measured, our breaths held tight in our chests. With every stair we descended, the air grew colder, thicker.

I pulled my vampiric cloak tighter around me; the fabric did little to keep the chill from seeping into my bones. Serika's murmurs threaded through the dark, soft consonants and old words that left faint, spinning runes on the floor. The wards coiled and paled, consuming stray echoes, dulling the creak of our boots, smothering the scent of us until our passage felt like a ghost passing through a tomb.

Then, through the damp hush, I heard it: a rasp of breath too small for the space, a sound so familiar it landed like a second heart. Mick.

She lay at the far end of the chamber behind a grille of rusted iron. Curled into herself like a broken bird. The bars made her prison look almost ornamental in the torchlight, but the wounds were real: deep crescent bites along her arms, places where the skin had been torn and was already blackening. Her chest rose in a ragged, shallow rhythm.

She coughed and a wet, bitter sound left her, and when we surged forward I felt the world tilt. Thalon's hand tightened at my shoulder, stopping me from touching the cage where she lay. His shadows uncoiled, long fingers of living dark that slid beneath the lock and braided into the mechanism. The iron shuddered; then with a soft implosive snap, the lock gave. As if the lock itself was relieved to be free. The sound was miraculous and obscene all at once.

I couldn't push the door open fast enough. I crawled into the small space, scooped Mick's head into my lap, and the motion sent a hot wave of tears burning into my throat. She smelled like damp straw and old fear. Her eyes fluttered open to me. Seeing, and then sinking away as weakness closed over them again.

"Mick," I said, voice raw and uselessly small. "It's me. I'm here. You're safe." My words felt like a lie and like a promise at the same time.

Elias's face was a map of rage. His veins standing on his temple, fists clenched like he wanted to tear the stone itself apart. He slammed his fist into the nearest wall; the echo answered across the passage in a long, hollow boom.

Thalon moved to my side, his eyes scanning the chamber for any sign of danger. Even in the dim light, his features were stone, barely contained fury. "We have her," he said, low and controlled, each syllable measured, though the tremor in his hands betrayed him. "But we cannot stay. We're not ready to bring the full weight of this against him. We go. Now."

Serika and Cerys knelt beside us, their palms pressed briefly to Mick's skin as they both intoned a soft string of words. Protective wards over her body. Tiny lights, like moths of warmth, briefly threaded through Mick's wounds and around her ribs. The queen's face, stark just moments before, softened into something maternal and fierce.

"She will live," Cerys promised, voice steady as iron. "We will take her from here. My husband's cruelty will never touch her again."

My fingers combed the damp hair from Mick's brow, the motion trembling. Every scar, every ragged mark flared inside me like a promise. Relief roared through me, but it rode on a tide of anger so hot it made my hands shake. Elias gathered Mick in his arms with clumsy tenderness and began the careful, ward-respecting way out. Every movement deliberate so as not to fray Serika's protections.

I slid to my feet, lungs tight with a new kind of resolve. Mick was alive.

That fact burned through the fear and grief, turning every nerve in me to steel.

We moved as one. A band stitched together by blood and promise, and headed back into the breathing dark, away from the cage and toward whatever storm Cerys would unleash to pull the King's reign down.

Mick's shallow breaths rattled against Elias' chest while he cradled her. The dungeon around us smelled of stone and despair, the darkness thick with the echoes of suffering. Every second we stayed here was another moment of danger, yet even as my fear roared, a strange calm settled over me. Serika's wards pulsed faintly along the walls, shimmering with a protective light I could feel as much as see.

"We move now," Serika whispered. "The King has not yet sensed the removal of the tracker spell, but time is short."

Thalon rose, shadows coiling around him like living smoke. He motioned for Elias and me to follow. I tightened my hold on Mick's foot, the only part I was able to touch while Elias held her close. I needed her touch, needed to know that my sister was alive. I could feel the pulse of life in her body, so weak and fragile. Something within me stirred; a warmth that rose from my chest and spread through my arms. I hesitated for a heartbeat, unsure, and then it came… A flicker of power, a thread of energy I had faintly felt before. The faint glow of life spread from my hands, brushing against Mick's bruised skin. I whispered her name softly, willing my energy to knit together torn tissue, soothe the bite marks, and strengthen the fragile rhythm of her heart. Almost like a prayer.

Serika glanced at me, eyes wide. "You… you're using it. Carefully. Focus, Leyla. Let it flow."

I felt the warmth settle in Mick's body, like sunlight reaching cold stone. Her breathing deepened slightly, a little steadier, and her eyelids fluttered. Relief threatened to break me, but we had no time to linger. Cerys moved ahead, her presence commanding, guiding Thalon and me through the twisting corridors.

"The King's hunters will not expect movement from here," she murmured, "but we cannot linger. Keep her close, Elias. His patrols are light here, but deadly."

The climb to the surface felt endless, shadows stretching and contracting under Thalon's control. His focus was sharp, ensuring our group remained hidden. I kept my hands on Mick, channeling small pulses of energy whenever she faltered, each touch knitting strength back into her battered body. She stirred more, a faint murmur escaping her lips. I felt hope bloom cautiously in my chest. Finally, we emerged into the open air atop one of the city's lower bridges.

The sky was darkening, the last shards of sunlight reflecting off the glass towers around us. The city shimmered like a frozen river of crystal, brilliant and deadly. Thalon's shadows wrapped tighter around us, blending seamlessly with the darkness. Cerys scanned the rooftops and streets below.

"We move through the alleys here. Guards patrol these routes, but not all at once. Shadow and ward will continue to shield us." I clutched Mick's foot tighter, whispering her name, willing her to hold on, willing my energy to flow. It was exhausting, pulling from some deep reservoir I hadn't fully tapped into. But, I felt a connection. A thread from me to her, from me to the city itself, from me to the promise of life I carried.

"Leyla," Elias said suddenly, his voice sharp but urgent. "Focus, she's counting on you. And we don't have long."

Thalon growled from ahead. "Watch it, Elias. She's doing more than we could have hoped for."

I nodded, drawing in a deep breath, and let my hands glow softly again. Small, broken shards of light seemed to rise from the ground around us, stirred by my presence, reflecting in the city's towers like sparks in a dark river. Thalon's shadow stretched over us, protective and alive, and I realized something terrifying and exhilarating at once: My power was stronger than I had imagined, especially here, in a city alive with its own energy. We descended the final steps toward the outer streets, keeping close to the walls, moving in rhythm with Thalon, following Cerys's precise directions.

Every corner was a potential trap, every window a watchful eye, but the wards and shadows held. Finally, we reached the relative safety of the outer district, the glittering towers now behind us. Mick stirred in Elias's arms, her eyes half-lidded, breathing more steadily. The bite marks now just bruises fading under my touch.

I pressed my forehead to hers as we slowed to a stop. "You're safe now… We have you."

Cerys walked beside us, her face a mask of satisfaction and relief, yet her eyes burned with purpose.

"We have completed the first step," she instructed. "Now we take her somewhere she can heal fully, and we plan for the rest. The King cannot stop what is coming."

I nodded, exhaustion and relief washing over me, but beneath it, a silent thrill. I could feel the pulse of my purpose stirring. The bridge between realms, the power to restore life, to bring hope, to make children laugh and play again. Mick's safety was just the beginning.

And I would see it through, no matter what came next.

Chapter Thirty-Four

Leyla

Cerys moved ahead with unwavering confidence, her steps echoing faintly against the darkened alleys. Every now and then, she paused, whispering directions that only we could hear. The City of Glass stretched behind us, glittering and deceptive, but in front of us was a path only she knew; a path that would take us into safety, into shadows unknown to the King.

"I've led others here before," she said quietly, glancing at me with softness. "Those who oppose my husband, who understand that the King cannot be allowed to rule unchecked… They are waiting. You will be safe there, for now." I swallowed, gripping Thalon's arm.

My chest ached, but I let myself focus on the thought of sanctuary. Safe walls. People who would fight for her, for us. Cerys led us through a narrow passageway hidden beneath a collapsed building, one that glimmered faintly with runes Serika had traced moments before.

"The city above may shine, but down here, the King has no eyes," she explained. "These tunnels were built long ago, before he seized power. I maintain them now for those who need refuge."

The descent was steep, winding downward until the sounds of the city—the crystal towers, the distant hum of the hunters—faded into muffled echoes. The air grew cooler, heavier, tinged with the scent of stone and underground earth. I could feel my pulse in my throat, each beat reminding me of the danger Mick had just endured. Finally, we reached a set of reinforced doors. Cerys gestured for us to stop.

"They are expecting us," she whispered. "Keep her calm. And follow my lead." The doors opened to a vast underground chamber, far larger than I had expected. Warm light glowed from sconces along the walls, reflecting off low ceilings and carved stone. Figures moved quietly in the shadows. Fae men and women, all alert, all armed, all clearly waiting for someone to guide them. This was her secret army, her rebels. The resistance she had built in silence for decades. One of the figures stepped forward—a young fae woman with sharp eyes, moving with purpose.

Cerys spoke quickly, her tone one of authority. "We have one who needs immediate care," she commanded.

The fae woman nodded, motioning toward a corridor to the left. Before I could protest, Mick was gently lifted from Elias' arms by two of the rebels. My heart lurched.

"No!" The word ripped from my throat before I even realized it, raw and desperate. Panic surged through me like wildfire.

"Leyla." Thalon's voice cut through my chaos—the anchor I didn't want but needed in that moment. "She's in good hands. You've done what you can. Let them help her."

I wanted to argue, to claw Mick back from the arms that carried her away. My fists clenched at my sides as the rebels moved swiftly, their movements efficient and practiced, and vanishing down the corridor. I followed, my steps unsteady, my mind reeling.

The passage opened into a wide chamber bathed in amber light. Bundles of dried herbs hung from the rafters, with scents of lavender and sage mingling with the faint tang of smoke. Rows of shelves lined the walls, each filled with glass vials that shimmered faintly from within. Warmth radiated through the room, not from fire, but from the slow, steady pulse of healing magic woven into the very stones. This wasn't just an infirmary, it was a sanctuary. A place that remembered life even in the shadow of death.

As they carried Mick through the winding corridor, I caught sight of the others. Rebels already filling the infirmary's shadowed corners. Some lay on cots, their bodies twisted in feverish pain, the marks of the King's cruelty carved into their skin. One man's arm was covered in bite wounds that still smoldered faintly, as if the venom inside refused to die. Another woman's eyes glowed faint red in the dim light, her pupils flickering like embers, half human, half something else. There were more, too many, each bearing signs of experiments gone wrong: veins that shimmered faintly with magic, scars that pulsed like living runes, whispers of those who had been touched by the King's twisted alchemy. My stomach turned.

Near the far wall, a woman sat propped against the bedframe, her trembling hands pressed to her abdomen. Her belly was swollen, but not with life. With an experiment gone wrong. The veins along her arms glowed a faint, sickly blue, pulsing in uneven rhythms that made my skin crawl. Cerys paused when she saw her, and for the first time, I saw something flicker behind her composure—sorrow.

"She was part of his fertility trials," Cerys said quietly, her tone laced with fury beneath the calm. "He sought to create heirs infused with demon magic. Because our magic is dwindling in Orrynne and life can no longer be created. But the body cannot bear what was never meant to live inside it." These were survivors of his madness, his proof that power could be warped into cruelty. And now, Mick was one of them.

Cerys then followed in silence, her gown whispering against the floor, her sharp gaze cataloging every corner of the space as though committing it to memory. When she finally spoke, as we approached Mick's bed, her voice was quiet but unyielding. "You will have your time with her," she said, turning her piercing eyes on me. "But now, you must rest and prepare. The King will not wait. And neither can we."

Her words hit like cold water. Thalon came to stand beside me, his presence steady but his expression conflicted— frustration warring with relief.

"You're needed here," his hands softly captured my face. "For her... and for what comes next."

I nodded, though my gaze remained fixed on the doorway. The sight of Mick—broken and blooding... but, breathing— had carved itself into me like a scar I would never lose. My heart ached with it, but beneath the ache was something else. Something fierce.

The pulse of my power stirred, faint but insistent, whispering through my veins like a promise. It was the same warmth that had carried me through the dungeon, the same light that had found her in the dark. It hummed now with purpose, telling me I could do more.

Heal. Protect. Restore.

Cerys stepped closer, her presence commanding, her gaze steady. "This is only the beginning," she said. "Mick will recover here. And when she does, the fight continues. You, Leyla, are the key. The Bridge of Realms. You must train for the war that will come. I will see that your accommodations are prepared."

Her words fell over me like a mantle… heavy, inevitable and stitched from both fate and fear.

Thalon's voice broke the silence that followed, quieter but certain. "We'll be sleeping in the same room, Mother." Leave it to him to ensure that no matter what was going on around us that he would lay his head by mine at night.

Cerys's lips curved in the faintest acknowledgment. "Of course, as you wish, my son."

And then she was gone, her footsteps fading into the hum of magic that filled the air.

I stood there, rooted, watching the last flicker of her silver gown vanish beyond the corridor. The scent of herbs lingered, the light of the potions flickered softly, and in that moment I knew.

There was no turning back.

Mick was alive. And the King was waiting.

Chapter Thirty-Five

Leyla

The infirmary was quiet except for the soft hum of magical wards lining the walls. Thalon was out inspecting the rebel grounds. Mick laid on a cot, pale and trembling, her arms bruised and bite-marked. My chest ached just looking at her. She had been the one to ground me through everything, my anchor, my chosen sister.

I knelt beside her, letting my hands hover just above her skin. I drew in a deep breath, focusing on the warmth that pulsed inside me; the energy I had felt in the dungeon, the spark I had only just begun to control. Slowly, deliberately, I let it flow through my palms, threading into her bruised arms and battered body.

A soft, golden glow emanated from my hands, subtle at first, like sunlight filtering through glass. I whispered Mick's name, coaxing life back into her, drawing strength from the connection between us. Her breathing, once shallow and uneven, began to stabilize. The dark bruises along her arms softened, the fresh bite marks fading into painful memory.

Serika hovered nearby, murmuring quietly, adjusting the wards as I worked.

"Focus, Leyla. She needs your energy to guide her, not to overwhelm her." I nodded, concentrating, feeling the threads of life responding to my presence.

Mick stirred, blinking slowly. Her eyes met mine, half-lidded and dazed, but recognition came.

"Ley…?" she whispered, voice weak. Her cracked lips trembled around my name, and for a heartbeat, I forgot how to breathe.

"I'm here, Mick. You're safe now," I brushed aside damp hair from her face. Relief mingled with exhaustion, but I kept my energy steady, steadying her heartbeat, easing the pain, strengthening her body with the flow of life I could summon.

Once Mick's breathing evened and she fell back asleep, I allowed myself a moment to look around the rebel base. Elias stood guard with Mick.

The rebel sanctuary spread out around us like a world carved from forgotten legend. The air smelled of old stone and warm spice, of earth and embers. Enchanted lanterns hung suspended from the arched ceiling, their light rippling like captured sunrise across walls etched with ancient runes. Crystals embedded in the rock pulsed faintly, feeding power into the wards that kept the King's magic from seeping in.

The space was vast, large enough to house hundreds. Its tunnels branching like veins beneath the city above. Figures moved in the distance, shadows wrapped in quiet purpose. Some bore swords and sigils on their armor; others carried trays of herbs and glowing potions that shimmered in their wake. It was not the cold discipline similar to the military back on Earth, but the heartbeat of a people rebuilding themselves. Each motion careful, reverent, and alive.

Cerys led me forward, her steps soundless against the smooth stone. Her gown swept behind her like a trailing storm cloud, and wherever she went, light seemed to bend subtly toward her. "You will be safe here," she said, her voice carrying softly through the chamber. "And you will heal. The King's reach does not extend below ground. Not yet."

A figure detached from the shadows ahead, tall and broad-shouldered, moving with the ease of someone accustomed to both command and danger. His silver hair was tied back in a braid that gleamed in the lamplight, and his eyes, amber and unflinching, found me with unnerving precision.

"Leyla," Cerys said, inclining her head toward him. "This is Briar. He oversees security and training for the rebels. His experience will keep us one step ahead of the King's hunters."

Briar's gaze lingered, his expression unreadable. "I've heard of you," he said at last, his voice deep and even. "The girl who bridges realms. Your power hums through the wards themselves, your presence already subtly increasing our magic. I felt it before you entered."

Heat crept up my neck. "I'm still learning," I admitted. "I didn't even know I could heal like this… not until my sister." Briar studied me for a long, quiet moment, the kind of silence that felt like being measured and understood all at once.

"You will learn," he said finally. "But understand this—your gift is not only healing. It is creation. Renewal. It is the opposite of what the King stands for. And that kind of power that will not stay hidden for long."

Behind him, Cerys stood watching us both, her composure steady but her eyes sharp, as if she were already calculating the threads of a thousand unseen outcomes.

When she finally spoke, her tone softened, but her authority did not. "I must return," she said, her voice calm, measured. "The King expects me to attend to him, to play the indifferent queen. But I have left instructions. Your accommodations have been settled. Briar will guide you to your rooms after I leave. Mick will heal here, and you, Leyla, will begin to understand the true breadth of your power."

Cerys placed a hand briefly on my shoulder. "Remember this," she said softly, her eyes locking with mine. "You are the Bridge of Realms, Leyla. Life flows through you. And soon, you will need to wield it not just to heal, but to restore what has been lost."

Her words settled over me, a weight to them I could feel in my core.

Chapter Thirty-Six

Leyla

B riar showed me to my room, or rather Thalon and I's room after Cerys' departure. He seemed kind enough, if not a little stiff. Thalon and I decided to make our way to the main hall after knowing where we would lay our heads that night. Best to know who was surrounding us while we slept.

The underground chamber hummed with life. Quite energy, purposeful motion, and the faint scent of herbs and smoke from the warding fires. The rebels had gathered in a large common room, tables arranged around a central hearth, and as I stepped in with Thalon, I could feel every pair of eyes on us. Some were curious, some suspicious, and a few openly wary. Serika was there, standing near the back, her sharp eyes scanning the room, her hair alone attracting the attention of the rebels.

"Welcome," Briar said simply, gesturing toward the empty benches. "Sit. Eat. Talk. This is your home, for now." I didn't miss how Briar's eyes subtly remained on me as we walked away. With the tension in Thalon's body, I am fairly certain that he didn't either.

We sat at a long wooden table, the benches rough but sturdy. For a few moments, the room was silent as the rebels studied him, noting his posture, the way he carried himself… the unmistakable aura of power that came with being the King's son. One of the men, broad-shouldered with a scar across his cheek, finally broke the silence.

"You expect us to trust the son of the man we've been fighting for decades?" he asked, voice low, wary. "You bring danger with you. His kind brings only death." I felt a shiver. Knowing that Thalon was in the mood to rip a fae's throat out.

Thalon's expression darkened for only a heartbeat before he leaned forward, his voice calm but fierce.

"I am the King's son," he admitted, "but Leyla is my mate. My fated. I would choose death a thousand times over before letting anything happen to her. I am not here for my father. I am here for her. She is my life."

The room froze. Murmurs ran through the rebels, disbelief and awe mingling in the air. Eyes darted between him and me. I felt heat rush to my cheeks as I met Thalon's gaze. His dark eyes held mine, unwavering, protective, fierce.

A rebel stepped forward, her expression a mixture of astonishment and delight.

"A true fated mate… in the flesh?" she whispered, almost reverent. "It's been six hundred years since the last fated bond was seen. It has only been chosen mates. The Gods themselves have blessed you."

Other rebels began nodding, murmuring to one another. Thalon's declaration had shifted the atmosphere instantly. Where suspicion had lingered, awe and admiration now took root. They were no longer seeing him as the King's son; they were seeing him as a man utterly devoted to the woman beside him, a man willing to die for the first fated mate in centuries.

I swallowed, emotion welling in my throat. To hear Thalon declare me like that, in front of these fae who had fought for so long, who had lost so much—it made the weight of my role as the Bridge feel more real, more vital. I could feel the pulse of magic in the room shifting, small threads of recognition brushing against me as if even the rebels' very energy acknowledged the significance.

Thalon relaxed slightly, leaning back on the bench, and for the first time since Earth, I saw him laugh softly, a private, easy sound that drew a few smiles from the surrounding rebels. I laughed too, letting myself breathe. The tension in the room broke, replaced by cautious warmth. Soon, conversations started, jokes exchanged, and stories were shared. I listened to tales of lost battles, small victories, moments of levity that had kept these people going all these years.

One of the fae women nudged me with her elbow, smirking. "So, you're the bridge, huh? The Bridge of Realms they've whispered about?" I smiled, feeling a blush rise.

"Yes… I'm Leyla. I'm still learning. But I will be honored to fight along yours and the rebels cause." I said it simply.

Thalon turned his body towards me, guided my hair behind my ear, and rested his hand on my thigh. His voice was for my ears alone. "Do you mean that?"

I lean away from him, looking into his eyes. "Yes. I do."

His storm gray eyes smiled at me, beaming with something that looked like pride.

I laughed nervously again, a little louder this time, joining in the stories, the teasing, the camaraderie. Thalon's gaze followed me. His shadows swirling around us always. I felt the tension between us deepen, simmering beneath the surface. And for the first time in my life, I felt a flicker of something I had thought not possible: belonging.

As Thalon and I made our way down the corridor, the hum of the sanctuary faded into a low murmur. Voices softened and footsteps retreated until it was only the two of us. The air was warmer here, heavy with the scent of herbs and old stone. I stopped briefly by the infirmary door, needing to see Mick one last time before we went to our room.

She lay beneath a haze of healing light, her skin less pale now, her chest rising in a steady rhythm. Elias insisted he was fine to stay the night with her at her side. The sight should have soothed me. Instead, something restless coiled deeper inside. Relief mingled with exhaustion, and beneath that, something far more dangerous. Anticipation.

When I turned back, Thalon was waiting just outside the threshold, half-shadowed in the dim corridor light, watching me. His eyes glowed faintly beneath his dark lashes, his expression unreadable. I reached for him before I could stop myself.

My fingers brushed his, and it was as if the world exhaled. His shadows stirred instantly, rising from the floor like smoke, wrapping around us both in a shiver of warmth and danger.

"Thalon—" I barely got his name out before the breath left my lungs. In one fluid motion, he had me pressed against the wall, his body caging mine without touching—at least not yet.

The cold stone at my back met the heat radiating from him, and the contrast made my skin burn. His shadows slid along my arms like silk, curling around my wrists and waist, pulsing in time with my heartbeat.

I could feel his breath ghosting over my lips, steady and slow, as though he was trying not to lose control. The faintest movement would have bridged the distance between us. My name caught in his throat, unspoken. The sound of our breathing filled the space, the magic between us humming like the build before a storm. He lowered his head, his mouth hovering just above mine as his words were a whisper against my skin.

"You have no idea what you do to me." And maybe I didn't. But I felt it, every bit of it. The hunger in him wasn't just want, it was gravity. Ancient and inescapable.

Then—footsteps.

They broke the spell like a crack of thunder. Briar appeared at the end of the hall, his tall frame cutting a silhouette against the golden light. His gaze flicked toward us, sharp and knowing. Thalon moved before I could react. His wings burst outward, black and magnificent, filling the corridor in an explosion of shadow. They curved around us, sealing the world away. All sound dulled. The air itself seemed to hold its breath. Inside his cocoon of darkness, I could feel the rumble of his chest against mine, the restrained fury radiating off him in waves. There were muffled voices outside.

Briar's tone was low, apologetic. I couldn't make out the words.

Thalon's wings folded back slowly, retreating into his body like they never existed. My dark angel a seemingly normal man again with slightly pointed ears. The magic dissipated, but the air still hummed with its echo. My heart thundered in my chest, and his breathing came rough and uneven.

"He's stepping on territory that isn't his," Thalon said finally, his voice dark and dangerous.

I whipped my head toward him. "Territory?" The word cracked between us, sharp as a blade. "Excuse me?"

His jaw flexed, but whatever retort he might have given was lost when a sound from inside the infirmary made us both turn. Mick's cough broke through the air, weak but real. The fire in my chest faltered, replaced by cold dread. I pushed past Thalon, back into the room, my anger momentarily forgotten.

This conversation, and whatever it would have became, would have to wait. But it wasn't something I would forget.

Chapter Thirty-Seven

Leyla

I was wrong.

So very wrong.

I'd told myself I'd stay angry at him. That I would demand an explanation for his words, for that possessive spark that had flared behind his eyes. But when we met back in our quarters, all of that resolve fell apart like smoke.

He hadn't said a word at first. Just brushed past the doorway's shadow and slipped into bed beside me. The heat of him was immediate, curling around me before his arm even found my waist. His breath stirred the fine hairs along my neck, and when he finally spoke, it wasn't an argument. It was a whisper.

"I shouldn't have said it," he murmured against my skin, his voice low, rough, barely more than a sigh. His lips ghosted over the curve of my shoulder, soft, fleeting kisses like confession. "I only meant…" another kiss, slower this time, "…that I consider myself yours. In every way."

And just like that, my anger dissolved into nothing. I could feel every inch of him; the strength in his chest pressed against my back, the steady rhythm of his heartbeat, the warm weight of his hand at my hip. The boulder that seemed to get heavier with every passing second pressing into my lower back. I should have pushed him away, demanded distance, but God, I couldn't.

It was torture of the most exquisite kind, the kind that leaves you wishing the ache would never end.

And then, just when I thought he might pull me closer, might give in to what was sparking between us, he'd drawn in a slow breath and whispered, "You need rest, my little light. Training starts early."

And that was it. He'd gone still beside me, his breathing evening out within minutes. Meanwhile, I laid awake for hours. Caught between frustration and longing, his apology replaying in my mind until dawn finally pried me from sleep's edge. Now, standing in the small training room, that memory clung to me like a fever.

Thalon was already there, stretching in the soft gold glow filtering through the narrow windows. The light caught on the dark strands of his hair, making them glint like obsidian. His bare forearms flexed as he braced against the wall, the movement drawing shadows across the sculpted lines of his back and shoulders. The curve of his jaw, the easy control in his movements; it was all maddeningly deliberate. My pulse quickened.

He turned at the sound of my footsteps, a faint smile tugging at his lips. "Ready?" he asked, his voice low and teasing.

But beneath the lightness was that same undercurrent I had felt the night before. That magnetic pull, quiet and relentless. I nodded, though my throat was too dry to answer. My hands curled into fists at my sides, not from nerves—but to keep from reaching for him. I nodded, tightening my fists.

"I think so," I said, though my voice wavered. The exercises were simple. Focus, control, and balance. Serika's instructions at Hollow Vale had given me the basics, but Thalon's presence drew out a different intensity. Every glance, every brush of his arm as he demonstrated a motion sent sparks along my skin. I tried to focus on the energy thrumming inside me—the pulse of life waiting to be awakened.

"Leyla," he said softly, circling me, "you're stronger than you realize. Let it flow."

I let the energy hum faintly, letting small tendrils of magic brush against the stones beneath my feet. At first, nothing seemed to happen. But then… a thin green sprout emerged from a crack in the floor. My eyes widened. I lifted my hands slightly, concentrating, and tiny tendrils of moss and small shoots began to curl upward. The hall was still mostly stone, dark and heavy, but pockets of life were returning, responding to me in tiny, fragile bursts. Thalon moved closer, his presence magnetic.

"Careful," he murmured, his shadows brushing against my fingers.

Heat surged through me, and I had to fight to focus on the magic rather than the desire it stirred. I let the energy flow in short, careful bursts. Patches of life appeared: a small cluster of glowing mushrooms, a few tiny flowers, even a faint shimmer along the edges of the floor like the pulse of sunlight. It wasn't full restoration, far from it, but it was a start. The world around me was noticing me, responding to me in whispers, hints of life returning. Thalon's shadows swirled protectively around us, responding to the subtle pulse of energy.

"You can do more," his eyes dark and intense. "I can feel it, mate."

I exhaled, trying to steady the tremor in my hands. His hand pushed back a strand of hair that had fallen from my braid. His breath hot on my neck as he leaned down to kiss my pounding pulse.

"It's… small," I admitted. "But it's happening, I feel more in control." A faint blush warmed my cheeks as he rose. I could feel the tension between us, the desire, the unspoken pull that had begun at *Eleanor's*, growing stronger as we trained side by side.

But I had to focus.

Mick was healing in the infirmary, the world itself was broken, and I was the key. I allowed myself one more pulse, letting tiny tendrils of life curl through the hall, just enough that the stone seemed less dead, the air a little warmer. Children would one day play here again. Magic would grow stronger. The Bridge of Realms was stirring, threads of portals forming in the corners of my vision, glimpses of a connected world waiting for me to open it fully. Thalon's hand brushed mine again.

"You've taken the first step," he whispered. His nearness made my heart race, and for a moment the tension between us flared—desire and admiration, worry and exhilaration—but I forced myself to focus.

"Yes," my hands still glowing faintly. "Thank you, Thalon."

A clap came from the center of the arena. Slow. Deliberate.

"That is great, Bridge of Realms. Truly." Briar stood. "Though, what should happen if the King himself or one of his hunters comes for your neck?"

Thalon tensed, his fingers suddenly gripping around mine with more strength than he had before. "Then they shall die at my hands."

"You can't be everywhere at once, Prince. Let's have our Bridge learn a few moves to make sure she can protect herself, what do you say?" He glanced at Thalon, but his eyes landed on me. "Bridge?"

Chapter Thirty-Eight

Thalon

The small training arena was alive with heat. An inferno of torchlight and sweat, where the scent of steel and stone clung to every breath. Shadows rippled across the walls, restless as much as the crowd of rebels that now circled the ring. They were eager for blood or brilliance, whichever came first. But I only saw her.

Leyla.

My anchor.

My undoing.

Across the ring stood Briar, the fae leader that radiated arrogance. From the way his mouth tilted when he looked at her, I knew he scented that she was unclaimed. He wanted her.

"Ready?" he asked, voice a low, taunting hum that carried across the arena.

Leyla nodded, chin lifting, eyes bright with defiance and something far more dangerous—trust. The sight of her standing there; barefoot in the dust, light catching on the fine sheen of sweat along her collarbone—stirred something primal inside me. My shadows responded before I could stop them, coiling low, pulsing in rhythm with the thrumming of my heart beat. The fight began.

Briar moved first. Swift, fluid, likely from his years of battle. His strikes were clean, his balance near perfect, his control infuriatingly precise. And yet Leyla… She matched him. Every blow he threw, she countered; every step he took, she turned into a dance. Her magic flared faintly with each movement, silver veins of light chasing up her arms. She was breathtaking.

The rebels cheered as the two circled, steel clashing, sparks leaping in the air. Briar laughed—a sound full of thrill and admiration—and for the briefest moment, his gaze softened when he looked at her. It wasn't the respect of a leader. It was hunger. My shadows wanted death.

He swept her legs; she twisted midair and landed light as ash. He smiled, low and appreciative.

"You learn fast," he murmured, circling closer.

"Maybe you're just slow," she shot back, breathless but grinning.

The crowd laughed.

I did not.

The way he looked at her, like she was something wild he longed to tame, set fire to the hollow places inside me. Jealousy was not a thing I allowed myself. It was reckless, mortal. But watching him test her, toy with her, admire her—it crawled beneath my skin like poison.

Briar feinted left, caught her wrist, spun her around—too close, far too close. His body pressed behind hers, a whisper of movement, his voice ghosting over her ear. "You could be dangerous, little bridge."

That was it.

The shadows in the arena surged with my fury, black smoke curling outward from my boots. Several rebels stepped back as the temperature dropped, frost threading through the air. Leyla broke his grip in a single burst of movement, magic flaring silver and bright, and slammed her elbow back into his ribs. He grunted, stumbled, and she pivoted, eyes flashing with wild light.

"Don't call me that," she hissed.

Briar only laughed, still breathless, still grinning. "You hit like royalty."

Something in her snapped. Her fist flew, clean and perfect, and connected squarely with his nose. The sound echoed through the stone chamber, sharp and final. Blood dripped down his face. The rebels went silent. Briar stumbled, one hand to his face. But instead of anger, there was delight in his expression—feral and fascinated.

"Gods, I see why you're his."

Before he could take another step toward her, I was there. Shadows rippled out of me in a wave, clearing the space between us in a blink. I caught her around the waist before she could fall back, her breath hot and fast against my neck.

"That's enough," I said, my voice edged with death.

Her magic still hummed, wild under her skin. Her pulse thundered against my chest. I turned my gaze on Briar, who met my glare with a knowing smirk.

"She learns fast," he said, rubbing his jaw. "I'd say she's ready for more."

"Touch her again," I warned softly, "and you will meet your Gods."

He lifted both palms in mock surrender, the ghost of amusement tugging at his bruised mouth.

"Duly noted, Your Highness." I didn't wait for a reply. The crowd parted as I carried her out of the ring, her body still trembling with adrenaline, her scent tangled with sweat and magic and fury.

"Thalon—put me down!" she demanded, though her voice wavered.

"No." My tone left no room for argument. "You're done for the day."

"Briar was just—"

"Looking at you," I cut in, sharper than I meant. "Like he didn't know I'd kill him for it."

Her breath hitched, caught between indignation and something else, something that made her eyes soften, even as she glared. When we reached our quarters, I set her down gently, shadows still flickering at the edges of my vision. She stood there, chest rising and falling, cheeks flushed, a faint smile tugging at her lips.

"You're jealous," she whispered.

"Obsessively," I admitted.

Her lips parted—maybe to argue, maybe to breathe—but I didn't give her the chance.

Every step I took toward her made the pulse of her magic thrum stronger, like a heartbeat I could feel against my own.

Her energy was wild, alive—magnetizing, intoxicating—and it called to me. Demanded acknowledgment, demanded me.

I leaned down, brushing my lips against hers, tasting the heat, the faint salt of sweat, the hum of power that ran through her. Her magic surged, small sparks dancing along my arms and across my chest where my hands pressed against her, responding to the pull of my shadows, intertwining with mine. The connection was electric, a living tether that made my body tighten with every pulse.

Her lips moved against mine, soft, uncertain, searching.

And then I heard it, her quiet, almost breathless words: "Thalon…. I…. I've never…"

The words made my heart clench. Not from pride, but from knowing she was mine alone. My shadowed hands moved to steady her, brushing a trembling strand of hair from her head. Every pulse of her magic, every flutter of life energy against mine, made me ache to protect her, claim her, and show her exactly what she had never known.

I deepened the kiss, guiding, patient but insistent, letting our powers mingle. Her life-magic pulsed brighter under my touch, weaving through the shadows that clung to us, teasing and testing, connecting us in ways beyond mere flesh. Every spark, every tremor of energy that flared when our breaths mingled, every flicker of magic sliding along our skin—it confirmed it. She was mine. Completely.

Her hands moved, tentative at first, then bolder, pressing against my chest, brushing along the lines of my shoulders, and I responded instinctively, letting the shadows twist and curl around us, enhancing the warmth, the intimacy, the shared pulse of our energies. Every beat of her magic against mine, every flutter of life-magic entwined with shadow, drew me tighter, closer, until it felt as if the room itself had melted away, leaving nothing but this, this connection, this claiming.

I leaned her back and all of my senses were overwhelmed with her. Her arousal. Her need. Her arms wrapped around my shoulders, clinging to me in every way. My lips moved down to her neck and Gods I have never tasted anything so sweet, her entire body trembled in anticipation. Small bumps forming along her arms. When my fingers untied her laced tunic and I saw the milky white flesh, my mind went blank. Pure need.

Her breath hitched when my thumb began to trace her pink nub in slow, determined circles. I looked up from her lips, and her eyes were hooded with desire. A groan escaped me as I bit down on her bottom lip. Slowly, I moved down to her nipple, hard and waiting for my tongue. Her soft moans only encouraged me.

When I felt her fingertips, so subtly and so hesitantly reach the top of my pants, searching for release… I came undone. I picked my mate up, her legs wrapping around me, her tongue relishing the taste of my own. When I lay her on the bed, to my ultimate amusement, my little minx yanked me down by my neck demanding to continue her exploration of my mouth. Of my body.

And Gods, I can't not get enough.

My hands found the last barrier between us and started to trace the outlines with my fingers.

A whimper escapes. "More, Thalon. I need more."

"Then you will have it, *mate*."

I tear them off and have my shadows save them for later. A prize of sorts. Perhaps I'll have them framed.

My tongue immediately found her center, and how wrong I was earlier when I thought the taste of her skin was immaculate. The taste of my mate, of her desire, is something so utterly addicting it cannot be described. I would stay here for hours. For days if I could. Her screams tore through the air.

"Thalon, please."

I could ram through a wall with how hard I was for her. For my mate. I wrapped her in shadows once more, knowing that it would bring a cooling to her while this may cause her pain.

"Do not be gentle with me, Thalon. I want it now. I want everything you have." I smirked at my little mate. So eager.

I slammed into her. Her cries of pleasure rippled through my soul. She was soaked. She was mine. Her legs began to shake as she began to take more of me, the pleasure building. She brought her hands back to my shoulders and nudged me towards the bed. All at once, she sat on top of me, riding me like her life depended on it. My hardened length only grew.

"Fuck, Leyla." I withdrew and thrust again, getting deeper. "That's it, give me Heaven."

Her body, covered in sweat. Her hair, sticking to her body.

I have never seen something so beautiful. When she let out her final scream, I plunged fast and hard. Taking her as she rode her waves.

I drew back only far enough to breathe, our foreheads still touching, our breaths tangling in the narrow space between us.

Her eyes found mine—wide, with vulnerability and trust. The sight of her unraveled something deep inside me.

Her name slipped from my lips, a whisper edged with devotion and danger. "Leyla…" My voice roughened, the sound closer to a growl than speech. I brushed my thumb along her jaw, feeling the quick pulse beneath her skin. "My little light," I murmured, every word a vow. "You are mine—always."

"Always." She echoed, her breaths already deepening as she lay on me. My shadows wrapped tighter around us, a living shroud, protective, reverent. And in that charged silence, I could feel it—the bond solidifying completely, the magic linking us, the promise unspoken but undeniable.

She was mine. My mate.

The Bridge of Realms.

And the world could wait.

Chapter Thirty-Nine

Leyla

The night was quiet. After what felt like an earth-shattering collision, the silence that followed was sacred—gentle, infinite. I lay suspended in it, cradled by the steady rise and fall of Thalon's chest, his warmth soaking into my skin until it felt like I'd never be cold again.

The air smelled faintly of rain and smoke; the remnants of magic still shimmered in the air, faint and silver, like the world itself was reluctant to let us go. Then it happened.

It began as the smallest ripple—like a fingertip tracing the inside of my mind. The echo of a heartbeat that wasn't mine.

Leyla?

My breath caught. My eyes flew open, searching his face in the half-light.

"You're… in my head?" I whispered, hardly daring to believe it.

Yes.

The thought was low, confident, possessive.

And it felt amazing. I shivered, leaning slightly closer, trying to make sense of it. I'd never imagined anything like this; not in stories, not in the magic I'd begun to understand. I could feel his presence, the strength of his shadows, the pulse of his heartbeat echoing through my own thoughts.

I didn't… I didn't know this could happen.

Neither did I, he said. His voice in my mind was dark, steady, possessive, and it made the small hairs on my arms rise. *But now we know. And this… This is ours.*

I reached for his hand, letting my fingers brush against his, feeling a spark of electricity as his shadows curled around me like liquid night. Every pulse of my magic responded instinctively, threading into his, humming along his energy. It was overwhelming, and yet… Perfect.

I'm here. Always. I flushed at the possessiveness in his mind, at the certainty in his tone.

The shadows wrapped tighter around us, but not threatening—protective, intimate.

And now nothing—no one, no magic, no army—can take us apart, my little light. I gasped softly, the thrill of this new connection coursing through me.

A tremor escaped me, half gasp, half wonder. The connection between us sang through every cell of my body, powerful and frightening and beautiful. I pressed my palms against his chest, feeling the steady, immortal rhythm beneath my fingers. Our heartbeats had found each other, merging in perfect synchrony.

We were the first fated pair in six hundred years. Our bond alive and ancient. The first time since setting foot in Orrynne, the weight I carried no longer felt unbearable. The world, fractured as it was, felt whole again in his arms.

I leaned into him, surrendering to the pulse that now bound us, feeling his warmth bleed into mine, our energies intertwined like light and shadow in endless dance… And fell asleep in peace.

The underground hall was waking slowly, sunlight catching the hidden runes and bouncing off the polished stone walls. I could feel Thalon's presence even before opening my eyes, the steady pulse of his magic like a heartbeat in my mind. It was still surreal, still thrilling, to realize we were linked—not just by flesh or destiny, but by thought, by energy, by everything between us.

Morning, he teased, and his voiced flared against my thoughts, Seductive… Wanting. Needing. My chest flushed.

Morning, I replied, smiling despite the lingering heat from last night.

I rolled onto my side, pressing a hand against his chest, feeling the warmth, the strength, the pull of shadow beneath. He hummed softly, a low vibration that made me shiver. Every heartbeat, every thread of energy we'd woven together—the hum of life, the pulse of magic—it wasn't just him. It was us. Together.

We agreed to get the day started, knowing that the rebels needed us in what was to come. Outside of our room, Briar's gaze immediately found us. I could sense his curiosity, his admiration—and something else. Something personal.

Thalon's voice snapped into my mind, low and firm: *Back the hell off.*

I startled, knowing it wasn't intended for me but shaken to hear his voice sound like death. Briar's shoulders stiffened, then relaxed, respect written across his features. He inclined his head, a silent acknowledgment of the boundaries Thalon set. Elias was leaning casually against a stone pillar, smirking.

"Wow," he said aloud, voice carrying that perfect mix of teasing and sarcasm. "Already establishing power hierarchies before breakfast? And here I thought this was a rebel hideout, not a mating ritual convention."

I shot him a glare. Thalon growled softly at him from across the hall, and I felt a fondness, a thrill, in the mind link as we exchanged unspoken amusement. The rebels were gathering near the hearth, murmuring to each other, stealing glances at us—Thalon and me.

I could sense their awe, their cautious trust, the recognition that we weren't just survivors or fighters, we were leaders. Already, their loyalty seemed to lean toward us. I felt Thalon's shadows coil lightly around me, protective and intimate. Reminding me I wasn't just Leyla, The Bridge of Realms… I was Leyla, his mate, and together we were stronger than anything the King could throw at us.

They sense that our bond was sealed.

I nodded, now understanding why we had so many more blatantly obvious stares than even yesterday.

We have to keep training, he whispered in my mind, voice low and teasing.

I laughed, feeling a rush of warmth. *You're the one who keeps distracting me.*

Maybe I like it, he admitted, and I felt the tug of his grin, the pulse of his energy through our link. *Maybe I like seeing you this alive, this powerful.*

The afternoon sun slanted through the hidden runes, painting faint patterns across the infirmary. Mick sat on the edge of her cot, pale but stable, though her movements were sharper, more alert than before. Her eyes danced around the room, a subtle tension in her posture, a quiet hunger lingering beneath her calm. I knelt beside her, brushing a damp strand of hair from her face.

"You're awake." I whispered, though a knot of worry tightened in my chest.

She shook her head slightly, lips pressing together. "I… I feel different," she admitted, voice trembling. "It's like… something inside me has changed. I want… I don't know. I feel… hungry. I feel… Wrong."

My stomach dropped. I looked up at Elias, who stepped closer, his expression calm but serious.

"Leyla… Michaela. The bite marks were not just injuries," he seemed to brace himself against the weight of what he had to say. "The King… He tried to make her the first mortal vampire. Experimenting on mortals and other creatures is one of his past times. The healer confirmed yesterday. Michaela transformed… Changed, fully." I blinked, trying to process what I was hearing.

"Changed… how?" I asked, the healer walking in behind us. Elias crouched beside Mick, gently resting a hand on her shoulder.

The healer spoke, an older fae woman with long gray hair and longer skirts. "She is a vampire now. That is why she's so… alert. Elias's blood has kept her sated so far, that is why she is not experiencing the endless hunger at the moment. We had a theory yesterday, and went with it. His blood, it healed her almost immediately."

She raised her hands as if not wanting to offend me. "Your life magic, your connection to the Bridge helped. But it could not give her what every… Vampire requires. Animal blood can help, but she'll need guidance… Someone to teach her how to feed without harming others."

Mick's lips quivered, her gaze dropping to her hands. "I… I don't want to hurt anyone. But it's… God, I am so thirsty." I pressed a hand over hers, feeling the subtle tremor of hunger beneath the surface.

"I am so sorry, Mick. I…I should have been there. I should have protected you. I'm so, so sorry." I cried into her hands.

"Leyla, you couldn't have stopped it." Her voice was raw with emotion.

"I will kill him, Mick." A vow. An oath. "I will kill him for what he has done to you."

"I know, Ley. I know you will."

"You won't be alone. We'll find Gyor. He'll teach you their ways—how to feed, how to survive, how to control it. You'll be okay, Mick. I promise." Thalon's shadow coiled around me as he stepped closer, his presence grounding, protective.

She will be okay, his thought came to mine through our mind link, steady and commanding. I nodded, letting his strength flow through me.

Mick looked between us, consumed by fear. "Leyla… I don't think I can do this."

Soft, deliberate footsteps echoed from the stairwell above. Shadows shifted, moving like liquid, and a figure stepped into the hall. Tall and commanding. With a presence that radiated power and centuries of experience. Gyor. And with him, a group of vampires—his own, disciplined and loyal, here to join the rebel cause against the King. My chest tightened at the sight of him.

Mick's gaze widened, hope flickering despite her lingering hunger. I felt Thalon tense beside me, shadows swirling protectively, but there was no fear. Only recognition.

The rebels had just gained new allies.

And together, we would face the King, stronger than ever.

Chapter Forty

Cerys

The palace had always been a gilded cage. Every corridor echoed with hollow politeness, every smile was a lie, and every glance at him, the King, as a reminder of the life stolen from me. I had spent days now walking among courtiers, gliding past servants and guards alike, my expression composed, indifferent. A perfect mask of the queen who had long since surrendered to the monotony of court life.

But beneath the surface, the fire never died. He had killed them. My oldest friends. The ones whose laughter had once filled summer gardens, whose whispers had spun dreams of hope. I had watched him extinguish their lives because they refused to bend, because they believed in a future he could not tolerate. Leyla's parents had been brilliant and radiant… and now, gone. Their deaths were not a tragedy; they were a calculated erasure. And the only reason I did not murder that bastard in his sleep is because of the hold he had on our son. Because of the Binding Sigil he demanded the Mage to do when our son was just a boy. Killing him would kill my son. Unless the sigil was broken, I was stuck.

For years. Years, I have led the rebels to make small acts against the King. Little did they know, I would never kill him. Never could because of his hold on Thalon.

Now, the bastard's plan has finally bit him in his ass and Thalon is mated to the person he was supposed to kill. I am taking full advantage and wasting no time in doing so. Thalon's binding sigil is no more. And I will see to it that my husband is finally killed. Even if I have to do it myself.

I lingered near the barracks tonight under the pretense of idle curiosity, letting my ladies-in-waiting chatter about inconsequential court gossip fill the air. My ears, however, were attuned to the careless, revealing words of his hunters. Demons trained to obey without thought.

"They'll strike tonight," one murmured to another, lacing his boots with practiced ease. "Rebels think they're hidden, but at nightfall we move. We take them all."

A thin smile curved my lips—not of pleasure, but of anticipation. Over twenty years of planning, waiting, sharpening every thought and skill to the edge of a knife, and now the arrogance of my husband, the murderer, had gifted me the perfect opening. I left my companions behind with a light bow, sliding into the shadows of the palace. Every step was measured, every wall and passage familiar beneath my touch. The air smelled faintly of wax and smoke, the lingering traces of a palace too grand for its own secrets. Each corridor was a channel for my intent: a subtle gesture here, a ward there, ensuring no eyes followed.

I moved like the ice in my veins, invisible but palpable. Every heartbeat a drum of anticipation and restrained fury. By the time I reached the outer streets, the sky had darkened into an obsidian velvet, the city lights like scattered jewels beneath me. I allowed myself the tiniest exhale; no one trailed me. The King's hunters were confident, overreaching, blind to the shadow moving beneath their noses. My anger, honed into precision over decades, pulsed in my chest, cold and ready.

Inside the rebel sanctuary, the air was alive with tension and quiet energy. Torches glimmered against stone walls, casting long, wavering shadows, and the scent of herbs, smoke, and iron filled the air. Serika, ever watchful, was the first to notice my entrance, her sharp gaze assessing every subtle motion I made. Relief and wariness wove together in her expression.

"You shouldn't—" she began, but I cut her off with a lift of my hand, a small, authoritative motion that silenced the room.

"I should," I said, my voice calm, steady, tempered with the weight of years of hatred and patience.

"The King's hunters are moving tonight. At nightfall, they strike." The room froze.

Even the faintest flicker of doubt vanished as I let the words hang, heavy with truth. This was not a panic I offered, but a plan. Rebels live and die by focus and precision; fear would not serve them.

Thalon emerged from the edge of the group, every muscle taut, every sense on alert. His dark eyes, shadowed by his hair, found mine, and I allowed him the faintest acknowledgment of my presence.

He understood.

He always understood.

Thalon pulled Leyla with him to my side. He began to lay out the positions, the likely approach, the timing — precise, unwavering, delivered in clipped sentences that left no room for argument. My husbands strongest weapon, now plotting his demise. I couldn't be prouder.

"They will move from three directions. They expect us in the lower chambers. They expect complacency."

I let my finger trace lines along the map, emphasizing vulnerabilities and opportunities. "We will use their confidence against them. We will force them into a trap of their own making."

Leyla stood nearby, her posture tense, her blue eyes sharp. "How do we stop them?" Her voice carried strength, but I glimpsed the spark of worry flicker beneath it.

Her mother's courage reflected back in her gaze, reminding me of the years lost, the lives stolen.

"We do not merely stop them," I said softly, letting the weight of my years, my knowledge, and my hatred infuse each word. "We make them pay for underestimating us. We survive tonight, and we strike back with every advantage we have." Whispers passed through the room.

The rebels shifted, absorbing the information, adjusting positions, and exchanging quiet nods. Thalon's gaze lingered on me, sharp and assessing, measuring the danger I carried. I saw him recognize it: the lethal patience, the unyielding rage, the careful planning that comes from twenty years of restrained vengeance. He nodded once, the kind of acknowledgment that tells me we are in this together.

For a heartbeat, I let my thoughts drift to Leyla, to the child sent to Earth, hidden and protected, and now standing fierce in a room of warriors who had fought too long to be free. Her shoulders were set, her dark hair catching the torchlight. She would survive. She would grow. And she would help restore what the King had destroyed.

"You will not be alone," I whispered to her, letting my eyes lock with hers. "Not tonight. Not ever." Her eyes went wide with shock, but she managed to bow her head the slightest in a show of respect.

It wasn't needed.

Not from Thalon. Not from her.

I would make that known after tonight. My careful planning is coming to fruition and after this war was won, I would ensure that I was the mother they both needed. I owed my friend at least that.

But tonight, the King's arrogance would be his undoing. His men would walk straight into the traps we will set, and the fury I had carried for over two decades would move through me with every strike. For twenty years I had waited.

Soon, the King would learn that debts long owed cannot be ignored.

Chapter Forty-One

Cerys

I did not linger to watch them move. Orders given were not comforts to be clung to, they were seeds planted, and I had to trust the ground to take them. Still, I paused long enough to let the sight of the rebels shifting into place burn into me. Hands that had been idle for years taking up axes and spears, younger faces tight with concentration, older faces hard as flint. They were not victims tonight. They would be the hunter's undoing.

"Briar, half the archers on the eastern ledge," Thalon said, voice low and exact. His jaw set; he nodded and moved like shadow.

"Serika, you take the western flank. Lay wards at the second approach and loose the flare-lines on my mark. Elias—cover the rear with the rebels who can fight in close. Leyla and Thalon, you'll hold the center and bait them toward the pit." They accepted each instruction the way soldiers accept breath: because it steadies them and gives purpose.

No one questioned us. Which was a courtesy earned over two decades of careful subterfuge and knowledge the King could not buy. We worked quickly. My hands, which had once been adept at tying ribbons and arranging courtly finery, were steadier with ropes and iron than I had expected.

I guided wards myself where I could; old magics responded to my touch. I could already feel my magic getting stronger being around Leyla. I am certain the others could as well. On the outer approach I traced sigils barely larger than a coin. They were quiet things that would snag boots, mute breath, and whisper false sounds down one path while letting the real one ring out. Where the stone was thin, I buried iron snares and soft stones that would sound like footsteps, then held them in place with an anchored rune that would loosen at my command.

Serika moved with me through the shadows, a silk-limbed current of power. She sealed weak points with braid-work runes; three small knots of ward-stitching that looked like children's knots but would tear armor straps and twist helmet crests at a touch. Her breath was even, precise; her muttered phrases had the sharpness of a surgeon's scalpel. Where she could not be, I left instructions in tight script upon the old maps. We placed caltrops where the hunters would most likely funnel — shallow valleys, broken paving, the single bridge the main road funneled through.

In the undercroft, Thalon had men hollow out false steps that could tilt under weight; a light enough hunter would cross and clatter through, while a heavier one would slip and find himself caught in netting below. The netting had been doubled and waxed to hold, and below that, ropes attached to stone anchors would jerk taut at the pull of a hidden mechanism. Good metalwork is quiet until it is splendidly loud.

"Timings," I said, pin-pricking the air with a finger to show the lines on the map. "They will move at dusk. The first wave will scout with three pointed parties. One will take the bridge and cut the eastern approach, one will sweep the western flats, and the others will probe for an exposed entrance. The bridge golems will knock at cadence two; that's our mark to fire the flares."

Briar knuckled the strap of an archer's quiver over his shoulder and met my eyes.

"What about prisoners?" he asked.

"The King's hunters are trained to follow order. There will be no prisoners. Only death." Thalon answered.

We moved through the sanctuary as if through a living organism. Sparks of gossip flickered and died as the fae men and women double-checked knots, sharpened blades, and breathed soft prayers to Gods who had long ago stopped answering. I ran my hands along stones that still remembered the hands of those who saved us once, and I whispered a name under my breath, a benediction and a vow. By twilight the sanctuary hummed with the low, mechanical music of readiness: arrows twitched in their sockets, wards pulsed faintly like a heartbeat beneath the floor, and the scent of oil and pine smoke filled the air.

Leyla walked among them, checking on the archers, kneeling to steady a fae whose fingers shook at the bowstring, brushing flour-dusted palms with hers as if the touch might bring courage. Thalon stood at her side, a dark monolith of watchfulness. I saw his eyes linger on Leyla the way a man's eyes do when he knows something holy is in reach. He is fierce and fatal and loyal to an extent that would have frightened me if it were directed at anything but her cause.

I loved him even more for it.

As dusk pooled into night, I repositioned the last of the wards. The calm before the strike has its own violence. We breathed it in as if it were air.

Chapter Forty-Two

Thalon

Leyla was pissed. Simple. I would have to deal with her anger later. I would not have her in danger. My mother stood by my mate, warding her and ensuring her scent was undetectable by the hunters.

The first warning came. A single crack from the tree line. A scout's call.

"Positions!" I shouted.

The command echoed through the stone corridors, sharp enough to cut through the drumbeat of boots and the scrape of armor. The rebels moved like they'd trained for this all their lives, because they had. Torches flared to life along the valley wall, spilling firelight across rock and iron.

Beside me, Elias adjusted his gauntlet, eyes scanning the dark.

"They're early," he said, voice low, steady.

"They're testing our defenses; he sent only one battalion," I replied. "He's sending a taste before the feast."

Elias smirked, one corner of his mouth lifting. "Let's ruin their appetite, then."

A thin ripple brushed through the wards, a whisper of power like cold wind over water. The hunters had arrived; moving along the eastern rise, silent and sure.

"At my mark." Serika loosed the signal flare. Blue light ripped the sky open, scattering sparks across the clouds. The first volley of arrows flew. The sound was immediate; a rush of air, the sharp percussion of impact. Bodies dropped before the hunters could blink.

"Shift left!" I called. "Cut off their retreat to the lower path."

Elias was already there, blade drawn, shadows dancing at his heels. He didn't hesitate; he never did. When one hunter broke the line, Elias met him halfway, steel flashing, quick and efficient.

"Try harder!" he yelled after the next one fell.

The ground trembled — then gave way. The nets I'd ordered sprung tight, yanking half their formation into the pit. Cries echoed through the canyon. The rest scattered, archers cutting them down like wheat.

"Push them west!" I ordered. "Make them think we're falling back."

It worked. Hunters surged forward; right into the illusion wards my mother had strengthened earlier. They stumbled into smoke and phantom soldiers, swinging at ghosts while our real fighters closed in from the flanks.

I felt her before I saw her—Leyla.

Her magic was a soft hum beneath my ribs, steady and fierce. I told her to stay behind the ridge, within the wards. Guarded and unseen with my mother. But there she was; bow in hand, firelight painting gold across her face, defiance written in every line of her stance.

"Damn it," I muttered. Elias followed my gaze, brow raising.

"You're losing that argument, brother."

"Not the time," I growled.

"Noted," he said, grin widening as he deflected a blade. "But I'm enjoying it."

The battle raged, quick and brutal. Briar and his squad struck from the right, their blades moving like a single thought. Hunters dropped in clusters. The night smelled of smoke and blood.

By the time the moon crested the ridge, the valley was ours again. Bodies littered the dirt. The King's banners burned. And the screams had long since gone quiet.

Elias wiped his blade, eyes scanning the horizon.

"Small force," he said.

"The real strike comes next."

He looked at me, jaw set. "Then we make sure we're ready."

When it was done, I found her again. Leyla stood beside the remnants of a broken cart, breath steady, bow still clutched in her hand. Her eyes met mine—unflinching, proud, and most importantly... Alive. And Gods help me, I couldn't even be angry.

Elias clapped my shoulder. "She's not hiding anymore."

"No," I said quietly, watching the flicker of torchlight across her hair. "And she shouldn't be hid either." The shadows stirred at my back, restless and sharp, like they knew what came next. This wasn't a victory. It was a warning.

I nodded once at the rebel. "Signal the fires."

Blue flame ignited along the cliffs; a chain of light, one torch sparking the next until the entire valley glowed like defiance.

Send the bastard a message he can see from his throne.

The bridge lives.

And his son was done obeying.

Chapter Forty-Three

Leyla

Smoke hung thick in the air, sharp with iron and ash. The screams had stopped, but the echoes still lived in the walls. The King's hunters were dead. Their armor glinted in broken heaps where the rebels had dragged them aside. It was over… for now. I should've felt triumph. Instead, I wanted to scream.

"Don't touch me," I snapped, shaking off the healer's hand.

I could still feel the press of the ward Thalon's mother had locked me behind at his command. My magic had battered it until the walls themselves groaned. He'd sealed me in like I was a child. Like I was fragile. And while I'd clawed at the wards, they'd fought without me.

Across the room, Thalon stood among his soldiers, the torchlight painting him in shadows. Elias was beside him, blood streaking his cheek but wearing the same crooked grin he always did. And it infuriated me.

"Coward," I muttered under my breath. Elias turned first, hearing me before Thalon did.

"Oh, Saints," he groaned, looking toward Thalon. "Best of luck, pal."

I stalked toward them, stepping over the body of a downed hunter. "You locked me away."

Thalon's head lifted. His eyes. Those deep, dark things, met mine. I saw the flicker of guilt there.

"You weren't supposed to be on the field, Leyla."

I stopped a few feet from him. "You don't get to decide that."

"You think I'll watch you walk into their blades?" His voice was low, rough with exhaustion and anger of his own. "You are the Bridge of Realms, Leyla. You cannot be risked."

The shadows at his feet stirred, curling and tightening like they felt the tension between us.

Elias stepped between us, his grin now gone. "Alright, maybe we save the lovers' quarrel until after the next attack?"

Neither of us moved. That's when Cerys descended the stairwell, her armor immaculate, her silver hair untouched by ash. She looked at Thalon first, then at me.

The expression on her face wasn't surprise, it was calculation. "You needed to be kept safe, Leyla. You would have made yourself a target being on that battlefield."

"I am a target," I said. "And if I'm one, I'd rather face it head-on than wait in the dark." Her head tiled slightly, as if she was considering my words.

A thin smile curved her lips. "Spoken like a true queen. But even queens must know when to listen." Mick stumbled forward then. Ashen, trembling, and her eyes faintly rimmed with gold. She'd fought tonight too. Barely controlled with her new instincts, but she'd fought.

"She saved two of our rebels," Elias said quietly. "Dragged them out herself."

Cerys looked her over once, then inclined her head. "Then she's earned her place."

My blood burned hotter. "And I haven't? Weeks of training! Weeks. And for what?"

Thalon's voice was softer now, almost weary. "The King sent a test, not an army. His next strike won't be this small. We cannot risk you for such a battle."

He wasn't wrong. I hated that he wasn't wrong.

Thalon looked back at me once more before following his mother to speak to the rebels. "This isn't over."

"You're damn right it isn't," I said.

When he was gone, Elias let out a slow whistle. "You've got fire, Leyla. I'll give you that. Remind me never to get on your bad side."

"You already are," I said, but the edge of my voice softened. He grinned, wiping blood from his jaw.

Mick leaned her head against my shoulder, her voice barely a whisper. "You know he only did it because he's terrified to lose you."

I watched Thalon's retreating form vanish into the dark. "He's going to have to learn that loving me means bleeding beside me."

Chapter Forty-Four

Thalon

I stood at the edge of the chamber, arms crossed, watching the aftermath of the ambush unfold. The fires of the flares were dying to embers, the wards still pulsing faintly with residual energy. I allowed my shadow to stretch and coil around me, a silent acknowledgment of control and presence. And yet, all of my focus wasn't on the battlefield. It was on her. Cerys. My mother. For years, she had been distant, reserved, unyielding. A woman who demanded obedience but offered little warmth in return.

And yet, watching her tonight and even this past week, the truth pressed itself into every corner of my understanding: she had been preparing for this for decades. Every cool glance, every word measured and restrained, every silent distance between us, it had been strategy. A lifetime of hidden preparation. I admired her now, not as my mother in the way the world imagined, but as a warrior, a strategist, a force that had carved power from shadows and patience alike. That same woman, whose orders I had bristled against as a boy, had orchestrated a near-perfect ambush on the King's hunters, all without ever showing the slightest tremor of emotion.

Turning back to the rebels, I let my voice cut through the heavy air of the chamber—steady and commanding. Alive with the hum of victory. "Listen to me. Tonight was only the beginning. The King will retaliate. He always does. But we are done merely surviving." The shadows curled tighter at my feet as I stepped forward, letting their pulse echo the conviction in my words. "We take back what was stolen. We strike with purpose. We fight with precision. And, we protect the Bridge, my mate, at all costs."

A ripple of sound moved through the rebels, half a growl, half a cheer, the kind that carried equal parts exhaustion and defiance. Blood stained the stone beneath our boots, and the scent of magic and smoke still lingered. I could feel the heartbeat of the chamber itself, thudding in rhythm with my own.

I glanced again at my mother, who watched from a raised platform near the rear of the chamber, her posture as immaculate and measured as ever. Her eyes met mine briefly, and I felt the unspoken acknowledgment between us: she had laid the path, but I would now walk it forward, carrying the torch for the rebels, for Leyla, for what had been stolen, and for what must be reclaimed. I drew a slow breath, feeling the shadows pulse in response to my heartbeat.

"We have work to do," I murmured, half to myself, half to the room. "And no one will falter. Not now. Not ever."

Beneath that declaration, I felt her. My mate.

The pulse of her magic brushed against the edges of my mind, faint but insistent. The Bridge of Realms. My fury and my heart.

And Gods, was she angry with me.

I'd protected her. But I'd also silenced her.

And with the rebels dispersing into the shadows to ready for the next strike, I knew the next battle wouldn't be with my father. It would be with her.

Chapter Forty-Five

Leyla

The firelight had burned low by the time I found him. The hall was quiet now, wounded tended to, the dead counted, the armor stacked in blackened heaps. Even the shadows had gone still, heavy with exhaustion and smoke.

Thalon stood alone in our room near the balcony doors, shirt discarded, hair still damp from washing away the blood. The muscles in his back shifted with every slow breath. I'd seen him fight before, but never like tonight. Every movement had been pure command, dark and dangerous, and yet all I could think about was the moment he'd ordered his mother to seal me away.

I stepped inside. The doors closed behind me with a soft thud. He didn't turn, but I knew he'd sensed me the instant I entered.

Thalon turned to me first, eyes shadowed but steady. *Leyla,* he entered into my thoughts.

"No," I snapped, the word sharper than I intended. "You had me caged. You do not get to be in my head right now."

He didn't flinch. "I was protecting you."

"From what? From fighting? From being YOURS out there?" I moved closer, anger vibrating through my magic. "You think I can't handle what you face? You think I'll break?"

His jaw flexed. "No. I think I'll break if something happens to you."

The words hit harder than I expected. I froze, the edge of my fury caught between the weight of what he meant and the sting of how he'd done it. He took a careful step closer. "I should've spoken to you first," he said, voice low, rough with something real. "I should've trusted your training. I should have trusted that you were ready. I won't do it again."

My heart stuttered. The fight in my soul was giving away. "You made me look weak, Thalon."

"I swear it." His hand found mine, his eyes exploring my own. "You will fight beside me, like my Queen, or not at all. But never behind walls again. I'm sorry, Leyla."

The silence stretched, thick with so many unspoken things. The scent of smoke and shadow wrapped around us, and for a moment, I forgot everything but him. The warmth of his skin, the ache behind his eyes, the way his power reached for mine like it couldn't help itself.

"Thalon…" I whispered, but I didn't finish. I didn't need to. He closed the space between us in a heartbeat. His hand slid to the back of my neck, his forehead resting against mine.

"Say you forgive me," he breathed.

"I shouldn't."

"I know." His lips brushed mine. "Say it anyway."

His lips found mine, deliberate, exploring the edges where anger and desire met. My hands threaded into his hair, tugging him closer, and the shadows around us seemed to lean in, as if aware that the bond between us was no longer just of desire, but of hearts, fire, and something more primal. He eased me back against the bed, never breaking the kiss. I arched into him instinctively, letting every frustration, every longing, every unspoken apology flow into that connection. The air was thick with heat, with magic, with the promise of something sacred and dangerous.

"Nothing else matters right now," he murmured against my lips. "No battles. No hunters. Only us."

I let myself believe it, if only for tonight. My hands roamed his shoulders, down his arms, feeling the taut strength of him, the life that was his, the shadows that always followed him even here. His hands returned the favor with careful urgency, tracing my curves, memorizing the lines of me, the places that had been shielded all day, by walls I refused and wards I had broken.

We moved together, slow at first, testing the rhythm. Letting the ache of unspoken emotions dictate our pace. And then, when the distance between us dissolved entirely, when the night and the world outside the walls ceased to exist, we surrendered. To desire, to love, to the need that had been waiting beneath every glance, every fight, every whispered warning.

The shadows of the ward, the smoke of the battlefield, the tension of the fight; all of it dissolved into the heat between us. Every heartbeat, every sigh, every whispered name became a promise: that whatever storms came tomorrow, whatever armies, whatever hunters, we would face them together.

Chapter Forty-Six

Leyla

The training hall was quiet, shadows stretching along the walls like liquid ink. Sunlight filtered through the hidden runes carved centuries ago, faint golden light pooling across the floor. Thalon stood at the far end, his dark eyes fixed on me, shadow coiling around him like a protective cloak. The tension between us hummed almost as strongly as the magic that pulsed beneath my skin.

"Focus, Leyla," he said, his voice low, deliberate. "Let the energy move through you. Don't force it, guide it."

I nodded, closing my eyes and letting the now familiar warmth coil inside me.

This time, I didn't just try to coax life into stone. I let the energy flow deeper, feeling the threads of the sanctuary itself respond to me. The air shimmered faintly as heat and power pulsed outward, and for a moment, I thought I could feel the heartbeat of the underground cavern, its ancient stone and wards, responding to my presence. Small threads of light leapt across the room, swirling around my hands, then branching out, dancing across the walls. I opened my eyes and gasped. It wasn't just life anymore. It was awareness.

The magic itself seemed to be alive. Shapes formed in the air, fleeting images of the worlds beyond, faint glimpses of realms.

"Keep it steady," Thalon said, stepping closer, his shadow curling protectively around me. "You're doing more than you realize. You're touching the Bridge."

I shivered, a mixture of awe and fear prickling my skin. The threads of energy pulsed wildly, tugging at me, demanding more control than I had yet mastered. My knees wobbled. My vision blurred. I stumbled back, the light threading around me like tendrils.

"Leyla!" Mick called from the stands.

Thalon caught my elbow.

The shadows tightened, anchoring me. But the energy inside me surged, overwhelming my senses. My legs gave way, and I collapsed onto the floor, the golden light spinning and fracturing around me.

"Focus on the pulse… The heart of the Bridge," a soft, melodic voice murmured. Serika knelt beside me, her hands hovering just above my shoulders. "Do not fight it. Let it show you."

Through the spinning haze of consciousness, I saw visions—not just of the sanctuary, but of the world above, of the fractured realms. Threads of energy stretched like veins through the earth, connecting kingdoms, forests, oceans, even the skies. I could feel the broken seams in the fabric of the world. My power, the life magic, was the key to stitching them together.

"You are the Bridge," Serika aided gently, pressing a hand to mine. Her voice was both command and comfort. "You feel the threads. You know what must be done. Let them guide you."

Images shifted in my mind: portals flickering open in distant lands, the faint glow of life returning to deadened areas, children laughing in fields that had been barren, magic humming stronger than ever before. It all swirled together, a vision of what could be... If only I could harness it.

I gasped, my chest heaving. The spinning light calmed slightly, coiling around me like a living ribbon. Thalon's darkness pressed closer, wrapping around me, steadying me.

"You're doing it," he whispered, his voice deep, full of pride. "Leyla, I can feel it. You're... beyond anything I could have imagined."

I shook my head, weak but resolute. "It's... it's too much."

"No," Serika said, her eyes glowing faintly. "It's enough. Enough to show you the path. Rest. Breathe. And when you wake, you'll know what the Bridge asks of you."

I felt the energy settle, withdrawing and folding back into my body, leaving me exhausted but alive, aware of possibilities I had never imagined. The threads of magic hummed faintly, a pulse beneath my skin that promised that I could—no, would—restore what had been taken from Orrynne.

Thalon lifted me carefully, his shadows guiding us both as we left the floor.

You're almost there, little light, he murmured into my mind. *And I'll be with you... Every step of the way.*

I nodded, barely able to speak, but a small, fierce spark of determination burned in my chest. I was the Bridge. And the realms were waiting.

Chapter Forty-Seven

Thalon

She was drained. Even as she smiled, a faint flush on her cheeks, I could see it in the slump of her shoulders, the slow rhythm of her breathing, the faint tremor in her hands. The Bridge had taken more from her than anyone could imagine, and yet she'd emerged from it stronger, brighter, alive in ways that made my chest ache. I carried her quietly towards the quarters set aside for us, my shadows flowing beside her, protective, almost sentient. I had learned to read her energy, the delicate pulse that told me when she was exhausted, when she was overwhelmed, and when she was scared. And right now, she was all three.

"You've done well today," my words for my mate alone as they brushed her ear. The warmth against her skin made her shiver slightly. Leyla looked up at me, a small, tired smile curving her lips.

"It's… different. I can feel it now, Thalon. The Bridge… it's there. I know what to do." I reached out, taking her hands in mine, feeling the residual energy still humming along her skin.

"Then rest. You've earned it."

The flickering light from the sconces in the hallway cast soft shadows across her face, highlighting the exhaustion, the fierce determination, and the quiet magic that radiated from her. I couldn't resist running a thumb along her jawline, marveling at the warmth and softness beneath my calloused fingers.

"Get a room," a voice called from the doorway. Mick, standing just outside with her arms crossed, gave us a sly grin. "Honestly. You two don't even try to hide it anymore."

I growled low in my throat, pulling Leyla closer instinctively. "Out of the way and we plan to," I said, though the corners of my mouth twitched with amusement.

Leyla just laughed, I could feel her relief through our bond as she thought of Mick. For weeks, worry had shadowed her every thought, a quiet ache beneath her strength. But now… now I could feel the shift. Gyor's methods were working. Whatever he'd done—whatever balance he'd struck with Mick's new, unnatural state—it was holding. And the fact that her appetite seemed to lean toward Elias, and now animal blood, had made things easier for all of us.

Elias certainly didn't seem to mind being her donor. If anything, he wore that faint, infuriating grin each time she fed, like he'd been waiting to play hero to a vampire. Unconventional, yes. But effective.

Once, the thought of a vampire's fangs sinking into fae flesh would've sickened me. Politics and old scars had left our kinds wary of one another, our alliances fragile at best. But now… with Mick… It was different. Everything was different.

The door shut behind us with a soft, final click, the sound sealing us away from the noise of the world beyond. I turned to her then, really turned—and the breath caught in my chest.

Those bright blue eyes lifted to mine, shimmering with the remnants of her magic. Stray strands of hair clung to her temples, damp with sweat from training, and the flickering torchlight kissed her skin in molten gold. Power still pulsed faintly beneath her surface, alive and thrumming, and Gods— she was beautiful. Fierce and fragile all at once.

I crossed the space between us, slow, deliberate. My fingers found her waist, tracing the curve of her body as if to remind myself she was real. That she was mine. Her breath hitched under my touch, and I felt the shiver that rippled through her.

"You pushed yourself hard today," I murmured, my voice rougher than I intended.

"I don't mind," she whispered back, her voice a haze of exhaustion and quiet satisfaction.

The sound of it slipped beneath my skin. My chest tightened, something raw and protective rising inside me. My shadows stirred in answer, unfurling around her like a living thing—dark tendrils of loyalty and want, wrapping her in a cocoon of warmth and claim. They danced across her shoulders, her arms, the edges of her pulse, until she was bathed in their faint hum. And then, with a sound like a breath pulled from the heart of the night, my wings tore free. Black as ink, they unfurled behind me in a slow, shuddering sweep, stretching wide enough to darken the walls.

The air shifted with the motion, carrying the faint scent of magic and storm. Leyla's eyes widened, and I caught the flicker of awe there—just before her fingers brushed one of the feathers, reverent, trembling. My wings moved instinctively, folding forward slightly as if to shelter her, to draw her closer. My own pulse stuttered at the sight of her surrounded by my darkness, her light glinting against it like starlight swallowed by night.

I leaned in until our foreheads touched, her breath mingling with mine. My hands lingered along her sides, memorizing the rhythm of her breathing, the steady beat of her heart.

"You're mine," I whispered, the words more vow than possession. Her pulse answered beneath my fingertips. "And I'll guard you. Always."

Her magic curled through mine, silver and shadow entwined, warm and pulsing with life. The air thickened, filled with that electric hum that always seemed to follow when we were this close. She tilted her face up to me, the faintest tremor of need threading through her, and I couldn't resist.

My mouth found hers—slow at first, reverent, then deep and consuming. Her lips were soft and sweet, tasting of warmth and salt and the faint tang of spent magic. She pressed closer, her small hands sliding up my chest, fingertips tracing the scars and sigils etched beneath my skin. Every touch sent heat spiraling through me, coiling low and fierce.

"Thalon…" she breathed against my mouth, my name breaking like a plea and a promise all at once. The sound of it undid me.

I closed what little space remained between us, until her heartbeat thrummed against mine. My wings curved around us, a blackened shield against the world, feathers brushing her shoulders like whispered vows. The rest of the world fell away—the looming war, the blood on my hands, the weight of crowns and realms.

The girl who had become my world, my undoing, my salvation. And when her quiet gasp of surprise slipped through the kiss, I smiled against her lips, tracing my thumb along her jaw.

She was mine.

She always has been.

Chapter Forty-Eight

Leyla

The hall felt impossibly still, as if the stones themselves were holding their breath. I knelt, hands hovering over the floor, my fingers trembling with anticipation. This wasn't like coaxing life into plants or cracks in the stone, it was the flow of existence itself. Threading together worlds, uniting the broken seams between realms, was heavier, denser, alive in a way that made my skin prickle. I drew in a shuddering breath and let my magic radiate outward. I could feel the thin veil between this world and the others—fragile, almost invisible, fraying in places from the King's corruption.

That was where I had to reach. My power wasn't just about creating life, it was connecting. Pulling threads across space and energy, stitching together realms that had grown apart.

The first step was sensing the threads. They were like faint silver lines, almost intangible, winding through the unseen corners of reality. I let my awareness stretch beyond the hall, beyond the sanctuary, feeling the pulse of distant forests, oceans, and cities that existed only in fragmented realms. Each pulse was a heartbeat, a memory, a fragment of what life could be. I focused, allowing the threads to brush against my consciousness. Light flickered in the corners of my mind as I reached, stretching my magic along each line, touching it, coaxing it awake.

It responded to me because I was the Bridge, the point where worlds could meet and enjoy the fruitfulness of my life-magic. I didn't force them; I invited them. My intent was the key. Thalon knelt behind me, his shadows coiling protectively around us.

"You're doing it," his voice low. "I can feel it… stretching out, reaching farther."

I exhaled, and a faint vibration hummed through the hall. The threads of life I had touched began to pulse in harmony, tiny sparks of energy flowing from one realm to another. I could see it: a faint shimmer of light in the air, like a network of glowing veins connecting invisible worlds. Each pulse carried energy, a whisper of possibility, a promise of restoration.

Mick hovered beside me, her hand lightly brushing mine. "Ley… it's… incredible," she whispered. "I can feel it too… Something shifting."

Her eyes widened, betraying her awe, but I could sense the hunger still lurking beneath her calm, the reminder that even in this moment of beauty, our battle wasn't over.

Serika's voice, calm but insistent, continued to guide me. "Leyla, you are the nexus. Each thread you touch, each connection you reinforce, allows energy to flow between realms. Think of it like weaving: strands of existence, faint and delicate, must be threaded with care. Your mind, your intent, your focus, they are the needle and the loom. Let the magic flow naturally; it will respond to your will if you guide it."

I closed my eyes tighter, feeling my own heartbeat sync with the pulsing of the threads. My body trembled as I wove, one hand tracing arcs of energy in the air, the other coaxing the threads beneath me into alignment. Slowly, I felt the first tangible effect: the faint rush of wind through the hall, carrying the scent of wildflowers and distant seas, though none existed here. It was as though the realms themselves were breathing, awakening in response to my touch. A bright pulse radiated from me, small at first, then growing. Like a ripple in water.

Life began to stir in subtle ways, cracks in the stone glimmered faintly, tendrils of energy dancing over the floor, the scent of rain and soil filling the space. I could see the outline of distant forests, oceans, and cities flickering like ghostly mirages along the edges of my vision, slowly connecting to the energy of the sanctuary.

"I... I think I can keep it stable," I whispered, my voice trembling. My energy surged outward, threading across realms, each one answering my pull with a soft glow. "I can do this..."

Thalon's hands rested lightly on my shoulders, grounding me. "You can. You're the Bridge, Leyla. You've been made for this. I'll hold the rest for you."

I gasped as exhaustion hit, my vision swimming with pulses of light, life, and possibility. The threads were alive, humming through me and out into the worlds beyond. But I could feel the cost already; my magic burned through me like fire, draining my strength even as it expanded. Serika stepped closer, her expression solemn.

"You're ready," she said. "The Bridge is forming. But know this; every connection, every thread you weave, carries weight.

Life will respond, but it will demand energy from you. Thalon, Mick, you must guard her, guide her, and trust that she knows when to push forward." I sank to the floor, trembling but exhilarated. Thalon knelt beside me, wrapping me in a protective shadow cocoon. Mick hovered close, her eyes wide in awe and admiration.

I felt the threads humming beneath my hands, faint connections now flowing outward into the unseen worlds, sparks of life beginning to bloom, rivers of energy starting to pulse with potential.

"We're ready," I whispered, voice weak but resolute. Like a prayer I knew would be answered.

"The Bridge… It's waking."

Thalon brushed my hair from my face, his gaze steady and intense. And then there was nothing, only darkness.

Chapter Forty-Nine

Leyla

The sanctuary was quiet the next morning, but alive in a way that felt foreign yet familiar. I could feel it: the threads of life I had coaxed awake yesterday pulsed faintly beneath my skin, tugging gently at the edges of the world. Outside, tiny green shoots continued to twist through the ruins, the faint shimmer of magic a constant reminder that the Bridge was forming, fragile but real.

The days were passing by quickly. I was forced to eat by Thalon, trained, and then my body gave in to the darkness. I hardly knew what else existed outside of my training sessions, they were my only focus. And Mick. She was doing much better, nearly fully recovered… And now a vampire. Her mom would have had a cow.

Thalon stood nearby, shadows curling subtly around him, protective, coiled like a living thing. His dark eyes never left me, scanning my every movement, every flicker of energy. There was pride there, yes, but also hunger, something raw and intimate, and I felt it brush against the pulse of my own magic.

Briar emerged from the shadows, eyes sharp and assessing. "The threads are spreading faster than expected," he said, voice low. "If the King catches wind of this before we're ready…" He shook his head, but there was a hint of wonder in his expression. "He won't know what hit him."

Cerys stepped into the room, regal as ever, her presence commanding without demanding. "He'll know soon enough," she said, voice calm but tinged with anger that simmered beneath her polished exterior. "But we have time. He will try to ensure that his next attack does not end like the last. Leyla, you are the key. The Bridge can't be rushed, but it can be protected… and guided."

I nodded, feeling the weight of her words settle over me. This was bigger than any of us. Even bigger even than the rebellion. I was the Bridge, and the threads of life needed my guidance. Thalon stepped closer, letting his shadow weave around my wrist, a subtle, grounding pressure.

"I'll keep you safe," he said quietly, voice low, almost intimate. "No one touches you while the Bridge grows."

I lifted my hands, continuing to let the threads of the Bridge swirl gently around us. Tiny flashes of color, subtle hints of growth, shimmered through the air. Flowers blooming along cracks in the stone floor, the faint pulse of life brushing the walls, whispers of other realms tugging softly at the edges of perception.

"It's time to sleep now, my love. You've done enough for today". The last words I heard before I saw nothing.

Today, was the moment I would finalize the Bridge.

Every fiber of my being thrummed with energy. The threads of life around me pulsed like veins of light, invisible yet tangible, connecting the stones beneath my feet, the walls around us, the anchors the rebels had formed around the courtyard… and reaching far beyond, into realms I had never touched. Thalon's shadows coiled around my ankles and wrists, a tether as protective as it was intimate. He didn't speak; he didn't need to.

The bond we had forged hummed between us, a constant reminder that he could feel every heartbeat, every pulse of energy. Mick sat nearby, fangs sheathed but alert, leaning against a bench with Elias hovering beside her, watching me like a hawk. I took a deep breath, closing my eyes and letting the threads respond. This is it. This is the connection I've been preparing for. I visualized it like an intricate lattice, threads running like silver filaments from me to every anchor, to the sanctuary itself, and finally to the worlds beyond. Threads that could bend, stretch, and interweave without breaking. I reached out mentally first, sending a pulse of thought and intent along the threads. The anchors responded instantly; the rebels flinched slightly as the energy brushed their minds, then relaxed, breathing deep as if the threads were soothing rather than intrusive.

Good, I thought, letting a tremor of relief pulse through me.

Then, slowly, deliberately, I extended the threads further. I pictured the other realms: the deadened plains outside the kingdom, the far reaches of our world that had been hollowed by the King's reign, even distant realms. My energy reached for them, bending the threads toward them, whispering to them, letting them feel the pulse of life again. And it worked.

A faint hum vibrated in the air as tiny motes of golden light began to stir, almost like fireflies awakened from centuries of sleep. Threads of energy shimmered along the edges of my vision—full realms responding, alive and rippling with potential. The Bridge was active, a living conduit between worlds. I opened my eyes. Thalon's dark gaze was fixed on me, and I felt the unspoken approval, the connection vibrating through our mind link, soaring with pride.

"You've done it," he said softly through our bond, his voice thick with pride. *"You're the Bridge, Leyla. You've actually done it."*

I exhaled, trembling slightly, my hands still hovering in the air as energy hummed across them.

Life was responding. Not just plants, but animals, distant threads of consciousness that had been trapped or dormant, even echoes of magic from the people who had lived and died here. The Bridge was alive, and it was mine to guide.

Mick stood, eyes wide. "I can feel it," she said, voice trembling. "Like the world is… breathing again." She glanced at Elias, who gave an approving nod my way, his usual smirk softened.

Cerys stepped forward, her presence regal even in the underground light. "It is as I suspected," she said quietly, almost reverent. "You were always meant for this. Leyla, your parents would be so proud."

I nodded, feeling the pull in my chest… not just exhaustion, but a deep, resonant ache as the energy flowed through me. Thalon placed his hand on my shoulder, grounding me, his own power flowing into mine.

I laughed weakly, exhausted but elated, letting the energy settle and pulse gently beneath the surface. The Bridge had been finalized. Threads connected worlds, life stirred where it had been absent, and the realm itself whispered back to me in faint, encouraging hums. And then, as quietly as she had appeared, Serika stepped forward. Her red eyes scanned the courtyard, sharp and measured.

"My role here is complete," she said, voice calm but firm. "The Bridge is stable. You have learned what is needed. I will take my leave. I have my own agenda I need to see to before the King arrives. The threads, the energy; the very life force of this realm and others… they are responding to you. But remember: every connection comes at a cost. You will feel it. And when the time comes, you will know what to do."

I blinked, momentarily stunned. "You're leaving?"

She nodded once. "I will not linger where my presence is no longer required. Remember what I said the cost was. Trust in your connections, Leyla. Trust in them—and in yourself." With that, she disappeared as suddenly as she had arrived, leaving the warmth of life, the pulse of magic, and the weight of responsibility in her wake.

Thalon pressed close, shadows enveloping us as she left the rebel sanctuary.

I let myself lean into him, tired but exhilarated, the threads of the Bridge humming faintly around us, promising that the realms would listen, and that the world might finally begin to heal.

Chapter Fifty

Leyla

The sanctuary shimmered in a golden glow, enchanted lanterns casting dancing light across the carved stone walls. Tonight, the rebels were celebrating… not for a battle won, not yet at least, but the first real touch of life and fertility returning to Orrynne. For the first time in decades, magic hummed through the air like a heartbeat, and everyone could feel it, subtle and intoxicating. Tables were draped in soft fabrics, fae wine glimmered in crystal goblets, and music floated faintly from enchanted strings.

The aroma of herbs, sweet spices, and baked bread mingled in the warm air. Laughter echoed off the walls, lighter than I had ever heard in this sanctuary. For a few hours, they could forget the King, the fear… they could just be alive. Thalon stayed close beside me, his gaze never leaving me as if I alone held all the light in the room. Every flicker of magic, every playful sway of my hair, every motion of my body in the dim glow held him in rapture. I could feel it, the way his shadows danced around us, protective and possessive, yet reverent.

"Leyla," he murmured, his voice low, almost lost in the music, "you are… everything."

I reached for a goblet of fae wine, letting the warmth seep through me, a tiny indulgence in this fragile peace. Around us, the rebels laughed, sang, and embraced the magic awakening in them.

It was surreal, seeing the fae move freely with the sense of fertility and life, some swaying to the music, others holding hands, sharing smiles they hadn't dared in years. Mick, never one to hold back, even apparently now in her vampiric state, had indulged too heavily in the fae wine. Her pale skin flushed pink, fangs peeking slightly as her eyes danced mischievously. Before anyone could stop her, she leaned over and planted a teasing kiss on Elias's lips. I watched as he froze for a second, stunned, before smirking and shaking his head.

"I think the wine is winning, Michaela," he said dryly, though amusement lit his eyes.

Mick laughed, nearly toppling over, and Elias caught her just in time.

I smiled softly at them, but my attention was drawn back to Thalon. He stood just a few steps away, shadows curling around his feet like a cloak. Even in this joyful chaos, his focus never wavered from me. I felt the pull of our connection, the mate bond, the mind link that had strengthened after our first night together. My chest warmed at the thought of him, and I leaned closer, my fingers brushing his.

"You're… mesmerizing," he whispered, hand grazing mine, thumb tracing circles across the back. The shadows responded, tightening slightly, as if recognizing their mistress's worth. "Every motion, every laugh, every spark of magic—it's all because of you, Leyla."

I swallowed, heat rushing to my cheeks. He leaned closer, the faint pulse of his magic mingling with mine, and I felt the connection thrum, deep and alive. We moved to the side of the hall, letting the music, laughter, and Thalon's shadows swirl around us, a private bubble in the chaos. My hands found his, his eyes dark with desire and awe. Every glance, every brush of his fingertips over mine, sent shivers through me. I let myself melt into him, the world beyond this our temporary sanctuary—danger, the King, the hunters—fading to nothing.

His gaze was all-consuming, and I felt the heat between us spike as if the very magic of the Bridge pulsed in tandem with our desire. "Tomorrow," he murmured against my hair, voice rough, "will come soon enough. Tonight… we are here. You and me."

I closed my eyes briefly, letting the words settle, the warmth of his hand, the pull of our connection.

As the night stretched on, laughter and music wrapping the rebels in a protective cocoon, I let myself savor it.

For a few hours, the world outside didn't matter.

For a few hours, life, magic, and desire were ours.

And when dawn came, we would face it together. But for now… for now, it was the night of life, the night of celebration, and the night of us.

Chapter Fifty-One

Thalon

The pounding at our door came hours after the celebration. In the early hours of the morning, the darkness still thick. The scent of smoke and steel hung thick in the tunnels long before the first blade was drawn.

The air was tight, electric, the kind of silence that always came before the kill. I'd learned to read that stillness, to feel the pulse of battle before it began. The torches burned low along the stone corridors, throwing long shadows that clung to the walls like ghosts. Rebels moved through them in tight formations, weapons drawn, eyes sharp. Their whispers faded as I passed, some out of fear, others out of respect. I didn't need their words.

The Bridge thrummed in the air like a distant heartbeat. Leyla stood beside me at the mouth of the hall, her hand steady on the hilt of her blade, silver threads of light already whispering across her skin. She was calm—too calm. The kind of calm that meant the storm had already chosen its path.

"You're sure they'll come through here?" she asked.

"They'll come where the scent of rebellion is thickest," I replied. "And that's us."

A flicker of a smile crossed her face, there and gone like lightning.

Behind us, Gyor barked orders, his deep voice echoing through the cavern: "Archers on the west ledge! Keep the tunnels clear! Move, damn it!" His command carried the weight of a leader who had lost too much to hesitate now.

Elias adjusted the grip on his spear, standing near the rear guard; sentinel, steady and watchful. Mick perched high above on the jagged outcropping, her eyes glowing faint amber in the dim. Even from here, I could feel the hunger pulsing through her, caged and coiled, though fading.

And my mother, Cerys, she moved like a phantom between them. Blades drawn, hair braided tight, the faint shimmer of ward-magic glinting across her armor. It was all in place. Every line of defense, every spell, every heartbeat. And yet… I could feel it. The hum. The pulse of the hunters beyond the stone.

They were close.

When the first tremor hit, it was subtle; a ripple through the Bridge that we could feel in our souls, like someone plucking a string of fate. Leyla stiffened beside me.

I caught the faint glow of silver veins crawling across the wall, responding to her presence. The Bridge was alive, waiting. Then came the sound; faint at first, then deafening just as quickly. The heavy rhythm of boots, hundreds of them, pounding the ground in unison. The hunters. Trained, disciplined, and merciless demons. The King's elite.

"Positions!" I shouted.

The tunnels erupted into motion. Arrows nocked. Blades raised. The air thickened with the scent of ozone and burning oil. And then… Impact.

The hunters flooded into the passageways like a storm tide, their armor black as obsidian, faces hidden behind carved masks. Their swords gleamed with runes that pulsed like veins of fire.

"Now!" I barked, and Gyor's front line surged forward.

Steel met steel, and the tunnels filled with the sound of death. The first wave was chaos; the kind that separates soldiers from survivors. Rebels clashed with hunters, magic flaring in bursts of color and sound. The Bridge flared to life, threads of silver spreading through the stone like veins of living light. I could feel Leyla's magic moving through it—fast, bright, and alive—amplifying every fighter who stood with us.

I moved through the battle like shadow incarnate. My magic cut through the air in ribbons of darkness, consuming light, devouring flame. A hunter lunged for Gyor. I struck from behind, my blade finding the weak point in his armor. He fell without a sound. Leyla fought near the front, her magic lancing through the air, illuminating the tunnels with pulses of silver. I could feel her through the Bridge and our connection—every breath, every surge of power. Our magics wove together without effort, her life-force and mine moving like tide and moon.

"Left flank, down!" Elias roared, driving his spear through two hunters at once.

Mick dropped from above, landing with inhuman grace, tearing through the rear line with a feral cry. Blood streaked her jaw, but her eyes were clear… calculating and controlled.

Cerys was a blade of wind and steel, darting between bodies, cutting down those who slipped past the front line. Her voice cut through the roar, calling out to Leyla: "Bridge surge holding steady! Keep pushing!"

I could feel it—the energy building. The rebels were holding. For now. But the hunters were endless. Their discipline was frightening to see from the opposing side. I used to give them orders and now I faced them head on. There were no cries, no hesitation. They fought like extensions of the same body.

"Hold!" I commanded, voice echoing over the din. "Wait for the signal!"

The rebels hesitated—barely. And then, Leyla raised her hand. Light exploded from her palm, cascading down the tunnel in a wave of blinding brilliance. The hunters reeled. I unleashed my shadows in response, a countercurrent of darkness that crashed into them like a living storm. The explosion tore through the cavern. Rock cracked. Fire burst from the torches. The screams of dying fae men and women filled the air, mixed with the hum of magic unraveling. When the light cleared, the tunnel was littered with bodies, hunters and rebels alike.

Smoke curled upward, glowing faintly with the remnants of Leyla's magic. She stood at the center of it, breathing hard, eyes glowing with silver fire. I could feel her exhaustion through our bond, the toll of what she'd given.

I crossed to her, my hand brushing her shoulder. "Still with me?"

She nodded. "Always."

But I could feel the shift. The air grew colder. The shadows deepened. A sound rose from the far end of the hall, not boots this time. Something older. Something heavier. And then I knew.

He was here.

The King's presence pressed against my senses like a hand around my throat; suffocating and ancient, powerful beyond reason. Even the Bridge faltered under it.

"Fall back," I ordered quietly. "Get the wounded clear. Gyor, guard the exits."

Leyla turned toward the end of the tunnel, where the air rippled like heat over fire.

Her voice was low, certain. "This ends tonight."

I met her eyes—and for a moment, everything else disappeared.

She was light.

I was shadow.

And between us was the fate of everything that had come before.

Chapter Fifty-Two

King Vaeris

The wind howled like a living thing as I crossed the valley of ash. It stank of death and rebellion. A scent I had once admired for its rarity, but now it clung to everything.

My boots crushed what remained of my empire: the bones of deserters, the soot of burned banners, the blackened remnants of my reign.

They whispered my name even now, in the dark corners of the world.

Vaeris. King of the Rift. King of the Hunters.

But they no longer said it with reverence.

The torches ahead burned low against the mist, marking the entrance to the rebels' sanctuary, the last wretched den my queen had crawled into.

My queen.

The title turned sour in my mouth. Cerys had been nothing but beauty and defiance since the day I claimed her. I'd found her young—too young—her ice magic still untempered, her gaze sharp enough to cut. I had thought to tame that gaze, to bend it. The night I took her for my wife, the whole court had watched her kneel in silence, her crown of frost glinting beneath the torchlight. She had not wept, not even once.

I mistook that for strength bound to obedience. I was wrong. For years, I believed the boy she bore me had changed her. A mother's softness, I thought. A reason to live beyond her own cold pride.

And for a time, I almost allowed myself to believe in peace.

But peace is a lie the weak tell themselves to dull the edge of vigilance. Now, she leads the rebellion that dares go against my reign. She teaches my son to turn his shadows against me… The gift I forged in him.

The fire in my chest flared hot enough to burn through the armor on my ribs.

I can still see her the day I placed the binding sigil upon Thalon's heart. She fought my hold until blood poured from her eyes. I thought it was resignation. I thought she'd finally learned. But it wasn't surrender. It was patience—the venom kind, slow and sweet, waiting for its hour.

And now, the sigil will not hold. My own creation. My own failure.

The thought sent my hand shaking against the hilt of my blade, old runes etched deep into its surface, humming faintly in answer to my rage.

I passed through the ruins of what had once been a place of prayer. The Gods had left this realm long ago though. It was me they now worshipped.

The rebel markings painted across the stone walls glowed faintly. Each one seemed to sneer at me, whispering in the voice of my wife and my son.

You have lost them.

No.

I paused before the heavy doors that led into the heart of the sanctuary, running my palm along the splintered wood. The grain was slick with moisture, and beneath it, I could feel the pulse of the realm itself—the Bridge and that cursed girl that brought it back.

Inside, they waited.

My son and my queen.

My betrayals made flesh. I almost smiled at the thought.

There was a strange poetry in it. That the woman I'd stolen, and the boy I'd broken, would be the ones to end me. Or try. Because they would not take the crown while breath still stirred my chest.

The storm outside rose to a roar, and with it, my power answered. Shadows coiled up from beneath my boots, crawling up my arms, whispering promises in a dozen dead tongues. My sigils burned black, veins of power crawling beneath my skin until the air around me cracked and bled dark light.

Let them see me as I am. Not a man, but a God their rebellion had made.

I slammed the doors open. The sound rolled through the sanctuary like thunder, scattering the torchlight into shards.

"I have come for what is mine," I said, voice steady and cold as the grave.

The Darkness Saves

The words echoed across the hollow chamber, reaching the corners where my wife's ice met my son's shadow.

The war that would end everything had finally come home.

Chapter Fifty-Three

Thalon

He appeared. The King stepped forward, an aura of evil warping the very air around him. Shadows bent toward him, and the light dimmed in the tunnels as if the world itself recoiled. Cerys and I tensed, stepping in unison, prepared to meet him head-on.

He struck first, no hesitation.

The air exploded with raw energy, magic lashing like whips, twisting the stone walls, slamming against my defenses.

I met him blow for blow.

Darkness crashed against shadow in a storm of sound and fury, each strike reverberating through the hollow bones of the sanctuary. Sparks of corrupted magic scattered like burning stars, lighting the vaulted stone in sickly bursts of red and violet. My father's power was an avalanche—old, practiced, and merciless.

Every swing of his blade carved through air thick with smoke and blood, the force of it rattling my teeth.

But I didn't yield.

I couldn't.

Cerys moved beside me like a phantom made of ice and resolve. Her blades flashed in a dance, each strike deliberate, definite. She darted past my shoulder, slicing through the dark arcs of my father's magic, deflecting them at impossible angles. Frost bloomed wherever her blades met his flame, steam hissing between them in violent bursts.

"Thalon—now!" she hissed, her voice sharp, commanding, cutting through the roar.

I went without hesitation. My shadows coiled and surged, answering the rhythm of her call as though we shared one breath. They lashed outward in sweeping arcs, biting into the King's hunters, forcing him backward a step. He countered with the strength of centuries, his magic — a thing that tore through the world rather than shaped it. But the Bridge's pulse throbbed through me, steady and alive, amplifying my power.

Leyla's essence flowed like starlight beneath my skin, threading power into every strike. Each motion grew sharper, faster, more precise. Every wound I gave him pulsed with a silver undertone, her mark mingling with mine. From the edge of the chaos, I caught a glimpse — Leyla and Elias.

Their hunter lunged once more, desperate, monstrous. Together, they moved as one: Elias's blade flashed in a golden arc, Leyla's magic ignited silver-white, and the creature's roar cut short, its body collapsing into stillness. The clang of its weapon rang once, then died.

Leyla's chest heaved, her face pale but fierce, eyes blazing with exhaustion and power. I felt her through our bond before I saw her move… That heartbeat, that pull. She was ready.

Now, I sent through the tether, my mind reaching for hers.

Her head lifted. Her gaze locked on mine, resolute. Then, her magic answered. It poured toward me like a tidal wave—radiant, merciless, alive. Threads of silver light burst from her palms, slicing through the air, converging on me with a force that bent the very fabric of the chamber. The torches guttered, shadows twisted and bowed. Stone cracked beneath our feet.

And for the first time, Vaeris faltered.

His blade trembled as the twin surge of power hit him—my shadow and her light entwined, unstoppable, undeniable. His snarl turned to disbelief as the weight of centuries met the fury of what he had created.

The bond between us sang in my veins, a single, perfect note of defiance. We struck together.

Cerys spun into motion beside me, her twin blades carving an X of frost that caught the King off balance. I drove my shadows forward, shaping them into spears that cut through his defenses, turning his own energy back upon him. Leyla's power wrapped around it all, a web of light threading through every crack in his armor, every fissure in his control.

He roared, the sound a beast's death cry.

The walls shook, the ceiling wept dust. The air shuddered under the force of what we unleashed. And then, it ended.

The blow landed true.

My blade, wreathed in Leyla's light, pierced through the black stone of his armor and into the hollow beneath his ribs. His eyes went wide, disbelief shattering into something that looked almost human. His magic fractured outward in a violent burst, shards of darkness scattering into the air before dissolving into nothing.

For a heartbeat, he simply stood there.

The great King Vaeris, the undying tyrant.

Staring at me as though trying to remember my face. Then, his knees gave way. The sound of his body striking the stone was final, echoing like the toll of a bell. Silence fell.

The tunnels trembled with the memory of what had just occurred. The air hung thick, humming with aftershocks, the tang of metal and smoke stinging my tongue. My arms burned, my lungs dragged against the weight of what was done.

He was gone.

After all the years, all the blood, all the chains. He was gone. This was the culmination of everything: every scar carved into my skin, every scream I'd buried, every sacrifice made in the dark. The crown, the kingdom, the curse. All of it, done.

My senses screamed.

Leyla.

Something was wrong.

I turned to her, her knees buckling. The pulse of the Bridge began to tremble, the threads of her magic flickering and weakening. Her body sagged, trembling under the weight of everything she had given. My heart slammed against my ribs.

"Leyla!" I barked, my voice rough with fear.

I reached her as she wavered, catching her before she hit the ground. Her arms slipped around me, but she was too heavy, too spent. I pressed her close, feeling the rapid fading of her life through our bond. Her chest rose, shallow, and then faltered.

My hands moved over her, desperate, commanding, unwilling to accept what I already sensed.

Her pulse—It was gone.

I tightened my arms, holding her as though sheer force could bring her back. My jaw ached, my shadow coiled around us both in silent fury, but nothing could reverse it.

The world narrowed to her still form, the heat of her leaving, and the unbearable weight of loss that slammed into me like the collapse of a star. We had won the battle. The bridge stood. The King was dead.

But Leyla—My life. My light.

She was gone.

Chapter Fifty-Four

Thalon

This couldn't be what fate had in store for us. No. I wouldn't accept it.

"Leyla," I choked, shaking her shoulders. "Don't you dare. Don't you dare leave me."

Mick knelt beside us, her hands slick with blood, her face twisted in something beyond tears.

"Thalon…" Her voice cracked, breaking. "She's gone."

The words split through me. *Gone.*

No.

Something inside me tore loose. I pressed my forehead to hers, breathing in her scent, the faint remnants of her light.

"No," I said again, softer this time, deadly quiet.

"Thalon," Mick whispered, her voice trembling now, tears streaking her face. "Burn them. Burn them all."

And I did. My power, fully unrestrained for the first time in decades, erupted from me like the breath of the Gods themselves. Shadows twisted from my fingertips, shaping into beasts, wings, fire, smoke. The sky screamed with me. The earth opened.

I didn't stop until every last one of the hunters was nothing more than ash in the wind.

When the silence returned, I was standing in a field of smoldering ruin, the scent of blood and ozone thick in the air. My mother appeared not long after, answering the pull of my grief. She stepped through the smoke, her hair shimmering with frost. She looked down at Leyla's body, and for the first time in my life, her composure cracked.

"My son…" she whispered. "Her sacrifice… She saved us all."

I drowned out the rest of her words. No longer caring.

She wove the old words, binding Leyla's body in ancient runes of preservation. Ice grew over her skin, sealing her in a cocoon of shimmering blue, as if she had been carved from the stars themselves. It seemed my mothers full powers had returned as well, thanks to Leyla.

"She will remain untouched," my mother said softly, "for three days. Then, we return her to the Gods."

But I wasn't listening. I couldn't. I placed a hand against the ice, the chill biting deep into my palm until blood bloomed against the surface.

"You can't leave me," I murmured. "Do you hear me? I forbid it."

Mick turned away, her shoulders shaking. My mother said nothing.

The silence pressed down like a weight. The realm was whole again, the air thrummed with balance, every fae had their fully restored magic, but I felt none of it.

The world could heal a thousand times over, and it would never touch the wound she left behind.

I sank to my knees before her, covered in ice and looking at my mate. My heart. The firelight reflected in the crystal.

"If the Gods want her," I whispered, "then they'll take me too."

Chapter Fifty-Five

Leyla

The world around me was not the world I had known. It was neither light nor dark, neither warmth nor cold.

It was everything and nothing, a liminal space suspended between life and death.

My body was gone, and yet my consciousness floated, untethered. A soft glow emerged in the distance, familiar shapes taking form. My parents. My real parents.

My mother's warm smile, her eyes reflecting pride and sorrow. And my father's strong, steady gaze. My heart, or what felt like it, ached at the sight.

"Leyla…" my mother whispered, voice trembling with emotion I had only ever read about in old letters and stories.

"You… you did what we could not. You carried the world inside you. You were the Bridge. You were everything." My fathers voice beamed with pride.

I tried to move, to reach for them, but my ethereal form resisted.

"I… I'm gone, aren't I?" The words slipped out before I could stop them, fragile, terrified. My father shook his head, placing a spectral hand over mine.

"Yes, my child. But you are between. You have seen what the cost is. You fought, and you fell, and you saved more than you know."

I blinked, feeling the tears sliding down my cheeks.

"I can't leave… Thalon—Mick—the Bridge—" My voice caught on a sob.

"You will return, my child" my mother said, stepping closer, her hand brushing my cheek. "Your journey does not have to end here, if you choose. The threads of the realms still pull for you. The magic within you cannot be contained, not even by death."

A soft warmth began to rise in me, like sunlight on frozen earth. My parents' presence felt like a tether, a lifeline, and I realized that this in-between was not punishment, but preparation. A guide.

"Remember, my daughter," my father spoke, "Your purpose is greater than one life. The realms need you. Your magic, your bond… It is the key. You will return stronger, ready to bring life where it has long been absent. There will be some that come after you and what you treasure most. You defeat them. Your grandfather will come for you. He still lives. You do not hesitate. The realms depend on you, on our bloodline."

I inhaled deeply, or the closest thing to it in this space, and felt the threads of my Bridge flicker, pulsing with faint light. "I… I understand."

My mother kissed my forehead, her warmth flooding through me.

"We will be waiting. And we will always be with you." She paused and let out a breath she seemed to have held for centuries. "And please. Tell Cerys, it was never her fault."

The light intensified, surrounding me completely. A warmth that burned away the fear, the despair, and I felt my consciousness being pulled back, back to the world of the living, tethered to Thalon, to Mick, to the people I had grown to love.

A voice, not quite mine, whispered on the wind: *You are not done, Leyla. The Bridge is yours alone to wield. Remember this.*

And I felt myself falling… And falling… And falling.

Finally, a pure blackness embraced my vision once again. And the shadows I had grown to love pulled me back with a fierceness only one fae held.

Thalon.

Chapter Fifty-Six

Thalon

T he ice was beautiful. Cold. Perfect. It gleamed like crystal, carved to hold her still form within its frozen embrace.

My mother, Cerys, had woven her centuries-old magic through it, protective and ceremonial. Fae tradition demanded that a body be preserved for a time after death, a period of mourning and reflection. I knelt beside the crystal sarcophagus, my hands hovering over the ice, feeling her essence— diminished. My chest tightened so hard it hurt, my heart breaking in a way I had never imagined.

Leyla… My mate… My little light… Taken from me, even if only temporarily.

Because that is what this would be.

Temporary.

After we send her body to the Gods, I would find her soul again. I would murder the Gods that dared take her from me.

The annihilation of the remaining hunters did not fill my need for revenge. With my powers fully restored, I was able to transport to the City of Glass. Nothing remains of that Gods forsaken castle but ash.

Still—nothing.

Nothing would satisfy this need for revenge. Nothing, except being with her again.

Mick stood nearby, her amber eyes glinting with sorrow. Of nothingness. I clenched my jaw, staring at her frozen form. I reached out, touching Leyla's ice with a trembling hand, wishing I could shatter it, break it, take her back into my arms.

The night passed slowly, unbearably. Mick and Elias stood only feet away, Elias comforting her when she would scream.

When she would cry.

Shadows stretched and twisted around me, protective, responsive, as if the world itself mourned with me. Every sound, every whisper, every clink of armor or tool, made me flinch. I felt alone, and yet the bond we had forged, even now, was unbroken.

And then, a tremor ran through the ice.

A faint glow began to pulse within her frozen form, soft and golden.

My heart stopped.

Could it be? No. Impossible.

Slowly, imperceptibly at first, her finger twitched. Then, a shiver ran through her entire body. The ice groaned faintly, and I pressed my forehead to the crystal.

"Leyla… Come back to me," I whispered into threads, urging my shadows, my darkness to bring her back home.

A gasp echoed from within the ice. Faint and trembling.

Her eyes fluttered open. Light—the real, vibrant light— returned. Illuminating her face, her hair. The warmth of life surged back into the crystal prison, cracking it softly and releasing her.

I caught her as she collapsed into my arms. Wetness streaming down my face. "Leyla."

She gasped for a breath of air. As if she had been drowning.

"Don't you ever leave me again." I demanded into her hair. Demanded into her will.

Her small, exhausted laugh was a sound I would never forget.

"Miss me?"

And Gods, I have never heard sweeter words.

The End—
of the Beginning.

Thank you

When I first began writing The Darkness Saves, I wanted to tell a story about love that shouldn't exist, and what happens when two people risk everything to choose it anyway.

Leyla's strength, with her quiet hope, and Thalon's fight against the darkness in and around him are pieces of all of us.

This book was meant to introduce Orrynne to readers, introduce the characters and their back stories. So, thank you. Thank you for letting me share this world with you.

And if you're wondering whether this is the end of Leyla and Thalon's story... Let's just say the Bridge has only just awakened.

With love,

K.

About the Author

K.L. Rutledge draws inspiration from years of navigating the intricate web of human emotions and decisions, which she channels into her writing.

Her stories feature characters faced with tough choices and the kind of stakes that push them to their limits. When she's not crafting her next story, she can be found in her home in Indiana, surrounded by her husband, two kids, and an ever-present cup of coffee. And her bernedoodle, Tuno. He is the supervisor of all writing sessions.

Her days are filled with balancing family life and her love for storytelling. And, if you ask her, there's nothing better than getting lost in a good book or dreaming up her next great love story—because, in the end, truly the best tales are the ones that make your heart race.

K.L. Rutledge

9 798218 849672